Someone Is Out There
Kaye George

Cover Art Design by: Kelly Moran/Rowan Prose Publishing
Photo Credit: Adobe Images/Deposit Photos
First Edition
ISBN: 9781961967458
Rowan Prose Publishing, LLC; Sapphire Imprint
www.RowanProsePublishing.com
Published in the United States of America

ACKNOWLEDGMENTS

I owe Darla Taylor, the real one, many thanks for giving me permission to use her name.
It was perfectly suited. But I need to let her know I would never do any of this to her in real life!
My thanks also to the team at Rowan Prose Publishing for bringing my novel into the world.
I'm thrilled to be seeing it come into being.

Chapter 1

So far, the evening had gone well. But Darla Taylor predicted it would end badly.

She poked at the food on her plate, moving it around so it might look like she had eaten something. Bobby wasn't noticing what she was doing. He wasn't noticing her at all. But now he looked up from his own dinner, his meal nearly consumed. His head motion was caught in her peripheral vision. She didn't look up at him.

She'd been dreading this dinner all day and it was proving to be at least as bad as she had feared it would be.

"I thought you liked baked potatoes." He sounded puzzled.

Darla looked up now. Bobby's smooth, handsome face was tight. Did he know what was coming? Darla closed her eyes and swore she could sense the tension zapping back and forth between them.

"Bobby," she said, putting her fork down, giving up on pointlessly rearranging her food. "I have something I have to talk to you about."

He narrowed those clear blue eyes she had fallen for a few short months ago. They were still clear and bright, but something more came across to her. Something like jagged lightning.

Bobby threw his knife and fork onto his plate with a clatter and waited, silently, for her to go on. Utensils softly connected with china at the surrounding tables in the dimly lit, romantic atmosphere of the restaurant.

This had always been one of her favorite dining spots. Would this ruin that?

The smell of the garlic chicken threatened to turn Darla's stomach. She had to get this over with. The thought of the money being wasted on this night at one of Charity Ohio's most expensive restaurants gave her one more moment of pause.

"I don't think...I don't think this is working."

He stared at her plate. "You have to actually put the food into your mouth. That's the way it works." He took a healthy swig of his second beer after shooting a wry grin across the tablecloth.

The hint of a smile he gave reminded her how much she had always liked his sense of humor. But right now, she had to resist falling under that tantalizing spell. She had to get through this.

"No, I mean us. I think we ought to..."

"See other people? Isn't that the way it goes?" His smile looked more like a sneer now. "You had to make me buy you dinner so you could dump me? Is that it?"

"No, that's not how I meant it. I mean... You know what? I'll buy dinner. But can we just talk a little?" She had rehearsed her lines, but wasn't saying them. It was all flubbed up now.

"I don't think so." He stood, threw his napkin onto the remnants on his plate, and left. Sitting still as stone for a few moments, she didn't watch him go.

Then Darla allowed herself a breath of relief. Okay, that was over. She had done it. The butter was melting into her baked potato. It looked and smelled delicious, and she now realized she was ravenous. Now, she could relax. And breathe.

She shoved the garlic chicken aside and ate everything else on her plate. The potato had started out so piping hot, it was still warm and delicious. This place was worth every penny.

In the cab on her way home, she replayed the breakup. Driving with the windows cracked helped cool her temper off. The outside temperature was nearing fifty degrees this time of night in early April. That was about normal for central Ohio, finally. A cold snap two weeks ago had threatened to hang on forever, but it was letting up.

She lifted her straight, brown hair off her neck to let the outside air waft across her skin. *Ooo.* That air was too cold. The cold snap was gone and they were back to more or less normal, but normal April evening temps were not warm. She rolled up the window as the taxi drove toward her rented house on the outskirts of town.

Shuddering at an unbidden memory, a date from two weeks ago ran through her head. That hadn't been the first time Bobby had over-imbibed, but it had been the first time she'd seen what she later thought of as "the other Bobby Abbott," the one who reminded her of her father. Her mother's ex-husband now. Would she ever escape from his dark shadow?

She and Bobby had been scheduled to double date that night with her best friend Virginia, Gin to her and almost everyone else, and Gin's current beau, but he had become her ex-beau an hour or so before the date, so she and Bobby had gone ahead with the plans, just the two of them.

The first stop that night had been miniature golf. Darla always liked the faux sport. It seemed more like a little kids' game than an adult endeavor, and it was a fun, light way to be outside, doing something, but something that didn't matter. On the seventh hole, though, the one with the windmill blades rotating slowly to block the tunnel you had to shoot your ball through, she realized this game did matter—to Bobby. He failed to get his ball through three consecutive times. On his fourth try, she couldn't help but notice how grim he had started looking. His face turned red and the stringy muscles in his neck stood out.

She knew he had started drinking before he picked her up. She could smell the fumes the minute she got into his car, but he didn't seem drunk. His driving was okay. However, he'd brought along a flask and was swigging from it at least twice on every hole. By the fifth hole he was weaving a bit when he followed his ball to retrieve it from the hole. He stumbled picking up the fourth or fifth ball. She was afraid he was going to fall over, but he remained on his feet and straightened up with his ball in his hand.

Then, on the seventh hole, this one, the hole with the difficult windmill, he took a long gulp from his flask, slammed it back into his hip pocket, and whacked the little ball as hard as he could with the toy club. It hit one of the windmill blades, shattering it, and bounced back to smack him on the shoulder.

Darla flinched, then stared, her mouth open, as he bent the club over his knee and threw it to the ground. Trying to become invisible, a lesson she had learned as a child, she remained motionless as he stalked off. She had a clear view of the parking lot, since the seventh hole was near the top of a hill, and watched him drive off, squealing his tires and nearly sideswiping a couple of parked cars. Grateful she wasn't riding with him, she collected the balls and his broken club and made her way back to the clubhouse. The teen-age boy behind the counter had seen Bobby storm off and looked like he felt sorry for her. When she told him the windmill was damaged, he assured her everything was insured. She called herself a cab, breathing a sigh of relief she wouldn't have to pay for the breakage.

That was the night it had occurred to her, the night she'd known she would have to break up with him. That behavior reminded her too much of the trauma in her past.

Not only were there the reminders of her childhood, the bad parts of it, roiling through her head, her last failed relationship surfaced, dredged up by yet another one.

Zeke Underwood. She'd fallen for him. Hard. For the whole two years they had dated, he had seemed like a catch—kind, considerate, good looking. Until she found out, quite by accident, he was already caught.

They were nestled on her couch, watching the comedy show they both enjoyed. They laughed at the same parts and gave each other looks of disbelief at the ridiculous parts, the places where the situations and the humor were forced. As always, the nearness promised to lead to the next inevitable step. They got along so well and were simpatico in so many ways.

Zeke got up to use the bathroom. And, she knew, to put on a condom. She had always appreciated him looking out for her that way. In the course of their half-clothed fumbling on the couch, the precursor to the next event, his phone had fallen from his pocket.

His text messages were open and one caught her eye as she picked up the phone.

Honey, don't forget to bring home diapers. We're almost out.

Honey? Diapers?

She noted the name the text was from, Katy Underwood.

As she watched, another text popped up, noiselessly. He had the sound turned off. That was smart, she decided, when she saw the next message.

Harrison misses his daddy. Coming home soon?

She didn't need any more proof than that. This wasn't a wrong number.

When Zeke emerged from the bathroom, he looked puzzled at her expression. "You're still dressed. Are you okay?"

She handed him his phone and put her shirt back on. "I saw the texts. You were kind of careless leaving your phone open like that."

He looked truly bewildered. Until he saw the texts. "I can...I can explain this."

"So can I," Darla snarled and jabbed her finger toward the floor. "Pick up your clothes and get out. Don't come back."

Every time she felt herself missing him, his mind, his body, the way they were in perfect sync whenever they were together, either in bed or walking down the street, she stomped on her thoughts and locked them firmly away. She refused to miss someone who could cheat on his wife. And his infant. What a jerk.

Bobby had happened soon after. He was convenient, since they worked together. When they started dating, she didn't know about the drinking. He never showed up drunk at the hospital, or even smelling of booze. As they dated more, he relaxed, she thought, and showed her his true nature.

Tonight, trying to foresee how it would go, she had pictured arguments, protests, maybe even begging or bargaining, to put it off. The way it actually happened was probably the best way it could have gone. He must have seen it coming, too. It was as if he'd been expecting it.

Since the mini golf outing, they had gone out a few times as she waited to find the right time to give him the talk, but they'd merely been going through the motions. She'd even thought he might take the initiative to break up with her at one point. Then they had started revisiting some of their early dates, places where they'd connected, places where they'd always had a good time. Was he trying to prevent the breakup? Show her how they had fun together?

She leaned against the solid back seat of the cab, the memories flooding in. Back when Darla had been sure that Bobby Abbott was the one for her, they'd taken a bike ride through the cemetery, followed by a moonlight stroll through Cantrell Park. The first of those had been Bobby's idea and Darla had had to rent a bicycle for it. The second was a favorite place of Darla's for walking. Bobby wasn't an enthusiastic slow walker, more inclined to jog until he was winded, then call it a day. But they had accommodated each other and had found areas in common. They both liked to be outdoors, even when the weather was less than ideal, and he could identify as many trees and birds as she could. Maybe a few more.

They also talked a lot about them both being in the medical field. It didn't seem to bother Bobby that Darla was a nurse and he was a nursing assistant, although at first, she thought he was trying his best to impress her by being almost too polite and taking her to nice places—concerts, plays, movies with drinks and popcorn.

As time went on, Bobby seemed to relax around her. He stopped trying to wow her. Unfortunately, that meant he wasn't always on his best behavior. Not that drinking too much a couple of times was a deal breaker. She told herself that. A few times. Until the golfing explosion.

She blinked back tears, not sure if they were tears of anger or self-pity. After all, Zeke Underwood, like Bobby, had seemed like "the one." He didn't have drinking or rage problems, so she had overlooked some warning signs for way too long. Different warning signs from the ones Bobby threw up.

The dates, cancelled at the last minute. The holidays he seemed reluctant to spend with her. The reluctance, no, the refusal, to talk about their future.

When she had found out what was going on, she was angry with herself she'd been that stupid as to fall victim to an old cliché. The wife and kids, with her on the side. It was a wonder the jerk had found as much time to spend with her as he did. He would be Zeke Underhanded, not Zeke Underwood, in her mind forever. She knew she shouldn't be angry with herself. She bore no blame. But she couldn't help it. Maybe she should have figured it out sooner.

The cab pulled into her driveway, behind her own car parked under the carport, since Bobby had picked her up for tonight's date. As she finished paying and tipping the driver, three enthusiastic barks came from inside her house. A brisk breeze blew her hair into her face as she hurried to the side door into her kitchen. Moose greeted her with the noisy bouncing enthusiasm of the two-year-old chocolate lab that he was.

Her heart lifted, as it always did when she was with Moosie. She was so grateful for him. After he was let out into her fenced backyard, cleaned up after, then fed and watered, she called her mother.

"It's late, Darla," Amy Taylor said. "Is everything okay?"

"I'm fine, Mom. I just...just wanted to talk to you." She shrugged out of her spring coat, still on from taking the dog out, got a cola from the fridge and pried up the tab top with a pop and a slight fizzing sound.

"So, something is not okay."

Darla smiled at that. Her mother was so perceptive. She could tell her daughter's mood, even over the phone. Who needs a *boyfriend* with a mother like that? "I think it's much better now. I just broke up with Bobby."

Her mother was silent for a moment. "You haven't been getting along well lately, have you? Did something happen?"

"No, no. Just cumulative, I think. There's no connection between us." She wandered into her cozy living room and perched on the couch with her cold can. Moose, done taking his usual three seconds to scarf his dinner, trotted over and laid his silken head on her knee. The couch was old and brown, a hand-me-down from her mother when she had gotten new furniture. Moose's fur blended into the weave, which was convenient for a casual housekeeper like Darla.

"There was once, as I recall you telling me. What happened to it?"

"Fizzled out, I guess." She wasn't going to bring up the drinking or the disastrous date tonight. She wouldn't do that to her mother. Wouldn't bring up those awful memories. Awful for both of them. The parallels between the drunken behaviors of the two men were incomplete, but some of the behaviors were eerily similar. Unconsciously, she stroked Moose's head.

"That's going to be awkward at work, isn't it? Is he upset? Angry?"

"A little." Darla recalled his sneer and him stomping out of the restaurant. Yes, he was upset. Yes, he was angry. Yes, it would be awkward at work. But she would deal with that. It would be better than continuing to date him as he drank more and more in front of her. He had never come to work drunk. And the "good" Bobby wasn't hard to get along with at all.

As she hung up, she felt a slight bit of guilt for not telling her mother everything.

She was still tense. Her body, tight all over, zinged with it. Whenever she needed to let go, to undo her tension, she turned to her favorite—her only—sport, archery. She didn't usually do it that late in the day, in the dark, but she would tonight. She collected her gear and went to the backyard to shoot at the all-weather target on the stand she always left there, at the far edge of her property. It only took two ends of six arrows each, before she was able to feel calmer, more relaxed. Then she let Moose out, since he was pent up in the house while she shot, as always. He plunged down the back porch stairs loped around the yard, his tongue hanging out and giving him such a sweet, goofy look. She collected her arrows before he could fetch them to her and gave him his yard time.

Three rose bushes, leftover from the previous owner, were showing signs of the budding they would be doing in June. It would be futile, though, since Moose would chomp on all the blooms he could reach, which would be most of them. How he avoided getting thorns in his mouth was a mystery to Darla.

After she came in and stowed her equipment, Darla switched her television on and surfed as a mindless diversion while she plopped on her comfy sofa and drained the cola to finish washing the taste of the date out of her mouth. "What Ever Happened to Baby Jane?" was playing on the old movie channel. She had seen it long ago, and started watching it, then remembered Baby Jane was tragically injured and left crippled for the rest of her life in the movie. That was too much like her mother's situation. She wasn't going to put herself through that right now.

Instead, she got up and ran her thumb along the spines of the mystery books on her shelves. She started to pull out one of the Lincoln Rhyme novels, thinking to reread it. It had been years since she devoured that series. But Jeffrey Deaver's character was wheelchair bound. Another reminder of her mother. She pushed it back in.

Was everything tonight going to remind her of what had happened to her mother?

She tossed the empty can into the recycle bin and poured a glass of wine. After wandering the few rooms of her small house, shadowed by her faithful canine, she grabbed the bottle and went to the bathroom. She drew a hot bath, pouring plenty of jasmine scented oil into the steaming water. She lit a candle and lowered herself into the welcome warmth. Finally, after her third glass was empty, she felt her shoulders completely relax. Maybe she'd be able to sleep tonight. The irony of relaxing with a glass of wine after ditching a guy for his drinking—and his behavior—was not lost on her.

She crawled into bed while Moose circled, then landed, with a plop, on his doggie bed on the floor beside her.

Her mother was right. It would be tense working with Bobby Abbott tomorrow. At least the break with Zeke had been completely clean. They had never encountered each other again. Darla was one of several nurses currently assigned to the recovery area of the hospital, where Bobby also was now.

They had worked well together on the children's floor for a few months before it occurred to either one to start dating. It had never been a problem because Darla outranked and out-earned him. So far. She expected everything would change now.

Chapter 2

Unlike the people who disliked the antiseptic odor of a hospital, who even felt sick from the smell of it, Darla loved it. It comforted her to know things were clean here, that people were working to keep—to make and then to keep—others healthy. The smell was part of the process, after all. Faire County Hospital never smelled bad to her, what she would consider bad, like urine, mold, dirty things.

The nurses rotated regularly and she had worked in a number of different areas. One she liked very much was recovery, she had found. In her hospital, recovery held two rows of curtained bays where patients stayed, lying on the gurneys, until they woke up from whatever surgery or procedure they had had done.

It had sounded boring at first, but it turned out that one reason she liked this area was it was one of the more relaxing assignments, in her opinion. Before rotations became so regular, she felt she had worked in emergency for too long, then she had done surgical assistance for several years after. Those were such tense situations, she was glad to now be keeping track of vitals, watching patients wake up, making sure they had pain meds and whatever else they needed, and letting the families in to see them. It was often a happy situation, with a problem having been taken care of.

There was something to be said for boring, but it wasn't that, she'd decided. It was just a slower pace than some of the other floors, with their excitement and exhilaration. There was usually no rush, and little tension. The patient was glad to have gotten the surgery over with, the relatives were happy everything had gone well, and they were all glad, if she were honest, that the patient had survived. It was rare they didn't, but it happened.

Like anything else, any other department, there were bad times, of course. When the patient and the family had to be told terrible news. Inoperable cancer had been found. An old cancer had spread. A scan had turned up problems that would be difficult to deal with. They weren't flat out emergencies, though, so that made the job, on the whole, less stressful.

She arrived at work that morning, taking in the familiar sharp, clean smell, walking down the brightly lit hallway, and anticipating a work day that would take her mind off her recent break up.

However, it wasn't long before her mood plunged. The very guy she'd broken up with last night, the one she'd made so angry, was waiting at the nurses' station. It shouldn't have been a surprise, since he worked here, but, even though she'd known she would probably see him, she hadn't thought how seeing him would make her feel. He gave her a hostile smirk and handed her a clipboard.

Her shoulders sagged. It was just her bad luck he was assigned to work with her this week. Bobby Abbot was a good nursing assistant, but that didn't make her want to work with him right now, today, after last night. It was true they had worked well together in the past. That was then. This was now.

She signed in on the clipboard at the nurses' station, as usual, and turned her back to him, wanting to concentrate on her work and try to ignore him.

Going to the medicine closet, she pushed the door nearly shut and began counting out her meds, the ones to distribute to the patients on her morning round, putting the pills in the little white paper cups and arranging them on the tray with the instructions. In ten minutes, she would start handing them out.

Stacy, at the nursing station desk, called her name. Darla came out of the med room and poked her head around the corner. Stacy looked up from the phone call she was on. "Darla? Someone wants to talk to you."

Bobby was nowhere to be seen. Giving a slight huff of impatience at being interrupted during work hours, and in the middle of her meticulous task, Darla walked to the desk and took the phone. People she knew didn't usually call her during her working hours. Giving a stronger huff of annoyance, she handed it back. "There's no one there. Do you know who it was?"

"Some guy, but he didn't say who he was."

"You didn't recognize a voice?"

Stacy shrugged. "It wasn't anyone I know."

Darla hurried back to her meds and halted just inside the medicine closet, her mouth grim and her eyes narrowed. The paper cups were upended and the pills were scattered across the tray. Her back had been to the closet for the brief moment she'd been on the phone so she hadn't seen who had been in the small room.

She had an immediate suspicion. Where was Bobby? Did he do this? She seethed as she straightened out the meds, again. First sorting them to determine which med was which, then putting the various sized and colored pellets into their neat white cups, then proceeded to hand them out late. Not very late, but a bit late.

The rest of the morning went smoothly, with Darla catching glimpses of Bobby here and there, but not encountering him again. At least he didn't show up to gloat. Her blood pressure rose a bit every time she saw him. And every time, as soon as she could, she paused to do a few deep breaths and calm herself before continuing.

He had to have made the phone call and dumped her meds. What a baby. This only made her happier about dumping *him*. If he could be this childish, it was a good thing she'd gotten rid of him before things got worse. If only she didn't have to work in the same area with him this week.

Throughout the morning, she got a creepy feeling every now and then. She would look up, expecting to see Bobby gloating or smirking. He would be good at both of those, she knew. Every time, she either just missed seeing him, or her apprehensions were unfounded. He was never within sight when she got those chills up the back of her neck.

At lunch time, Darla spoke to a supervisor and asked to be switched to another area next week. They were usually assigned to a specific area for a month. The supervisor said they needed someone in Emergency, Darla's least favorite department. She decided to think about it.

"Can I tell you later?"

"How much later?" the supervisor asked. "I need to know in a couple of days. Can you do that? I can hold it open that long, but I need to get the schedule set."

"Sure. I'll do that."

Darla took her break in the cafeteria, getting a soda and sitting at a corner table, and took her phone out of her pocket. She kept it mute during work, but she carried it. Right now, she had to talk to someone. Who better than Gin? When Gin answered, her spirits lifted a little. It always did her good to talk to her best friend. Gin Holland was an aide, a home health care worker. They had been friends for years and, after some other places, Gin had ended up working for the Only The Best Health Care company as a member of the team assisting Darla's mother at home. It was only because of Gin and the others on that team that Amy Taylor could still be living at her own house and not in "a" home, or "the" home, as Darla thought of it, and as her mother referred to it aloud. Often.

"Hey, do you have a minute?" Darla asked. She knew Gin was at her mother's today. Darla tried to keep track of the schedule, which her mother had a copy of, telling her who would be helping her each week.

"Sure. Your mom is watching one of her judge shows."

Darla chuckled. Her mother loved all the courtroom shows. Even the divorce court shows, which Darla couldn't stand. Although she did like some of the others. Amy had told her daughter once that she wanted to know what to do if she ever had to go to court. Or if she ever wanted to sue anyone. The woman could be a bit prickly and, when she thought about it, Darla didn't know why she had never yet sued anyone. She probably would someday. Although that didn't explain why she watched the divorce courts. She wasn't going to need those again.

"I did something last night," Darla said. "I broke up with Bobby."

"Huh. I can't say I didn't see that coming. Are you okay?"

She saw it coming? Huh? She had never said anything to Darla about it. "I am, but he—" Her phone buzzed with an unfamiliar number. "Someone's calling. I'll be right back." She switched over to the new call.

A disguised voice croaked, "Knock, knock."

"Who's there?" she answered, dutifully, a little annoyed that someone was playing silly jokes while she was at work. But who could resist saying, "Who's there?" Even if she said it impatiently.

The call cut off without the next line of the joke. That was strange. When she returned to Gin, she told her what had just happened.

"Probably a wrong number."

"Probably," Darla agreed. "Unless it's..." She didn't mention who she thought it might be, but Gin's "Huh" showed the notion had crossed her mind also.

During the afternoon she got three more of those knock-knock calls with dead air following. Was Bobby making these prank calls? Was he acting like a pouty young teen? Was he the biggest baby in the world? She went looking for him after the last hang up to ream him out, but he wasn't anywhere to be found. Hiding from her? That made her anger flare even more. That made her even more angry.

She was steaming as she went through the rest of her day, being extra careful not to make any mistakes with the IVs and meds. Feeling as distracted as she was, it would have been easy to do. Nurses couldn't work distracted. Lives were in the balance, after all. People in the hospital were often fragile.

At the end of her shift, she decided she would give it one more day before moving to a new work assignment. If Bobby was still being such a snot tomorrow, she would take the transfer to the job she liked the least. She didn't have to tell them until Wednesday, and today was only Monday. She got her paperwork for the day in order and retrieved her purse from the locked drawer. At least no one had broken into that and bothered her things.

On the way out of the building and across the parking lot, she kept an eye out for Bobby, still wanting to give him a big fat piece of her mind. Spring was taking its time coming to Ohio this year. Sometimes it was balmy and pleasant by now. The wind whipped up dogwood blossoms which had fallen and blown from a nearby park. She hadn't zipped up her coat, so she clutched it around her to keep the wind off her torso.

As she approached her car, she slowed. Huh?

It looked odd. It was tilting to the right. When she got close enough, she saw why. Her right rear tire had two deep, wide gashes on the sidewall and was perfectly flat.

Chapter 3

After staring at the tire, which remained slit and flat, and after fuming for a few more seconds, Darla whipped out her phone and called Gin again.

"Gin!"

"Now what? Don't shout."

"Someone slashed my tire. My tire is flat." Darla could hear herself still shouting. "Sorry, I'll try to calm down."

"Hang on. I left work half an hour ago. I'll put on my shoes and come over. Where are you? Still in the hospital parking lot?"

"Yes, I just got off shift." Darla stopped to collect herself for the space of a couple of breaths. "I have a spare. And a jack. I guess I could change it."

"Hey!" She jumped at the sound of his voice. Bobby was behind her. "What happened? You want me to change that for you?"

"Hurry," Darla said to Gin and closed the call. She whirled on Bobby. "You should change it, shouldn't you? Considering you probably did this!"

He backed up a step, shock on his face. "I would never do anything like that."

"Like what? Like tipping over all my meds this morning so I had to redo them?"

He hung his head. "Okay, that was me." The confession took her by surprise. She hadn't known, for sure, it was him. "I didn't do it on purpose. It was an accident. Honest. I had to get some saline for an IV and I bumped your tray. I was in a hurry. I'm really sorry."

"Too sorry to apologize?" She was screaming again.

He backed up another step. Maybe he *hadn't* slashed her tire. Maybe the spilled meds *were* an accident. She didn't trust him, though. How could she?

Still looking at the ground, he shook his head. "I know. I was embarrassed. I've been avoiding you all day. I'm really sorry." He looked up at her. "Can I change your tire? To make it up to you?"

It would be a lot easier than doing it herself. It would also be easier than calling her roadside assist program. She'd used them for a dead battery last summer and it had taken them forty-five minutes to arrive and jump start her car. She assessed the situation. This seemed to be the "good" Bobby, the sober one. The one she had always liked.

"What's that?" Bobby pointed to the windshield.

A small envelope was stuck under the driver side wiper blade. She snatched it, half expecting it to be a note from Bobby. She read it to herself.

Knock. Knock. I know where you live.

Darla frowned at Bobby. "Is this your idea of a joke?" She stuck it out toward him.

He read the short note. "No. That's creepy." He shivered and frowned and recoiled a bit. "My idea of a joke is something funny."

"Like calling me all day and hanging up?"

"Huh? Why would I do that?"

He looked truly puzzled at all this, Darla had to admit. But how good an actor was he? He had bragged about having parts in high school plays more than once.

Darla heard a welcome sound, the purr of Gin's Toyota approaching. Gin's car pulled up beside them, her tires crunching on the pavement with her sharp turn to get beside Darla's vehicle. She hopped out and looked at both of them. "Darla. Bobby, what are you doing here?"

Bobby pointed to the flat tire. "I'm offering to change her tire."

"That's nice of you," Gin said. "Why don't you do that and drive her car to her place afterwards. I can drive her home now. Is that okay with you, Darla?" Gin eyed Darla's clenched fists. "You need to get your dog fed. It's getting late."

Darla suspected Gin wanted to separate them as soon as possible. That wasn't a bad idea. Gin was good at reading Darla's mind. She always had been. Almost as good as her own mother. Darla took a slow breath, then took another look at the note. The handwriting didn't look like Bobby's writing. But she had never seen his block printing. She relaxed her jaw and her shoulders a bit.

Gin spied the paper Darla was peeking at. "Did someone leave a note? Offer to pay for it? Did your tire get cut accidentally?" Gin asked.

Darla handed it to her with a frown.

"Oh, no." She read the note, then pointed to the two deep, parallel cuts. Her eyes got wide. "So, this was not an accident." Gin whirled and squinted at Bobby. "Did you do this?"

He stuck his chin out at both of them. "I'm not a vandal and I'm offering to help you out. Do you want me to or not?"

Darla wordlessly opened the trunk and pointed, so he could get out the spare and the jack. When he didn't take the hint, she picked up the jack. The metal was cold on her ungloved hands.

Bobby shook his head and took it from her, then wrestled the tire out of the trunk.

Reluctantly, she told him thanks and handed him her key fob. She sounded sullen, even to herself.

"Don't be so grateful," he muttered as he squatted to start loosening the lug nuts, glaring at them like it was the metal fasteners that had offended him instead of her.

Gin whisked Darla away and they talked on the way to her house.

"What's going on?" Gin asked. "I don't think Bobby did that. He wouldn't leave a note like that. And, as little as I think of him, I can't picture him calling you and hanging up all day long either."

Darla begrudged him that. "I agree. It's not like him. It's just...the timing. We broke up last night, and now today someone is terrorizing me."

"Think about what the note says, though. It would be silly for Bobby to say he knows where you live. Of course he does. He's stayed over more than once." Gin peered at Darla's face. "Have you officially broken up with him? For real?"

"Yes. And I know. I'm not thinking straight. I need to clear my head. If it isn't him, who have I ticked off?"

"Someone at work? A patient or a family member? Do you work with any psychos?"

"There isn't anyone I work with who would do this. I don't think. And I see the patients for such a short period of time, their families even less. We've had a good string of recoveries over the past month or so. Everyone has left in pretty good shape. One family even came back upstairs and brought me the most beautiful bouquet of roses from the gift shop before they left."

"Someone, somewhere, doesn't like you. Somehow." Gin looked worried.

Obviously. But how could that be? She didn't have any enemies. Except maybe Bobby. Or Zeke. But she had much more reason to be angry with Zeke than he did to be angry with her. He was the one who had wronged her. No one probably wanted to think someone disliked them enough to terrorize them, she thought. But someone was doing this.

"Why did you break up anyway? I never thought he was right for you."

Really? She wished Gin would have told her and saved her some trouble. "We just...don't get along." Even with Gin, she couldn't go into the reasons right now, getting into her childhood trauma and the history she wanted to keep buried forever. Maybe later she would talk to her about that.

Gin pulled into Darla's driveway and she climbed out, ducking her head back in to talk. "Thanks for the ride. Do you want to come in?" Darla stood with the passenger door open. She was offering because that's what she knew she should do, but she actually wanted to be alone, as much as she usually liked Gin's company. Her whole day had been so stressful. She needed a long bath and a tall drink. Very soon.

"I'm beat," Gin said, to Darla's relief. "Go try to relax. Don't forget, Bobby's driving your car here." So, she would have to delay her long bath? "I'll sit in the car and wait here to drive him back. You go ahead and take care of yourself." Gin was such a good friend.

Darla was glad Gin wouldn't be coming in but she still didn't want to be in the tub when Bobby arrived. The long bath would have to be deferred, but not the tall drink. When she got inside, she opted for a strong one rather than a tall one, a tumbler of straight single malt Scotch. But only after tending to the needs of Moose, who was, as always, enthusiastically grateful for her attention. After the backyard outing, she sat at the window, the dog at her feet munching a chew toy, waiting for Bobby to pull up.

A half hour went by. The hospital wasn't far away. How long did it take to change a tire? Had something gone wrong? What if he wasn't okay? She wished she could quit feeling so jumpy.

At last, he arrived. He drove into the driveway, pulled around Gin's car, and put hers under the carport. He nodded to Gin as he got out, beeping the lock before walking to her front door.

She met him there, holding it open six inches to indicate she didn't want to invite him in. He held the key fob out wordlessly.

"Thanks, Bobby. I'm sorry I accused you."

"Your flat is in the trunk. Can I come in?" He didn't exactly look contrite. More grim than anything. He eyed the dog. Bobby wasn't fond of Moose, and Moose usually steered clear of him, too.

"You'd better not." Why would he want to come in? Gin was out there waiting to drive him home. With the key in her hand, she shut the door and turned the lock. She stood still for a moment, not hearing him depart. She finally felt his footsteps cross her wooden porch and walk down the steps. He had stood there a moment, though. At last, Gin's car drove away. Bobby wasn't dangerous, she told herself. Gin would be fine. She texted her anyway and asked Gin to let her know when she got home.

Pacing her living room, she was furious at someone, but who? That was a strange feeling. Was she ever going to find that "someone?" Zeke had been disastrous, of course, hiding the fact he had a wife and two small children. He didn't even use the fiction so many married guys used, that he was going to get a divorce any day and marry her. At first. She kind of *did* think they might get married at one point. They talked about colors, flowers, who to invite, where to have the wedding. Until she found out a wedding would make him a bigamist.

An unbidden thought sprang up. Would Zeke be the one bothering her? It had been over a year. Why would he do that, all of a sudden? She shook her head, rejecting that theory. It didn't make any sense.

Darla was ensconced in her warm tub, surrounded by bubbles and fragrant candles, by the time the text from Gin came. She noted the time, an hour after her own text. What was taking everyone so long today? Gin's explanation that she and Bobby got to talking didn't make her feel any better. Had those two been sitting around discussing her? She felt herself tensing up again. Closing her eyes, she sank lower in the hot water, pulled her shoulders away from her ears, and took five deep breaths. Then a satisfying mouthful of Scotch.

While Darla was dressing for work the next morning, her mother called. She often called around 6:30 in the morning and they would chat for ten or fifteen minutes before Darla had to leave for her shift, which started at 7 am. It had always been a nice way to start the day, Darla thought. Plus, she could keep track of how her mother was doing.

"Hi darling. How was work yesterday? Awkward?" And her mother could keep track of her, of course.

Darla debated telling her mother about the troubles that may or may not have been caused by a vengeful Bobby, but she didn't want to lie to her mother. "Not exactly." She shared nearly everything with her mom, always had. Nearly everything. Her mother could get on her case sometimes, so she didn't like to expose herself to that kind of scorn.

Her mother detected the hesitation.

"Oh dear. Not exactly, but...somewhat? What happened?" The "mom radar" had detected something.

"I didn't want to tell you, but I got a bunch of hang up calls at work. Well, one hang up, then some weird ones where someone said 'Knock knock' in a strange voice and hung up."

"At work? Do you think they were from Bobby? Was it his voice?"

Now dressed, she followed Moose into the back yard so he could do his morning business. "I have no idea. The voice was disguised. I don't know if the caller used something, or just croaked the words, I couldn't tell." She passed by the roses and the baby buds that would soon be lush, fragrant blooms. The roses, she was happy to see, held baby buds that soon would be lush, fragrant blooms.

"You didn't recognize the voice at all?"

"No Mom, I couldn't tell. It was so…low and gruff, like growling."

"So, it was disguised with one of those electronic things."

"I don't know. I think someone was just lowering his natural voice to frighten me."

"Darla, I'm so sorry. That sounds scary. Are you all right?"

"Yes, I'm fine. It was unnerving, but there weren't any real threats or anything. Nothing concrete was said. But it was scary." *Should she tell about the note on her windshield? That was threatening. Then she would have to mention the slashed tire.* Also, quite threatening. "Something else did happen. After work. I came out and my tire was…flat." No, she couldn't tell her about the note. She wanted to keep anything to do with violence far away from her mother. The woman had dealt with enough of that.

Back inside, holding her phone clamped between her jaw and her shoulder, she clattered dry food into the dog's dish and ran water into his water bowl.

"Do you think Bobby did that?" She kept harping on that.

"There's no way to tell."

"You're well rid of him. Except you still have to work with him." She had never liked Bobby after the one time he picked Darla up from her mother's house and Moose was there. Moose growled when he walked in, but calmed down when Darla told him to. That was curious, that Moose had never liked Bobby. Darla's mother took her cue from the dog and had never had anything good to say about him.

"I do have to, Mom, you're right. But he can't do anything out of bounds while we're at work, in the hospital. Everyone is usually so busy, anyway. He is too. He's very good at his job."

"Well, let me know if anything else happens. I'll worry about you." She didn't sound very convinced.

"No, Mom, please don't worry. I'm fine at work and I won't see him outside work anymore."

"Can you block Bobby's phone number?"

Darla was proud of her mother for knowing about blocking numbers. Just a few of years ago she had learned, with difficulty, to operate a smart phone. "No, I can't. These calls aren't from Bobby's number. Every call has had a different number." That was something strange she had noticed. *How sophisticated was it to use all those different numbers? Did a person have to have multiple phones, or could they clone numbers? Make them up? Did that cost money?*

"Maybe Bobby will quit bothering you after a while. I can't imagine what he's getting out of it."

She really thought it was Bobby. "Mom, I don't know if it's him. It wasn't him who left the note."

"Note? What note?"

Damn! She'd said it. Now she would have to tell her mother about the note. And about the tire being deliberately cut, not just accidently flat. She knew she would anyway. Eventually. But she hadn't wanted to today. It was too fresh. Darla sat at the kitchen table to talk about it and plunged in. "When I left work, someone had cut one of my tires and that's why it was flat. And there was a note on the windshield."

"Oh, that kind of a note. At least it's a good thing. Someone offering to pay."

"No, that wasn't it! No one was being nice. They were being awful." Darla's voice was getting shaky. She was frightened all over again. Being pretty sure it wasn't Bobby was scarier than knowing it was. That left a gaping unknown before her. If it was Bobby, she'd know what she was dealing with and how to avoid him. All she had now was uncertainty.

"What did the note say, dear? Was it threatening?"

"I think so. It said, 'Knock. Knock. I know where you live.'" She could kick herself for blabbing about the note to her mother. The woman knew how to draw everything out of her. She always had.

Her mother gasped. "That sounds like something a serial killer would say."

Right, a serial killer was her first thought. In addition to watching judge shows, her mother watched and read a lot of true crime. She used to use the term "axe murderer" a lot, but maybe the shows she watched were concentrating on serial killers lately. "Or a creepy stalker," Darla said, to bring it down a notch. "It's not something Bobby would write and it's not his handwriting." As far as she could tell.

"Do be careful. Someone is out there."

Darla knew that. Someone *was* out there. But who was it? She wished her mother hadn't said the words "serial killer."

Chapter 4

Darla's Tuesday went much better than her Monday had gone, once she got to the hospital. On the drive there, scary scenarios kept running through her mind. The day was warm enough to crack her windows open, so she did that, and cranked up a local music station so drown out her thoughts. She also tried some deep breathing. She had to admit, calming exercises were easier to do in a quiet, stationary place, but her mind was stabilized, to use a medical term, by the time she got to work.

Things went well that morning. Bobby gave her solemn nods whenever their paths crossed in the hallways of the recovery unit. Even better, she didn't get any knock-knock hang-up calls all day.

She was still thinking about Gin and Bobby last night and how long it had taken for her to call and say she was okay. So, on her lunch break she called Gin. "You okay today? Was last night...was it okay?"

"Hey, you know I don't mind helping you out. It was no problem. If I get a flat tire, I expect you to be there for me."

"No, I meant driving Bobby back to the parking lot."

"Oh, sure. He didn't say much. I think he was pouting. He's kind of like a four-year-old, isn't he?"

"Maybe he is. I didn't realize until Sunday night."

"A good-looking four-year-old, though."

Ah, now they were getting around to what she wanted to talk to Gin about. "So, anything happen? Between you two?"

"You mean, am I going to dive in for your sloppy seconds? Not yet."

Darla laughed. But she sincerely hoped Gin wouldn't take up with him. That would be beyond awkward. Friends didn't date exes. Or anyway, they shouldn't.

"Why did you say that?" Gin asked.

"Well, it just...took so long."

"That's not my style and you know it. I got home and had a message from my brother so I talked to him for a while. Sorry I didn't rush to let you know."

That was a relief. She would quit worrying about that, at least. "I was just worried about you. And wondering if I know Bobby as well as I think I do. I hope your brother is doing okay."

Gin said he was and Darla hung up and got back to work.

Soon after she got home that night, her mother called again. It was not usual to get two calls in one day from her. Darla snatched her phone from her purse to see if something was wrong.

"Mom? What's going on?" She had just followed the dog into the yard, but soon felt a few raindrops on her face, and retreated to the doorway until Moose finished. He was done in record time.

"There's something I should tell you."

"About my stalker? Do you think it's my father?" She used to call the man "Dad," until she was finally able to stop thinking of him that way. Calling him "Father" wasn't something she liked to do either, but that's what he was. Going back inside, she got a cup of yogurt from the fridge, peeled the top off, and stuck a spoon into it. Moose stayed close in case she dripped some onto the floor. He was only mildly damp and she didn't think she needed to towel him off.

"Your father? Why would you think that? No, I doubt it."

"Okay. What then?" Moose shook off some raindrops from his thick coat and Darla covered her yogurt cup with her hand so it wouldn't get wet. Maybe she should have wiped him down.

"I was thinking of my first husband, Elliot." The one she never talked about. Darla knew his last name was Ryan, Elliot Ryan, and they'd been married for a few short years, but her mother had always been unwilling to tell Darla much of anything about him. She paused, standing in front of the sink with a spoonful of yogurt halfway to her mouth. Was she finally going to find out something about this mysterious man? They had married young. Darla always assumed it had been a mistake and they both realized it, because they soon parted ways. That was about all she knew.

"What about him?"

"Oh, nothing. Except..."

"Except?" A dollop of yogurt made it to the floor, briefly, before being consumed by Moose.

"I've never told you he got sent to prison."

"No, you certainly didn't tell me. Did you just find out?" She leaned farther over the sink for her next bite. Her mother was doing what Darla always did. She was spilling secrets. These were long-buried secrets, though. Prison? How bad was Elliot Ryan?

"No..."

"You've always known? You never told me?"

"He was sent there before I married your father. You didn't need to know that."

Darla swayed. Her knees felt weak. She pulled out a kitchen chair and plopped down. Telling everything had obviously been a one-way street between them all this time. Moose, sensing her distress, put his head in her lap and looked at her with his deep, soulful eyes. She rubbed behind his silky ears. What would she do without him?

"What happened between you, anyway? I always thought you were just married briefly, too young, then divorced. But he went to prison?" She had to find out everything. Most importantly, what did he go in for?

"There was a bit more to it than that. I was completely blind when I fell for Elliot. I didn't see him for who he was. At all."

It must run in the family. The very-married Zeke flashed across her mind. "Who was he? Who did he turn out to be?"

There was a pause and Darla gave her mother time to unburden herself. She had kept this secret for a long time. Maybe it would be a good thing to get this out into the open. Whatever it was.

"So, you think he's the one harassing me?"

"No, no. It's just...this has all made me think of him. He was a cruel man. Through and through. He was handsome, dark, dashing, but cruel."

"How long were you married? Not very long, right?"

"A little over a year. Just long enough to... He did drugs, drank too much, and...other things."

So, he had some things in common with her mother's second husband, Darla's father. He was a drinker, too, and abusive. What had she just said? Just long enough to...to what?

"I never even knew anything about him until just now." Darla set her spoon down in the sink, too absorbed to eat just now. She had to concentrate on every word her mother was telling her, after all these years. "You've never told me anything. And you just now thought of him?"

"After we separated, while I was waiting for the divorce to come through, this is the kind of thing he did to me. It made me think of him."

"He called with knock-knock jokes and hung up?"

"No, not that. We didn't have cell phones back then. But he did slash my tires one night. All four of them."

"Did you call the police on him?"

"I didn't, because I was afraid of what he would do to me."

"But you said he went to prison. What for?"

"Our sex was...not good. Very rough. I guess you'd call it rape today. Only in those days, women didn't get raped by their husbands."

"Of course, they did, Mom. They just didn't call it that. So that's what he was convicted of?" She hated her mother felt that way.

"In a way. He raped several other women."

Darla would have dropped into a chair if she hadn't already been sitting. Or onto the floor. Even seated, her knees got weak. "While you were married?" Her voice squeaked. Moose flinched at the sound as he finished the yogurt cup dangling in her hand.

"Yes." Her mother's voice had never been meeker, as far as she knew. She wished she were with her right now instead of on the phone. Her mother needed a good, long hug from her daughter. She stood to rinse the empty container and put it in the recycle bin.

"Oh, Mom. How terrible that must have been for you."

"It was. It really was. I had to testify. Being in the court room with him staring at me was one of the worst days of my life."

"Well, being raped must have been another one."

Another pause. "It wasn't just once. I have always dreaded the day he gets out."

"Does he know about me? Does he know you remarried and had a baby?"

"I haven't communicated with him at all, but I suppose he could find out. Everything's on the internet, isn't it?"

"What do you have online, Mom? Do you have a Facebook profile? Twitter account? Instagram?" She didn't think her mother dealt with online things past email. Was she wrong?

"He's in prison now. Do they have computers in prisons?"

"I don't know, but they might."

"I don't think I have those things you mentioned. I have email."

"Yes, I know you have that. If you don't know about them, you don't have those other things." Still, he could find out about her family if he tried, if he did have access to a computer. "Has he ever contacted you?"

"No, and I hope he doesn't. If he calls me, I'll hang up."

"What will you do if he comes to your door? Will you know when he gets out?"

"Oh dear. Do you think he would? I'd have to call nine-one-one. They will let me know when he's released. That's what I was told."

"You let me know the minute you hear. When is his sentence up?"

"Not yet, officially, but they sometimes get out early, someone told me. Or I saw it on television. Darla, I'm sorry to dump all of this on you right now when you're under so much stress. But I felt you had to know this is a possibility, if he's gotten out and I wasn't notified. I'm supposed to be told, but maybe I missed a phone call or something."

Darla told her mother to keep her cell phone charged and with her, which she didn't always do. After they hung up, Darla kept turning over this new information in her mind. Her mother had gone through so much. More than Darla ever knew about.

She rarely used sleep aids, but tonight she took a Benadryl. She made a mental note to check her mother's phone for messages the next time she was there. Without the antihistamine pill, she knew she'd be up all night worrying about her mother and the memories being dredged up. After watching television for a half hour, she felt herself loosening, conking out. That medicine was almost always a sure-fire sleep aid for her.

Before she lost consciousness on the couch, she made her way to the bedroom, Moose padding behind her. She fell asleep listening to her dog softly snoring, a light rain on the roof, and the wind picking up outside, whistling through her bedroom window, open just a crack.

Chapter 5

It was Wednesday, the day Darla had to tell her supervisor whether she was moving back to ER or not. When she awoke, she fought the fog from having taken the sleep aid and took a zombie shower. Then she went through the familiar motions of tending to Moose and getting down a few bites of breakfast cereal after she got dressed for work. As she was putting on her shoes, it came back to her. It hit her this was the deadline for her decision and she groaned, at first.

She figured she would have to decide by the end of the day, though, not right away, so she put her decision off and went about her work after she got to the hospital. At least her day was unhampered by hang up calls. She had expected some, so she kept her phone on mute at the beginning of her shift. When she checked it a few times, there had been no calls.

Her shift went by quickly and smoothly. Bobby nodded to her whenever they passed in the hallway, as he had done the day before. She even needed to call upon him for assistance with shifting a heavy-set preteen from the bed to a wheelchair for his trip home because she and the aide couldn't quite handle his weight. Everything was professional that day with Bobby, no problems, and Darla was relieved. Maybe she would be able to stay on this floor after all.

An hour before her shift ended, she was called to the nurse's station.

"Can you stay on?" Stacy asked. She told Darla her replacement on the next shift had just called in sick.

"That's awfully late notice," Darla said.

"Just, can you do it?" Stacy asked, worry making her plead. Darla could hear the distress in her voice. Poor Stacy. She had a tough job. "I called two nurses who are off today and neither one of them is even in town. I just now called another one and I think I can get her to come in late, but it would help out if you could stay an extra three hours or so."

Her shifts were long without being extended, twelve hours for three days in a row, normally. She would then get two or three days off. Sometimes four. She liked her hours. Since they varied, she could get lots done on her days off. But twelve hours was already a long day without another three hours. At least it wasn't going to be a double shift.

"I should be able to. Let me see if I can get someone to feed the dog." Poor Moose couldn't be expected to put in a fourteen- or fifteen-hour day, after all. She called Gin, who said she would go over right after she got off work at OTB, their name for Only The Best, Gin's company, the one that placed home healthcare workers for people in their own homes. She and Gin had had keys to each other's places ever since they *had* places.

After the extra-long workday was finally over, Darla dragged herself home, late at night. There had been no flat tires, no windshield notes. She pushed herself up out of her car and walked to the side door. She started to put her key in the lock, but the handle twisted before she turned the key. Gin must have forgotten to lock the door, she thought. She hurried in, out of the cold.

The dog whimpered, his tail between his legs.

"Moosie, what's wrong?" His food bowl was empty and his water bowl completely dry. Right now, he was huddled next to the back door. When she opened it, he was out like a shot to pee.

What had happened? Gin hadn't been there, that was clear. Darla looked at her phone, frowning, ready to call her. The phone had been off for work and there had been a call from Gin she hadn't heard. Darla swore softly and dialed immediately.

"Gin, you didn't make it?"

"I left a message. You didn't listen to it?"

"No, I just now got home and noticed the call. What happened?"

"I couldn't find your key. I looked all over and I still don't see it anywhere. I must have put it in an odd place."

Gin had not left the door unlocked. I must have left it unlocked. It wouldn't be the first time. She reminded herself that Charity was a safe town, as her mother always said. Darla ran water into Moose's bowl and poured out his food. He was already back at the door, ready to come in and chow down. "When's the last time you used it?"

"Ages ago. It was the day I came over while you were at your mom's and I snuck in and decorated for her surprise birthday party."

That had been a fun day. Darla had taken her mother out for dinner to celebrate. Then they had driven to Darla's to finish there with some friends and a big cake. "Yeah, that was months ago. I'll get you a new key when I can."

"Is Moosie okay? I was worried about him."

"He was ready for me to be here, but he's fine. He didn't even have an accident." He had been left too long a couple of times in the past and he had once left a puddle right next to the back door, poor thing. He must be old enough not to do that now. Still, it wasn't fair to him to make him go that long.

"That's good. I'm glad. So sorry about that. Give Moose a hug from me."

Darla was even gladder Moose had fared so well. It would have been her mess to clean up. "Sorry, Moosie." She rubbed behind his ears. "I won't do it again." He always got lots of hugs from her and from Gin, which he seemed to appreciate. She would get another key made for Gin tomorrow, her day off.

She decided to pay her bills since it was April 10th and she usually did them about every ten days. Gin always paid everything online and didn't get paper bills, but Darla was superstitious about trusting electronics for her utilities, things she had to pay. Maybe this came from the couple of times her e-mail did go astray in the past and she got angry letters from the water and gas companies threatening to cut her off.

After she walked outside to get her day's mail from the mailbox at the end of the driveway, she went to her desk in the living room to pick up the pile where she kept her bills. She always left the envelopes for the bills to be paid in a neat stack. There was no neat stack now. There was no stack at all. The bills and envelopes were scattered across her desk, some right side up, some upside down.

Could Moosie have disturbed her mail? Not likely.

She dropped into the desk chair, putting everything together in her mind. She shivered in fear at the thought that her door had not been locked. It hadn't been her who left it unlocked. Someone had been inside her house while she was at work.

After jumping up and standing frozen for a few moments, she raced through the house, looking for more disarray. And she found it. The cushions had been pulled off the couch onto the floor in the living room. One table lamp had been knocked to the floor, but not broken. In her bedroom, the covers were turned down, not neatly. Her pillow had been thrown onto the floor. The bathroom was the worst. Half a tube of toothpaste had been squirted onto the mirror and into the sink. It was possible, just barely, the dog could have done everything else, except unlock the door, but he could not have squeezed the toothpaste out of the tube and onto the mirror.

She kept searching for another half hour or so, but couldn't find anything else out of place. She didn't find anything missing. What had been the point of this?

Nothing was ruined or damaged, except part of a tube of toothpaste. But she had been violated nevertheless. Whoever had been in her house wanted her to know they'd been here. They wanted her scared.

Should she call the police? She was undecided. What could they do? There wasn't any theft or real damage. She wouldn't just get another key for Gin tomorrow, she would change her locks. Someone must have Gin's missing key. But she couldn't sleep here in peace, knowing someone had been here. She made up her mind to call the police.

"Nine one one. What's your emergency?" said the calm, reasonable voice.

Darla's was shaky. "Someone's been in my house."

"Where are you right now?"

The operator got her address and asked if she was sure no one was there now.

She was pretty sure, but did she know, absolutely? "Oh my god, no, I'm not. What should I do?"

"Please wait outside until the officers arrive. They should be there in a few minutes."

Darla leashed Moose and ran out to wait in the front, grabbing her purse on the way out, just in case someone was still there and might steal it.

Soon a Charity police car drove up, the letters CPD prominent on its door in stark black on white, and parked behind hers in the driveway. They hadn't used the siren or flashing lights. She was glad of that, not wanting to alert the whole neighborhood. The person in the passenger seat glanced up and nodded at her, standing there in the yard.

Two uniformed people got out, one man and one woman. The petite woman had bright red hair, lots of it, which made up for the tall thin man who had none.

They asked her what she had noticed, and she told them about the messes, and also mentioned she had been getting some harassment at work. She couldn't answer their questions about who she thought might be responsible for this, or for the problems at her work. One of them made notes, then they both went inside. She was glad she'd gotten the dog taken care of before she noticed anything. After what seemed like hours, but could have been fifteen or twenty minutes, the police came back out her front door.

"Did you find anything? Any fingerprints?"

"We've checked out the house," the man said. "There's no one inside. We checked around the outside, in the back yard, but no one is there either. Your doors and windows all seem secure."

"You're not taking fingerprints?" Darla asked.

"No, there's no point. There aren't any in the crucial places. Whoever was in your house likely wore gloves. You're lucky you weren't home when this happened," the woman said. She handed Darla a business card. "You should think about a security system. Camera, alarm, something like that. I see you have a deadbolt on your front door. Maybe put one on your back door, too. Call us if you notice anything else, anything missing or disturbed."

"Okay, I'll look into installing something. That's a good idea. Thanks." Darla was glad they hadn't used fingerprint powder. They had done that at the hospital once since she started working there, when drugs were missing, and it made a big mess that had to be cleaned up after they left.

She thought about staying at her mother's, but she didn't want her to know about this. It would only worry her. Gin's apartment didn't allow pets, so that wasn't an option. Knowing the intruder was gone, and making sure the house was locked up, she decided to stay home. It wasn't ideal, but it was so much easier than figuring something else out. And she was so tired. She was starting to wilt from fatigue. The long work day, then this, all the tension.

She not only put the deadbolt on in front, she also jammed chairs under the knobs of the back and side doors.

She didn't sleep well that night, tensing at each tiny noise from inside and outside the house. Even though Moose was there to protect her, she had a horrible dream. The kind she used to have, years ago. The fact she hadn't had this dream in a long time didn't, apparently, mean it was over and done with. If she could choose, she would certainly never have it again.

In the dream, a dark shape stood at the foot of her bed. She opened her eyes and tried to see the face, but the shape was inky and opaque. And terrifying. A frightening scream brought her wide awake.

It was her, screaming. There was no one in the room aside from a worried chocolate lab, putting his front paws on her bed so he could reach her to lick her face.

Eventually, she rolled over and tried to resume her slumber. Moose settled down on the floor next to her. But, for the rest of the night, what sleep she did get was restless. She was afraid the dream would come back if she fell sound asleep. That dreadful dream had once been common, probably three or four times a week. Then tapering to three or four a month. Then, finally, stopping.

In the morning, Darla was shaky in mind and body, her mind jumbled and her thinking slow. It had been a mistake to spend the night here, she could see that now. Gradually, as she ate breakfast and did some deep breathing, she calmed enough to tamp down, to bury, all but an innermost kernel of fear, leftover from the nightmare.

Before she called a locksmith to rekey her doors, she called Gin to set up a dinner date. She urgently wanted to talk to her. They ate together often on Darla's days off. Gin's work days with OTB were much shorter than hers were and her best friend was almost always available for going out, so their get-togethers had to hinge on Darla's erratic schedule.

Over the phone, Darla related the events of the night before, the disturbances and the summoning of the police, and their actions. She didn't mention her dream.

"What do you think happened? You think someone else has a key?"

"The police didn't think there was what they called a 'forced entry.' I don't know who would have my key, though."

"I can't find mine, like I told you. I must have lost it and someone found it. But how would they know it was to your house? This is crazy."

"The locks will be changed soon and I won't have to worry about it. I'm having them rekeyed. At least nothing was stolen. I can give you a new key when we meet," Darla said, after asking her if she was up for burgers after her shift.

"Oh, not tonight. You'll never guess why."

That wasn't hard to do. "You're dating someone again." Gin hadn't been seeing anyone for a few months. That was a long time for her to go without a new guy. She didn't have many dry spells.

"Bingo. You got it."

"Anyone I know?" Please, Darla prayed silently, don't let it be Bobby Abbot.

"No, I doubt it. How about tomorrow?"

"Sure, I'm off then, too."

"Okay, bye."

Darla looked at her phone, puzzled. That had been strange. She was expecting Gin to tell her all about the new guy. Especially since it was someone Darla didn't know. Gin went through men like candy and was always enthusiastic about the latest—overly enthusiastic. Usually, she would let Darla know why this new one was the ideal guy, the perfect man, and she would never need to date anyone else again. Sometimes Darla thought Gin expected too many roses and rainbows each time. She was always disappointed. So, what was different this time? Why didn't she want to go into ecstasies about her new guy? Maybe it *was* Bobby.

Her next disappointment was the only locksmith in town couldn't come out until the next day. He was having vehicle problems and needed his transmission worked on. Darla was glad she had a big dog in the house. Moose *was* big, too. He had weighed a little over ninety pounds the last time they'd gone to the vet. She was glad she never had to lift him. She was strong, but that was a lot of dog.

Darla had read a book on picking out a puppy before she went to see the litter her neighbor's dog had two years ago. The book said to pick the largest dog in the litter so you could be sure to get a healthy one. Moose was obviously the biggest, about half a puppy larger than the next biggest one. When she was given the material for Moose's registration papers, her neighbor told her Moose's sire had been a Grand Champion Something and had weighed over one hundred pounds. At least Moose hadn't gotten that big. Yet.

Over the next year, Darla realized that, when you pick the largest puppy, you get a large dog. But Moose was healthy, and had been since she'd had him. No problems there. Just problems with furniture being chewed and one favorite area rug being torn to shreds.

Moose was presently zonked out in front of the door she would need to use when she left the house. He did that a lot, and always when she was about to leave. Did he plop down there on purpose so she would have a harder time leaving? Sometimes she thought he read her mind. She gazed fondly at the huge dog, guarding the door.

Then it hit her.

Why hadn't she realized this right away? Moose had been in the house when the intruder had been there. He—Darla thought of the person as a man—had been all over the house. It didn't seem that Moose had bothered him at all. There was no blood anywhere, no chunks of flesh Moose bit off and discarded while the man fled in terror for his life. Darla was angry enough at her intruder she would like to have seen that. But those police officers would have found it if there had been. The bad guy had taken a leisurely stroll through her house, obviously.

She recalled what the trainer had said when she had taken Moose to puppy obedience classes through the community center. The woman had told Darla labs were friendly and not dangerous to have around, as a rule. They were safe with small children and other household pets. The only time they would likely attack would be if someone were trying to hurt her. That was a good thing, Darla and the instructor agreed.

She imagined the bad guy bending over and rubbing Moose's warm tummy, maybe tossing him a dog treat from the cupboard. The more she thought about it, the more she fumed. She stood motionless, in the middle of her kitchen, getting hotter and hotter.

She had to let off some of her steam, relieve some of this tension. Her tried-and-true method was archery. Her mother had been a competitive archer, had even traveled with a semi-professional group when Darla was a little girl. So naturally, Darla had taken it up as soon as she could. Her mother taught her the basics, and when she was a teenager with a driver's license, Darla found a range in Dayton and took actual lessons.

Now, she grabbed her kit, always kept by the back door, slung her quiver around her waist, and headed to the backyard. Moose didn't like that, because she always left him inside while she shot, to be sure she never hit him.

It wasn't marked, but she knew from years of experience what the distance was. She liked to use twenty yards, which fit into her back yard well, if she used the whole yard, from nearly at the house to the target at the back fence.

The ritual of this hobby usually soothed her. Today, after she checked out her stuffed burlap target set up in front of a stack of hay bales at the back of her lot, she strung the bow with a slight grunt, put on her glove and arm protector, and nocked an arrow. Her arms were strong from years of stringing bows and pulling them. Today, though, her arms felt like strands of spaghetti. Nerves, she knew. Taking a calming breath, she let the arrow fly. It didn't even hit a hay bale, let alone the target.

Steadying herself, she reached into the pouch for another arrow and tried again. And again. She couldn't seem to hit the target at all today. Slowly, still trying to calm herself, she walked to the target and picked up the stray arrows. Two had flown over the chain link fence at the back of her yard. She had had a gate installed for the purpose of retrieving her stray arrows. On advice from the man who worked on the gate, she had also put a padlock on it. She unlocked it now. Both arrows lay at the edge of the woods that stretched out behind her yard. As she bent to pick them up from the tall wet grass, an eerie feeling came over her.

The woods were dark and dense. She knew anyone could be hiding there. Her tormentor could be watching her. She shook droplets of dew from the feathers at the ends of the arrows and hurried back to the spot she had shot from, closing the gate, but leaving it unpadlocked, in case more arrows flew over the fence.

She took a few more shots, but didn't do any better. After locking the gate, she jammed her kit back in the carrying bag and stomped into the house, more keyed up than she had been before she started shooting. That had not been what she had intended.

Moose was happy to see her, anyway. He wiggled in excitement when she went back inside. After a cup of coffee, and the adoration of her dog, she felt her tension ease slightly. Looking at Moose, she realized she would have to go out today, although her locks would not have yet been changed. Her nemesis could get back in again and do more evil. She was low on a few groceries and nearly out of dog food. For herself, she could make do with whatever was stashed at the back of the freezer, but Moosie had to have his kibble. He couldn't make do. Well, he could, but it wasn't healthy for him to eat scraps of people food.

Darla decided to run out to grocery shop right then and get it over with. She would make her trip as quickly as she could, and would do it immediately. Otherwise, she would hesitate, hem and haw, and worry about it all day.

She dashed to the small market a few blocks away and plucked a few things off the shelves as fast as she could, wheeling the cart so quickly around the corners, she did one on two casters. That made her slow down to make sure she didn't hit anyone, but she didn't go too much slower. She had to get back as quickly as she could.

When she returned, she didn't immediately see any signs of disturbance. She carried her bags in and put everything away, then let Moose out for a luxury mid-day back yard excursion, the kind that was only possible on her non-work days. It started sprinkling after a few minutes, though, and they both ran back into the house. More April showers, Darla thought, hoping the daisies she had planted in her back garden would flourish in a few weeks. May flowers, she thought. That's what should happen, right?

he took the time to inspect the house further. The papers on her desk weren't disturbed this time. The couch cushions were on the couch and her bed wasn't mussed. The tension left her stomach and she relaxed a notch.

Since Gin had stood her up, Darla had decided to make herself a special meal. She had bought a beautiful pink piece of salmon and some fresh asparagus just now. She made a small bit of sauce with butter and lemon juice and poured it over the salmon, then sprinkled it with dill and wrapped it in foil. She had wanted to grill it in the backyard, along with the asparagus, but the rain, now a downpour, was preventing that. So, the salmon went into the oven and the asparagus was sautéed on the stove. It would still be delicious. Those were two of her favorite foods.

Dinner had been as good as she had thought it would be. Her mother called as she was finishing up.

Before she could think about it, Darla blurted out everything that had happened, that her house had been entered and vandalized the day before.

"Someone broke in? Were you home?"

"I wasn't home, but it wasn't a break in. I called the police and they looked everything over, but couldn't say anyone had actually broken in."

"Did you leave the door unlocked?"

"Well, maybe, or maybe someone had a key."

"I had to find out if anything happened today. You changed the locks, right?"

Now what? Why did she want to know that, before she knew about the break in? "No, I couldn't get that done today, but the house is fine. I went out to the store for a few minutes and it doesn't look like anyone was here while I was gone."

"I called because, well, you know, Darla, there's something else I should tell you. "

"What do you mean? What should you tell me?" The little bit of mellow she had built up eating her lovely dinner evaporated.

"It's about your dad. I was thinking about this and I realize I should have told you about his behavior after we broke up."

Darla knew her parents had split up because Todd Taylor, her father, was an alcoholic. She had vivid memories of him coming home late, stumbling, and falling. Crashing into lamps and breaking them. Sobering up for short periods of time. Then falling off the wagon and getting worse every time he fell. Eventually starting to get violent with his wife, behavior that escalated bit by bit over time. Always followed, eventually, with abject apologies when he sobered up and she forgave him. Until he pushed his wife down the stairs and injured her permanently.

"How could it be worse than when he lived with us?"

"Not worse, just.... Scarier. To me, anyway. He would stalk me. It reminds me a bit of what's happening to you."

Strange. Her own father wouldn't stalk her. Would he? "Why didn't you say something? You think my father is doing this to me?"

"No, no, I don't. Not really. But it's...similar behavior."

Her mother had sure been terrible at picking men. She went for a type. An abusive, alcoholic type. And a stalker type, too, apparently. Darla was silent, fuming about her mother not ever having told her this. But why was she telling her now?

Her mother continued. "I don't see any reason he would do this to you. I mean, he bothered me because he wanted me to take him back."

"After he partially paralyzed you? Really?"

"Todd didn't think straight when he was drinking."

Which, Darla was pretty sure, had been much of the time at the end of him living with them. "Do you even know where he is? Where he lives?" He hadn't been in their lives for at least five years. Darla assumed she would never see him again after he missed two of her birthdays and two Christmases. She had stopped expecting to see him and had, mostly, succeeded in putting him out of her mind. The only thing that mattered was the settlement he had been forced to pay his ex-wife to cover her care and living expenses for the rest of her life. The assumption must have been, Darla always thought, that her mother would live a long life, because the settlement was more than generous.

He had once made an extraordinary amount of money from a clever idea he managed to find backers for. The invention was still advertised heavily for Christmas and the holidays. The idea his company implemented was making personalized covers for robot vacuums. The customer would send in a picture and a cover would be designed based on the photograph. They were wildly popular and wildly expensive. When he was forced to sell the company to give the money to his ex-wife, Darla had been astonished at how much it sold for. And happy for her mother.

There was a hesitation. "I...I'm...not sure. No, no. I don't. I sure don't know where he is."

"Are you sure? Are you not telling me something else?"

"I have to go, dear."

Darla analyzed the conversation after they hung up. That last bit, she was pretty sure, wasn't one hundred percent true. All that hesitation was a good sign she was lying. She knew her mother pretty well, she thought. Darla would bet money, not a lot, but some, on her mother knowing exactly where Todd Taylor was. Darla had a vague idea where that was, even. In this town. Close enough to stalk her. But why?

Chapter 6

Darla had picked out a book, a light cozy mystery, from the shelf in her living room and started toward her bedroom to read herself to sleep when Gin phoned. "Is it too late to talk?" she asked.

"Almost, but not quite." She would have taken Gin's call even if she'd already fallen asleep. Which she hoped she'd be able to do tonight. "I'm heading toward bed. How was your date? Where did you go?" *And who was the guy?*

"I think I could really like this guy. We click. We really do."

"That's what you always say." Darla had to chuckle just a bit, because it was true, almost word for word. Gin clicked with every guy she dated. Until she didn't.

"He's different. Honest. He's, well, he's older than the guys I usually date."

"How is that better? Is he well off?" She walked into the bedroom, shadowed by Moose. Talking to her best friend was so normal, so far removed from the scary things happening to her, it felt wonderful.

Now Gin chuckled. "We haven't gotten that far yet. But he's mature. Seems stable. Settled."

"No signs? Like an expensive watch? Or car?"

"Not really."

"He's not married? For sure?" Gin had also encountered men who were lying to her and cheating on their spouses more than once. Or twice. They were a modern-day scourge.

"We haven't gotten that far, either, but I don't think he is. He works for my company."

So, not wealthy. "Where did you go?"

"Oh, Darla, we went to the place we first met, Axe Me. It's this bar-club-type thing, a place where people throw axes at target. With a bar."

"Axes? Are you serious? You met him there?"

"Yeah, I was picking up my dad. He's on a team there and I met him that night. We didn't do anything official, like for a team, we just did it for fun."

"Is it like target shooting? You throw the axe and aim for the center?"

"You don't aim for the center, exactly. You're supposed to hit all the rings in a certain order."

"That sounds complicated."

"Not too much, once you get the drift. I mean, not complicated to understand. It's hard to do. I can't do it at all, but it's just fun to try. This place is a restaurant and bar that has lanes in the back, kind of like short bowling lanes, but with walls between them."

"That's good. So, you don't kill each other with bad throws."

Gin laughed. "I know. I think I would do that if the walls weren't there. He's teaching me and I'm getting a little better."

This sounded like an unlikely hobby for Gin, but maybe the guy was worth it. "Well, I'm glad you had a good time. I hope this works out for you, Gin. I hope this is *the* guy." She and Gin always hoped this. It might happen someday.

Darla wondered if this new guy was assigned to take care of her mother on some of the days. Probably not. Her mother preferred women and usually asked the service to replace any men they sent. After all, the aides had to help her shower and dress and she was too modest to have a man do those things. Even past that, the modesty, she could be particular. Demanding. Even prickly and unreasonable at times.

"Thanks. About time, right?"

"What does he look like? Tall, short? Dark, handsome?" Darla set the book on her nightstand and went into her bathroom, to be ready to brush her teeth after she had hung up.

"He's kind of tall, not gigantic. He's got a fine body. And a good—"

Darla screamed, cutting her off.

"Darla? What's wrong? Darla? Are you hurt?"

She hadn't dropped the phone, but almost. Her hands were shaking. "I'm okay. It's just...someone's been in the house again." The empty toothpaste tube lay, flattened, beside the sink. This time the "someone" had written on the mirror in large letters, nearly covering it, with the toothpaste. Not just a smear, like the last time.

Knock Knock I am coming

The letters were crude and barely legible.

"Do you want me to come over?" Gin asked.

"I don't know. I think I'll call the police." She was whispering as she spoke to Gin and described what she was seeing.

"That's creepy. I'll be right there. Call the cops. Now."

Darla used the number on the card the policewoman had given her. The number rang a few times, then switched to another one.

"Officer Morgan's phone. Can I help you?"

"She gave me her card last night. I had a break in, and I have another one tonight."

She gave the person on the phone her address and they quickly looked up her case. "Please wait outside while I send a detective. It won't take long."

Again, she leashed Moose and sat on her front steps. Darla gazed around at her front yard, the street, the neighboring houses. It had stopped raining, she was glad to see. If there'd been any wind, she and the dog might've gotten wet sitting on the porch.

There was a row of bushes, large box elders the size of small trees, between her house and the one to her left. A streetlight just beyond them threw eerie shadows across her own lawn. Moose sat beside her, calmly and obediently, his gaze intent on the bushes. Darla stared at them too. *Why was he concentrating on them? A person could easily hide in there.* A slight damp breeze wafted across the yard. She peered at the box elders as intently as Moose was, aware of the movement of each leaf, expecting someone to leap out at any moment. It felt as if it were taking hours for the police to respond. At last, a car came down the street.

This time a plain car and a plainclothes detective arrived, male and Black. It seemed she'd been upgraded to getting a detective working on her case.

"Detective Coleman," the man said, shaking her hand. He was a large man with a firm handshake. He didn't seem much older than her. She felt good that he was here to help. "I read over the report from last night real quick before I came. Can you fill me in on what happened today?"

"Well, I guess I had another break in, and I think it must be the same person."

"Why do you think it's a break in? I thought there wasn't any forced entry the other time, according to the report."

"Oh, I guess not really a break in, then, right? Well, last night the person squeezed out half my tube of toothpaste. Tonight...no, not tonight. They must have come in while I was gone this morning."

Another car parked behind his.

"You brought more people?" Darla asked.

"That's Crime Scene," Detective Coleman said. "CSI."

The official Crime Scene unit had arrived even before the detective went inside. They were getting more serious about her troubles. She wondered if they would be able to find incriminating fingerprints this time. At least they were looking for some with Crime Scene people, unlike the patrol officers from last time.

"What time did this happen?" The man whipped out a small notebook

"I think nine, or nine-thirty this morning. I got back before ten-thirty."

"Are you sure you locked your doors before you left?" He was a large man and his presence was comforting, calming, especially with his rumbling, soothing low voice.

"Yes, I'm...almost certain." She closed her eyes and pictured returning. She had used her key to get in. "Yes, yes, I did. I had to unlock it when I came home."

The look on his face as he wrote down her words said he wasn't convinced. The intruder could have locked it, she supposed.

"Anything else you can tell me?"

"That's all I've seen. But this time there was writing. On the bathroom mirror. With the toothpaste. Last time the toothpaste was just smeared on the mirror." Darla shivered, recalling the ominous message. She quickly told him about the phone calls and the note with her slashed tire, all of them repeating the words that were becoming threatening to her: *knock, knock.*

He wrote it all down, telling her to hold up a couple of times while his writing kept up with her narration. "I'll make sure the house is clear. This evidence is in the bathroom, right?"

He got directions to the bathroom, put on shoe coverings and gloves, and entered the house with the team of two from Crime Scene.

She waited some more with Moose. He chose that moment to take a dump in the wet grass of the front yard. Of course. She didn't have any bags with her. She'd have to remember to pick it up later.

Gin arrived while the team was still in the house. It was well after midnight by this time. The two friends hugged, Darla with desperate intensity. Gin squeaked under the pressure.

"Whoa, girl. I might need those lungs for something. Like, maybe, breathing." Gin gave her one last squeeze. Then she stooped to brush a few stray leaves and pieces of grass off the concrete and sat on the front steps beside her. She was still dressed in nice slacks from her date. "What on earth is going on?" She gave Moose a few strokes and he licked her hand in thanks. "I made a stop on the way here." She held up the bottle of wine she had brought, and the corkscrew and two plastic glasses.

"You thought of everything, Gin."

Gin opened the bottle and poured a bit into each glass. "To no more intruders." She raised her plastic glass and bumped Darla's.

"Yes, to that!" She took a sip and set the cup down. "They're taking me more seriously than they did last night. They sent a detective and some official fingerprint people—I guess that's what they are—and they've been in there forever. Last time the uniform police didn't think they should look very hard for fingerprints. I don't know why. They told me they thought the intruder probably wore gloves."

"That's crazy. They don't know that."

Darla nodded. "I don't know. That's what they said, though."

"You're getting the locks changed tomorrow?"

"Yes, he said he'll be here early. Figures, since I'd like to sleep in after two late nights."

"No, you wouldn't. You won't feel safe here until you get new locks and keys."

Darla had to agree with that. They both sipped the wine. Darla sipped, anyway. Gin was on her second glass. Darla figured she had warmed up on her date. Gin's breath had not been pristine when she arrived at the house just now.

Darla looked around the yard, wary. The bushes moved again. "Do you see someone there?" she asked, pointing to them. She was too weary to walk over there with Moose and find out what was there. If it was a night creature, Moose would be delighted. The wine was helping taking her tension away.

Gin squinted and considered them with her head tilted. "I don't think so. It's supposed to start getting windy tonight. We're in for some real storms tomorrow. Or maybe the next day. I forget which." She looked at Darla. "Are you imagining things? I do that when I'm scared sometimes."

Before Darla could deny imagining things, or ask Gin what she was scared of, the three men came out of the house. Two of them nodded at her in passing, stripped off some of their protective gear, got into the CSI car, and drove away.

Detective Coleman stayed on the porch, then motioned them both inside, stripping off his gloves and pocketing them. Darla gladly came in, away from the dark, spooky front yard. Her relief was short lived. The inside of her house was a bit spooky right now, with a lot of the surfaces covered by fingerprint powder.

After the detective found out who Gin was, noting her name and information in his notebook, he had Darla go over her timeline again as he checked his notes. "I'm sorry for the print dust. It should wipe off pretty easily."

"I'm grateful you took so many prints," Gin said. "She needs to find out who this is." She gestured around the room with her glass, not spilling any by some miracle. Darla was more and more aware this wasn't the first bottle of wine she'd drunk from tonight. Maybe she needed to have a talk with Gin. Maybe this new guy was not a good influence.

The detective shook his head. "I'm afraid we didn't get much evidence. All the doorknobs are wiped clean."

"How about the toothpaste tube?' Darla asked.

"That, too. Although they think they might have some partials that were missed on bottom end of the tube and on the mirror before. Can you come to the station so we can get yours for elimination? I don't have a kit with me."

"Now?" Darla was pretty sure she was going to fall in a heap if she didn't get to bed soon. Even Moose had yawned a couple of times.

"No, tomorrow is fine. Any time. Whenever you get there." He handed her a card. "Here's my number at the department."

Turning to Gin, he asked, "Are your prints likely to be here, too?"

"I'm sure they are. Unless they were cleaned up by this guy. So, I should come in to the station, too?"

He nodded. "Please."

"I have to work tomorrow."

"Whenever you can. No rush. Just within a few days."

He asked Darla who else would have left prints in her house. It gave her pause to realize not many people ever came into her place.

She gave them Bobby's name, since some of his might still be there. She couldn't think of anyone who had been inside her house recently. Zeke seemed so long ago. Maybe she should be more social. She was happy being alone with just Moose for company most of the time, though.

Her fling, if that's what it was, with Bobby Abbott had been brief. For the last ten years of her life, since high school, when she mostly ran around with a group, she had been without a boyfriend more often than with one. She had read it was healthy to be satisfied with your own company. But after being satisfied for a few weeks after a breakup, it always felt more like loneliness than satisfaction. Right now, though, she was in the relieved-it's-over stage, so that was a satisfied one.

"I know this is silly," she said to the detective. "But would you mind looking in those big bushes in the front yard? I'm feeling really spooked."

He smiled. Was he laughing at her insecurity? "No problem."

She walked out and watched him go over to the bushes from the porch. He rustled the branches and went the length of the row of bushes, chopping at them. With his dark skin and his dark clothing, he was almost hard to see. He didn't use a flashlight, she noticed. Should she offer him one?

"Nothing here."

"Thanks," she called. He had thrashed the bushes pretty thoroughly. There was no one there.

He came back to the step. "Feel better?" This smile looked warm. And friendly.

"Much."

Chapter 7

B ut after she'd been in the house with Gin for a bit, Darla asked her to come back outside with her. She had to examine those bushes for herself, to see if there was any sign someone had been there. The detective had looked in the branches and there was no one there at that time, but maybe someone had been there earlier. She grabbed her bright mag light from the kitchen drawer and they both went out, accompanied by the dog.

A cricket in the box elders ceased rasping as they approached. Gin, holding the light because Darla was holding the dog, shone the light into the bushes.

"Wait," Darla said. "Shine it on the ground. See if there are any footprints."

"Good idea." Gin moved the light methodically back and forth next to the bushes, then inside them, between the stalks. Dew began to fall and Darla could feel her hair getting damp. The air was heavy. The cricket had moved on and chirped from farther away. Or maybe it was a different cricket, working in relay, taking over for the one they had frightened in to silence.

Finding nothing, they gave up after ten minutes or so and went inside.

They were met with the sight of dust from the crime scene unit on nearly every surface. At first Darla frowned, thinking about the clean-up, but then realized she should be grateful the police were being so thorough. And she had to be hopeful some useable evidence would turn up. After Gin and Darla cleaned up most of the fingerprint powder, it began to feel like a pajama party. The wine helped contribute to that festive feeling, in spite of the circumstances. Darla suspected she'd be finding the powder in obscure places for days to come. It wasn't sticky or gooey, but it was there.

They soon got into gossip mode and talked a bit about mutual acquaintances, then Darla tried to find out more about Gin's older man. Darla was on her second glass, but Gin had emptied most of the rest of the bottle.

"So, how much older is he?"

"Oh, not that much. I think maybe eight or ten years. Or twelve. I haven't asked him how old he is."

That seemed like plenty to Darla. Especially if he was twelve years older. "Is he from Charity?"

"I'm not sure. Maybe he used to live here, but I don't think he has for a while. He didn't know about the new hospital wing."

"Does he have a name?"

"No, no name." Gin laughed. "Yes, silly, he has a name. Ned. Ned Farley. Are you going to look him up?"

"Should I?"

Gin laughed. "I already did. You should know that."

She did know that. Gin had gotten in the habit, after a few failures that bordered on disaster, of checking out the men she auditioned regularly for husband material.

"What did you find?" Darla asked.

"Not much. I mean, really, hardly anything. Most of what I find under that name is obviously not for him. There are a lot of men with that name, and none of them are him. He's totally clean."

"Maybe Ned is a nickname."

"I didn't think of that. Edward?"

"Edgar, Edwin. Probably a few things. Or maybe it's a middle name he uses for a first name."

Gin pondered. "Well, that makes it hard. I'll just have to search some more. I'll try it every which way."

"I'll do some searching too. What are friends for? I mean, no one has absolutely nothing on the internet. Something has to be there, somewhere. What about his family?"

"He says he doesn't have any. His parents are dead and his doesn't have any brothers or sisters."

This wasn't sounding good. *Was he hiding? Hiding from Gin? Or from someone else?*

"Gin, do you think he has my key?"

"Why would he have your key?" Gin looked at Darla like she thought she was nuts.

"Well, it's missing. And someone is..."

"Yeah, someone is a creep. It's not Ned."

Gin was annoyed, so Darla didn't mention Gin's missing key again.

Eventually, they headed for the bedroom. "Do you think you'll keep going axe throwing?" Darla asked.

"Sure, he likes it and so do I."

After they got under the covers, Gin fell asleep immediately, snoring softly. Darla, alert and spooked by every sound, lay beside her, wide awake. Darla thought about the "clean" internet searches. It was more than likely this Ned Farley was trying to hide something since there was nothing about him anywhere. Was he that guy who wormed his way into a woman's life and made off with her money, credit cards, personal ID? Darla's house key?

Moose set up a racket just as Darla was beginning to fall asleep a couple of hours later. She and Gin both jumped out of bed and followed him to the front door where the big dog stood growling and snarling.

Darla reached for the doorknob, but Gin stopped her. Gin had sobered up quickly for this latest alarm.

"Don't go out there. Call the cops," Gin said.

Darla dashed back to the bedroom, found the card for the detective, and called. She started to tell them who she was and the background of everything that had happened to her, but dispatcher already knew. Darla told them that now her dog was agitated by someone outside.

She hung up, as some of her tension started to dissipate. "They're sending someone right away," she told Gin. That was a relief. But it would take them a few minutes to get here. Would someone hang around long, with a dog barking, alerting everyone to his presence? It was unlikely he would be caught tonight.

Within a few minutes they both heard a car pull up. Maybe it was the police already. Maybe, if someone was lurking, the approaching police car, without lights or siren, wouldn't scare them off. She wanted the person to be caught.

When she heard car doors slamming, Darla cracked the door open to see two uniformed policemen walking through her yard with flashlights, shining them into the box elder bushes and into every other corner. One of them disappeared around the back and Darla opened the door and stepped out onto the porch.

Into a pile of fresh dog shit. She muffled a shriek.

The police in the front yard looked up, then kept sweeping the yard and the growth.

Gin peered over her shoulder and gave her a horrified look when she saw it.

At least Darla was barefoot, so her slippers didn't get dirty with it. "I bet that's the pile Moose did in the front yard today. I didn't clean it up because the crime scene people were in the house and I forgot about it later."

"Over here," Gin called, to show the police officer what had happened.

The taller one ran over. He shook his head and snapped a picture of it with his phone.

"It's mine," Darla said. "I mean, it's from my dog. I forgot to clean it up."

"And this is where your dog did it?" the shorter one said, having returned from the small back yard.

"No, no, he did it way out there." She pointed to the far side of the yard. "Someone put this here."

They both nodded their heads. "So, your dog barked at the person who did this? The one who moved it and put it here? Is that what you think?"

That's exactly what Darla thought, when they put it that way. They took very short statements from both women.

"Can you stay while we clean this up?" Gin asked.

They agreed to do that.

Darla groaned inwardly. She had been thinking of leaving it until the morning. Which was in a very few hours now. Gin ran inside and returned with a roll of paper towels, a large plastic bag, and a glassful of water. She did all the cleanup, including wiping Darla's foot so thoroughly Darla knew she would be able to walk back inside on two feet to use soap and water in the bathtub, instead of hopping on one foot, which she had been envisioning.

The two women closed the front door on the receding red tail lights as the police cruiser left.

"The dog poop didn't say 'knock knock' anyway," Darla said. Maybe the stalker had actually knocked this time. If so, she hadn't heard him.

"I don't see how anyone could do that. They'd need a lot more poop. They ought to post a guard on you." Gin frowned. "I'm scared about all of this."

"He's long gone.," Darla hoped it was true.

After Gin fell back asleep, Darla remained awake.

About a half an hour later, she saw a light on her ceiling. It went out, then back on for a second, then off, then on for longer. After a few seconds, the pattern repeated. A long beam, a short, then another long. She grabbed her cell phone from the night stand and looked up Morse code. Sure enough, her tormentor was flashing the letter K on her ceiling. He was far enough away Moose didn't wake up. After four repetitions, the lights stopped.

Her first impulse, after the initial flash, was to call the police again. But what could they do? They wouldn't catch him. What he was doing wasn't even leaving any traces. Unfortunately, she hadn't thought of taking a video of the bizarre display until after it stopped. She could kick herself for that. This was assault. She needed to be more alert, think on her feet, think faster.

She lay awake the rest of the night.

Gin left for work while Darla was still in bed. It was another day off for Darla Though she wasn't sleeping, she didn't have the energy to get out of bed. She would have to get up soon, though, since the locksmith was coming at nine. The man who was coming owned a shop his parents had owned before him, so Darla had known his family for years. In fact, their parents had been friends and played golf together. When he arrived, he and Moose greeted each other like old friends, also he had never met the dog.

He rekeyed her locks quickly, adding a deadbolt for the back door, and asked how many keys she would need.

A distant rumble of thunder made Darla glance out the window, but the sun was still shining on the front lawn. It would probably rain later, she thought.

"Three, I guess. Well, how about four? In case one gets lost." She would give one of the new ones to Gin and hope she didn't lose it again. She and her mother had keys to each other's places, but her mother would never be able to get to Darla's place on her own, so she didn't know why she did that. Her mother had asked and liked to have one, so Darla had given her one. She would make sure she had a new one, too.

"No problem." He filed the keys for her, tested them in the lock, and was soon finished. He gave the dog a goodbye scratch behind the ears and drove away.

The house was empty again. That made Darla slightly queasy, though she knew no one else was inside. She poured herself a second cup of coffee and took it to her comfortingly private backyard, letting Moose root around, patrol the fence and explore the one large tree and the few small bushes next to the fence.

She was glad she had thought to come outside with her coffee. The terror of the night seemed more remote now. Here, it was so peaceful. So quiet. There were four different kinds of birds chirping their small hearts out in the trees in her yard and her neighbors' yards. The thunder had stopped and wasn't bothering the wildlife at all.

After casting a glance at the fence and the small shrubs at the edges of her property, even though no one could hide in them, she closed her eyes and willed herself to relax. Maybe the worst was over. No one could get inside again and she wouldn't leave Moose's dog poo in the yard, front or back. Her tires could be punctured and flattened again, but he had already tried that. It had only happened once. Maybe he wouldn't repeat it.

Her phone rang, jangling her out of her reverie. The caller ID said it was Gin's older brother, Keith. She wondered why he would be calling her. They knew each other, of course, but never did things together and hardly ever called each other. Hardly ever spoke to each other, actually. And their social circles had never overlapped or interacted. She didn't dislike him. They just didn't socialize.

Keith was a much different person than his sister. Gin was petite, dark, shapely, and lively. Keith took after his accountant father. He was tall and thin, light complexioned, and bookish. They each took after one of the parents, who were as mismatched as the brother and sister. He had worn thick glasses since he was a child and now taught Economics at the Charity Junior College.

"Hey Keith. What's up? Everything okay?"

"Hi Darla. You doing all right? Gin told me what you've been going through."

"I think so. Having her stay here last night helped a lot."

"Let me know if you need anything. Look, I called to talk to you about Gin. About this guy she met at the axe throwing bar."

"She told me about that. I can't picture Gin hurling hatchets for fun, but she seems to like it. She said the place is called Axe Me? That's kind of funny."

"Yeah, you've probably seen it. It's the bar on Dayton Street. Used to be Bill's or Ed's or something. They renamed it when they put those throwing lanes in. She met this guy through our father. They've been throwing on a team together since Ned came to town. Gin got him his job."

"How long ago was that?"

"A few months. Not that long ago. I'm concerned."

"You know, Keith, she's told me next to nothing about him. It was like washing a herd of cats to get her to tell me anything. Have you met him?"

"I did. Once. For about five minutes. But I feel like she's keeping him away from me."

"Same here. I mean, I haven't met him at all and I wonder if I ever will. She did say she likes him an awful lot. But I can't get her to say much about him."

"Maybe because he's a friend of our dad," Keith said.

"Oh, maybe." Darla shivered at the thought. "I see why you're concerned."

Gin and Keith's dad had an unfortunate recent past. He had been an accountant for a non-profit called OASIS—Our Arts In Smithton, benefiting a small art gallery in a nearby town. The job didn't pay well, but the family had collected quite a bit on their mother's life insurance after she was struck and killed by a drunk driver. Their father, Gary Holland, had been an insurance salesman before the accident, so the family was well supplied with life insurance.

The most unfortunate part of Gary Holland's past, though, beyond losing his wife tragically when she was much too young, was what happened a few years after that. Gin and Darla had talked about it from every angle they could think of. Yes, his job didn't pay much. But the insurance money was plenty to live on. Yes, Gary was depressed, but did you commit crimes because you're depressed? Yes, he was angry. And that might have been what happened. He was angry at the world and felt it owned him something. He apparently felt the world owed him money from the bank account of OASIS, the non-profit group. By the time he was found out, he had been skimming for a few years, so he had raked off a substantial amount of money, nearly a million dollars.

People were astounded to know the group had that much to steal. People were also angry, at least as angry as the man who stole the money. His prison term had been seven years. After he got out, he tried working at several jobs, but none lasted long. Keith and Gin gave him money when he needed it and he seemed to get by. He seemed to love to go to the axe throwing bar and, fortunately, it was a hobby that didn't cost much. Keith and Gin even bought him an axe so he wouldn't have to rent one. Darla suspected Gary Holland might get be getting rid of some of his hostile tendencies doing that, so maybe it was a good hobby for him.

"Do you think Ned is the age of your father?" Darla asked.

"He didn't seem that old. Older than me, and older than you and Gin."

"So, there's not an obvious reason why she's keeping him such a secret. He doesn't have two heads or three legs, does he?"

Keith laughed. "No obvious physical defects. He seemed normally shaped when I met him, but it's hard to size up a person in five minutes. I just wanted to let you know how she met him, in case that means anything."

After they hung up, Darla pondered one obvious unspoken reason Gin might be reluctant to let her brother and her best friend talk to Ned for long. Simply put, Ned knew their father. How did he know him? Where had they met? At Axe Me, the hatchet throwing bar? Or maybe in prison? Darla was sure that was Keith's concern and now it became hers, too. Darla thought maybe she should try doing it, axe throwing, and get to know what kind of people hung out there.

She searched the internet for his name, but didn't find much at all. Why was that? It was too suspicious.

Chapter 8

Darla headed to the police station by eleven to give her statement about the events of last night. It was a simple procedure. She told a person at a desk what had happened, the series of events: the toothpaste with the message, and then the dog poop later. When she explained the "knock, knock" message had been used a few times already, that wasn't noted.

"Don't you think it's important this person is terrorizing me with this?"

The man squinted at her. "It doesn't sound like terrorism. It's not threatening. Saying he knows where you live—that's not threatening."

"And also, 'I'm coming.'"

"Yes, I guess that might be, a little. No real threats. Kind of vague. More of a nuisance, don't you think?"

No, she didn't think that. "But I'm frightened." Her voice rose in anger. "I'm being terrorized. Targeted. Shouldn't I get some police protection?"

"Ma'am, this is a small department. We can't really do that. But I'd be on your guard. Keep everything locked up."

She didn't even bother to mention the flashing lights on her ceiling after the team left. What good would that do?

She drove home frustrated thinking about what she could do. She didn't have a security camera, but maybe some of her neighbors did. Or maybe they had seen something. She drew into her driveway, determined to do something.

Leaving the dog in her house, she knocked on the door of her next-door neighbor, the one on the other side of the box elder bushes. The woman, Mrs. Silverson, answered the door. She and her husband were both in their sixties. She knew he worked retail somewhere, maybe in Dayton, Monday through Friday, but his wife was usually home. She baked a lot and sometimes brought things over to Darla.

"Hi, Mrs. Silverson. Could I ask you a couple of questions?"

She gave Darla a suspicious look. "Are you selling something, dear?"

"No, no, I wouldn't do that to you. It's just that…I've been having some trouble and wonder if you've seen anything at my house. Someone sneaking around."

Mrs. Silverson cocked her head in thought. "You know, we did. Last night." She emphasized this statement with her pointer finger.

"You did? You saw someone? In those bushes?" Darla pointed to the large box elders.

"Yes, right there. We couldn't see who it was, but someone was out there with a flashlight. That was after the police left."

Oh, she had just seen her and Gin. "Did you see anyone before that? Someone sneaking onto my porch?"

"No, we had gone to bed, then we heard the first set of police come. Then we noticed the lights in the bushes later. Then we woke up in the middle of the night when the second one came. They slammed the doors really loudly. Ivan got up to look and he was surprised to see the police car. What's happening over there, dear?"

"I've been having some trouble. Someone is bothering me, slashing my tires, putting dog poop on my porch, and they were even inside my house yesterday. You don't have any security cameras, do you?"

"We've never needed them in this neighborhood. Who do you think it is? Do you have a jealous ex-boyfriend?"

Darla shook her head. "I'm not sure. I do have an ex, but I don't know it's him."

The woman would have told her if she'd seen someone flashing lights into Darla's window later, but asked anyway. No, she hadn't seen any lights flashing. She left with Mrs. Silverson wishing her well and telling her to be careful. As if she wouldn't do that!

Next, she went to the neighbors on the other side of her house. They were a family with a younger girl and two teen-aged boys. Teen-aged or near that, as far as Darla could tell. She couldn't tell how old kids were. She could barely tell how old adults were most of the time.

The parents were both at work and two of the children at school. One boy was home alone, though. She suspected he had pleaded sick, but seemed to be happily playing video games, judging from the console noises which came from the front hall when he asked her in. He certainly didn't look sick. He wasn't the first kid to play hooky, play sick, or play video games all day.

She didn't know if he was Matthew or Michael. They were both about the same age and size. The younger girl was named Mia. It amused her the family had gotten stuck on M names.

"What did you want, Ms. Taylor?" He was being super polite. Maybe to make up for some of the minor vandalism he and his brother occasionally did around the neighborhood. It was never anything serious, or destructive. But they sometimes did things like TPing at Halloween, loud firecrackers on the Fourth, denting a few mailboxes with drive-by baseball bat swats. Hers had a small dimple from that pastime. Okay, that was slightly destructive. Their father had offered to replace hers, but she didn't think it was necessary. The mailbox still worked, after all.

"I'd like to ask you a couple of questions, okay?"

He shrugged and resumed his seat on the couch, picking up his game controller, but not operating it yet.

"Did you see anyone lurking around my house last night?"

That got his attention. He looked at her with interest. "Like, who? A cat burglar? A robber?"

"Someone broke into my house and disturbed some things."

His eyes got wider. "Like, leaving a dead animal? Painting on the wall with blood?"

Her intruder was no match for this kid's imagination. Thank goodness. "Not quite. Just minor things, but I could tell someone had been inside. I just wonder if you saw anyone?"

"When was it?"

"Actually, the first break-in was day before yesterday, Wednesday, in the evening."

"I was at football practice that day for a while. Didn't see anybody."

"Did you go to school yesterday?"

"Yep. Just sick today."

He would not have seen the daytime break in yesterday then. She had no way of knowing when the intruder was in her house during the day yesterday. "How about late last night, around three in the morning?"

"You've had a lot of this? I might have heard your dog. He doesn't usually bark in the middle of the night. But I didn't get up. Didn't see anything."

"And later on? Anything?"

"Nope. I was probably asleep."

She asked about cameras, but they didn't have any either. She thanked Matthew, or Michael, and left. She would go to the houses of the other neighbors when they were more likely to be home. In the middle of the day, most people were at work. Tomorrow was Saturday and that would be a better time.

Walking home, she was brought back to the phone conversation with Gin's brother Keith. Gin's new mystery boyfriend met her father before he met her. Ex-cons? Maybe they had served time together? At least he didn't seem to be as old as her father, according to Keith.

Walking into the house, she decided, on an impulse, to visit that place, Axe Me, this minute, and find out something about the sport Gin had taken up with this guy. Sport? Hobby? Game? She would see. It was something she knew nothing about.

In the car, she keyed in the name of the place and the address popped up on Dayton Street, just as Keith had said. There was a parking lot beside it with several empty spaces, so she parked and walked in. Like most bars, it was dark inside, even in the daytime. There were four or five tables along one wall, so she thought they must serve some food, too. The sign outside did call it the Axe Me Bar and Grill. She soon spotted the sign over a door in the back that said, "Throwing Club." Over the sounds of talk, some laughter, and glasses and bottles being set down, she heard some dull thunks from that area in the back. So that's where she headed.

Just inside the swinging door she pushed through was a stand, manned by a young bearded guy. Prices for rentals and times were on a sign behind him. Compared to the bar, this place was brightly lit. She could clearly see the lanes, only a half a dozen of them in the small space, and people occupying four of them. They were all young, men and women both, and the ones not throwing were generally clutching a beer. Darla wondered how safe it was. Drinking and throwing sharp objects.

She also wondered if she could do this alone, or if that would look strange. These people were all in groups, or at least couples.

"You wanna get some practice in?" the young man asked.

Since he asked, maybe it wasn't strange to be here alone. Maybe she would pretend she was doing just that, getting in some practice for, say, her team. Or something. He seemed to expect that.

"I'm sort of a beginner," she said in a gross understatement. "I haven't done this for a long time. Could you show me the basics?" The thunking sounds were a bit louder here, and the conversation a notch or two higher in volume than in the bar. Maybe that's because of the young age of most of the throwers here. Or the fact so many were holding those beers. The atmosphere was festive, it felt.

He said, sure, he could show her. He took her money for renting a hatchet, as he called it, and a fee for the lane. She followed him to an empty wood-lined lane on the end, where he stepped up to a mark on the floor and proceeded to demonstrate two ways to throw. Throwing with one hand, he brought the axe back over his shoulder and flung it, embedding the blade in the outer ring of the target. He retrieved it and walked back to her.

"That's the way most people do it. Or you can do it this way." He lifted it over his head with two hands and, hurling it just as hard as before, hit the target on the other side. "This way is better for beginners. Easier to aim, I think. You wanna try?"

Darla suddenly got nervous. What was she doing here? She had no idea how to do this. But it did look kind of fun. Taking a calming breath, she nodded and took the axe he was handing her, the one she had rented.

"Do you think I should do one-handed or two-handed?"

"Maybe two hands."

Yes, he had said, just now, that was the way a beginner should do it. Okay. One more deep breath. She gripped the handle like a baseball bat and brought it over her head. It was heavier than it looked. She threw it hard. To her surprise, it made it all the way, but the blade bounced off the wall and fell onto the floor.

"I'll let you practice for a bit. Your time is up in an hour."

After about twenty more throws, and not a single target hit, Darla decided she didn't want to stay for an hour. She picked a time when the guy wasn't at the stand, maybe taking a break somewhere, slipped the axe onto the counter, and slunk out. This was not the sport for her. Gin could have it.

She wished she could have worked in a way to talk about Gin's father and her boyfriend, the opportunity hadn't come up. The only person she had spoken to was the guy who took her money and showed her how to throw.

She played with Moose when she got home to try to take her mind off everything. Axe throwing and how not fun it was. Gin and Ned. And Gin's father. And her stalker. Whom none of her close neighbors had ever seen.

Moose was acting so cute, performing all his tricks. Darla dutifully rewarded him for them. He ran through the list. Sitting up, rolling over, shaking, begging on his hind legs. She reached into the box for another treat for that last trick, her favorite, and reached the bottom of the box.

"Oh no, Moosie! We're out of treats. You want a car ride?"

She patted her thighs with an excited look on her face, and he picked up on it. Yes, he did want a car ride. He almost always did.

She decided she would drive to the pet store, where he was welcome to walk the aisles with her, and she would buy him some more treats. He hadn't been in the car for a few days and he loved riding. She tried to give him frequent car rides to nice places—the pet store and the park—so the infrequent trips to the not-nice place, the vet's, wouldn't be such a trauma for both of them. She wanted him to keep loving the car.

Her house should be safe while she was gone, with the locks changed now.

Moose perked up at the words "car ride" and her antics and pranced impatiently while she got his leash off the hook and around his neck.

Outside, Darla approached her car, inspecting it with trepidation, grateful that it didn't list to one side, which would be the sign of another flat tire. She opened the rear passenger door so Moose could clamber in, then stopped, aghast, when she walked around to the driver's side. Her car had been keyed. The jerk was staying busy! Unless he had done it just now. Didn't he have anything else to do?

It hadn't been that way when she came home from the axe bar. She would have noticed. The damage wasn't subtle.

Her mind turned black with rage at whoever had done this and she stood perfectly still for at least twenty seconds. Who should she call? Would the police want to know about this?

She fleetingly thought of the two boys next door, but one was in school and the other had probably been inside all day. He was at least pretending to be sick. She remembered faking sick to stay home when she was his age. You had to play the part.

The black in her mind faded to a storm-cloud-like gray as she was overwhelmed with a paranoid feeling. What if the person who did this was hanging around to see her reaction? Was her nemesis hiding nearby? Watching her this very minute? She turned in a slow circle, scanning her house, her neighbors' houses, the car parked in the next-door neighbor's driveway, her arm hairs prickling and lifting. She even ducked down to see if there was a pair of legs to be seen under the neighbor's car. That large bush near the curb in the yard across the street from her—someone could be crouched behind it. Someone could be hidden on the other side of the porch of her other next-door neighbor.

Thunder sounded, but not far away like it had been the day before. This time the rain clouds, their bellies full of darkness, were skidding across the sky and were going to blot out the sun in a few minutes.

Moose barked impatiently. Not a fierce, warning bark, just an impatient, "Let's go!" bark. Surely, he would sense if someone evil were nearby. Wouldn't he? The guy must be gone now.

She got into the car, her hands shaking as she started it up. She had to leave, to get out of there where someone might be hiding and gloating, rejoicing in her anger, her pain. At least her locks were changed and she had made sure everything was locked up tight as she left. If the jerk had a key, he would find out how useless it was now. Had he already tried it and gotten angry he couldn't get in? And had keyed her car instead?

When she got to the pet store, she hesitated. She sat in her car, fuming. How could she just go in and shop? She had to make some calls. If she didn't tell someone about the latest outrage, she would explode. She dialed the number on the card the detective had given her first. She was transferred and told he was not available, so she left a message, then called Gin. Her call went to Gin's voicemail, which she knew Gin would never check. She could text her, but then Gin might want to come be with her immediately and Darla didn't think she needed that this time. There was nothing Gin could do.

She was cooling off a bit. Maybe it wasn't such a big deal. Maybe it was a neighbor kid and not her tormentor. Still, she had to tell someone.

Darla ignored the rain drops splatting onto her windshield.

So, she called her mother and described the marks on her car door. Two parallel lines, deep and obviously intentional. "This can't have been an accident."

"This isn't stopping, is it?"

"You agree with me this is probably the work of my stalker? No, it's not stopping. How do I get him to quit, though? I'm just a sitting duck for anything he comes up with. I can't defend against someone I don't know. I don't even know what he'll do next."

"I suppose you could get security cameras at home."

Darla had thought of that, fleetingly, but hadn't acted on it, for some reason. She was too frazzled to think straight. "That's not a bad idea. Maybe I should. I wonder how long it takes to get them installed." She really should, since she had found out her closest neighbors didn't seem to have any.

"Can you come for dinner tonight?" Her mother changed the subject drastically. "It's been over a week since I've seen you."

"Yes, it has. Sure, I'll come over, Mom. Can I bring something in?" She always asked, but she always ended up doing that, whether or not her mother told her to. "Wings? Tacos?" Those were her mother's two favorites. The aides always fed her healthy food, so Darla didn't feel bad bringing her meals that were missing all or most of their vegetables. The small town of Charity wasn't known for gourmet dining, so it had to be done in one of the larger towns nearby, Dayton or Springfield. Or Columbus if they wanted to drive farther for a special occasion.

The rain was coming down harder. The clatter on the window panes distracted her and she was so easily distracted right now.

"Wings. With that marvelous sauce." Her mother sounded happy and eager. It was good to hear that in her voice. It pained her to see her mother worried and distraught. Like Darla was now.

"Wings it is." Maybe she would try not to talk about the stalker tonight. There was no point, she had to admit. And it would be great if her mother maintained her good mood.

While she'd been on the phone, Moose had been whining even louder and was starting to yip now, so Darla proceeded to the pet store with a happy, wagging dog.

Chapter 9

As soon as Darla got back inside her home from the pet store, she dried Moose off. Running through the rain to and from the pet store had dotted his dark coat with raindrops that sat on his back like crystals. By the time they had exited the car, in the driveway at home, it was pouring, and they had to run. They made it into the house in record time. But she couldn't deny Moose his outing at that point.

That second outing, to the backyard, drenched him. That was another toweling off, this one more vigorous and thorough. She, herself, dried her hair with her blow-dryer, brushed it to a nice sheen, a paler, chestnut version of Moose's chocolate coat, and changed her sopping clothes. Moose stayed in the hallway every time she used the appliance. While not as noisy as a vacuum, he still regarded it as a scary beast, something to stay far away from.

Warm and dry, she sat at her desk and went online to see if she could obtain some kind of security system, or some cameras, or whatever, for her house. At least there wasn't a thunderstorm and the power hadn't been knocked out. Just unusually heavy rain. She learned she had to order them. Then she would probably have to have someone install them.

There wasn't any place close by to shop for them and pick them up. So, order them online, she did. She found a system that got good reviews, with an intercom for the front door. The intercom would be fine, but the cameras were what she wanted the most. She was able to order four of them and planned to put them at the corners of her house, with one covering the front door and driveway. Now, she thought, let that slasher/scratcher/note writer/flashlight shiner try to get away with anything unseen.

She then spent the afternoon in other earnest endeavors which all turned out to be fruitless. The rain had stopped abruptly, so she searched the backyard while it was still daylight, picking her way through the wet grass, for any tell-tale signs of an intruder. Footprints, broken bush branches, maybe a dropped wallet with an ID or a passport inside. She really didn't know what she was looking for, but she had to do something. She couldn't sit in her house waiting for the next attack. Moose didn't seem interested in any new smells. Maybe no one had been in the back yard today. After Moose was finished doing his business, she scooped it up right away, not relishing any more porch surprises.

She had already searched the thick bushes in the front, but she did that again. For this, she took Moose with her on his leash into the front yard. Maybe he would be intrigued by some smells there. Drops fell from the leaves as she shifted them, lifting some and pushing some aside, peering into the interior of the solid green wall. Moose did concentrate on one particular spot, sniffing much longer than anywhere else. The bushes were so dense at that spot that the ground wasn't even wet. Darla turned on her cellphone flashlight to inspect the ground in the darkness under the dense brush. Were there footprints? It was hard to tell. The dirt was hard-packed and littered with leaves that had fallen from the bushes in the fall of last year. Were they disturbed? Moose pawed at them, then quit. Had the mystery man been hiding here? Watching for his opportunity to torture her further? If so, he wasn't overly fascinating to Moose. The dog could be interested in a mere squirrel, or a chipmunk, for all she knew. If only he could talk.

When they got inside, she gave Moose a good brushing, getting ready for the visit to her mother tonight. Darla picked up wings, remembering to get extra packets of hot sauce, the regular kind, the ones her mother called "marvelous," and showed up at about six-thirty at her mother's house accompanied by Moose.

Darla rang the doorbell and saw her mother's wheelchair approach through the glass panes in the front door. Her mother stretched forward to open the door and greeted both of them enthusiastically. But she showed maybe a tad more enthusiasm for Moose. Darla was glad her mother loved the dog. She got so much joy from seeing him, it made another bright spot for her when they visited.

Darla considered her mother's life to be dreary, so she made it a point to try to visit regularly, bringing Moose to brighten her day. Her mother almost never went anywhere, just had aides come in to neaten and clean the house, to bathe and feed her, and sometimes entertain her when she got tired of reading and television. She would occasionally tire of even her true crime and judge shows. Amy Taylor also loved board games and the aides spent hours doing those with her. That was fine with Darla, as she disliked doing them very much. Sometimes she looked at her sedentary mother, sedentary through no fault of her own, and remembered what a terrific athlete she had been. As a child, Darla had accompanied her to many archery meets and had watched her win her many trophies, the ones that now crowded the shelf where they sat at her house, shiny and loudly proclaiming her former prowess.

"Did you get the sauce?" her mother asked. There was one time when Darla had forgotten it and her mother had asked her every time since then. Her view was that there was no point to wings without sauce, and Darla had to agree on that.

Darla fished the hot sauce packets out of the takeout bag and waved them for her mother to see, the packets making a crinkly sound. She was rewarded with her mother's beautiful smile.

The dining room table was already set, as if they were going to have an elegant dinner. Her mother's appetite didn't extend much past four or five wings—with the marvelous sauce, of course. A bottle of wine sat by Darla's place, a corkscrew lying next to it. Darla knew the day aide had to have done all of this preparation. Once again, Darla glanced at her mother's polished archery trophies, gracing the sideboard shelf, and glinting in the light from her chandelier.

"Was Gin here today?" Darla asked.

"Yes, she came this morning, her regular time, but she left a little early. Since she had set all of this up before she asked, I told her that was fine."

"Did she have a date?"

"I imagine so. She changed her clothes here and put on make-up." Amy rolled herself into place at the table and poured the wings from the sack onto the serving plate, which had been set where she could easily reach it beside Gin.

"Mom, do you know who she's dating?"

"His name is Ned. Ned Something, Far, Farney? Something like that."

"Farley? Ned Farley?"

"Yes, that's it. Help yourself, dear. Don't let these get cold." Her mother tore open a few sauce packets and accumulated a puddle on her china plate, which she immediately dipped her first wing into.

Darla followed suit, taking some wings and some sauce.

"What has she said about him? Do you know where he works?"

Her mother tipped her head sideways in thought. "No, I don't believe she's ever said."

"And you haven't met him?"

"Never laid eyes on the man."

So, he hadn't been here, working. Gin did say he worked for her company. Darla assumed he was an aide, but it was possible he might work in the office. He might even be the janitor, for all she knew. "Did she say he's a friend of her father?"

Amy sobered, holding a wing in the air, half-way to her mouth. "No. She didn't tell me that." She pursed her lips and shook her head. "She probably knows I would disapprove of that."

No one had been thrilled when Mr. Gary Holland had been sentenced to seven years in prison. He hadn't succeeded in making many good impressions since he'd gotten out three years ago either, drifting from job to job and losing all of them in quick succession. That was probably because he had acquired an alcohol habit since his release. At least alcohol, Darla thought. Maybe worse. Maybe much worse.

Thinking of Gin's father and his bad habits made something occur to Darla. "Mom, do you keep track of your pain medication?"

"Oh, the aides do that."

That's what Darla was afraid of. She hated herself for thinking of it, but could Gin be helping supply her father—or that new boyfriend about whom she knew nothing, given that her job was helping out disabled people who were often on pain medication? She usually tried not to think about Gin and Keith's father, Gary Holland, and had succeeded in that for a long time, but, now that she had been reminded of him, that awful thought sprang into her mind. Gin was being so secretive about her boyfriend, and that wasn't like her. Was it because he knew her father? How well did they know each other? Did they share bad habits? Share a drug dealer?

Darla kicked herself mentally about thinking such awful things of her friend—stealing medication from her own patients. How could she think that?

Still, she made a mental note to count her mother's pills before she left, and to do it every week thereafter.

"What's new with you, dear?" her mother asked.

Darla's expression gave her away.

"Oh no, what now?" Alarm raised her mother's thin eyebrows.

"Oh, Mom. Something else happened."

"Your stalker again, isn't it?" Her mother was calmer about this than Darla.

"I have to assume that. I ruled out the boys next door."

"Oh yes, they do get into mischief, don't they?"

"But they couldn't have done this. They weren't around, except the one who is home sick." Darla stretched to reach across the table to take another wing, leaving the serving platter where her mother could reach it.

"I hope...no, that can't be." Darla's mother dipped and bit into another crunchy piece of chicken.

"What do you hope? That this isn't my father? Do you really not know where he is?" She swirled the wing in the sauce. It *was* good sauce.

"Not exactly. It's just he did that same precise thing to me one time. Two long gouges. Up and down, just like yours."

"He did? Well, do you know approximately where he is, then? Is he around? Is he staying near here?"

"He...may be."

"Mother." Her fingers let go and dropped the wing onto her plate. "Have you seen him?"

"I may have."

Darla gave an exasperated huff. "Mom, you either have or you haven't. This is the man who put you in the wheelchair. If you've seen him, you need to let me know. And we should let the police know. I think it's time you got a protective order."

"Oh, I don't know if I need that."

"Mother! You do! And I might need one, too. I'm going to call someone about that tomorrow."

"Don't be too hasty, dear. Let's think about this."

"Why would you not want a protective order? It's to keep him away from you. Do you *want* to see him?" When she didn't answer, Darla had a suspicion. "Have you seen him? Are you seeing him?"

To be sure, her mother had made two disastrous choices for husbands. Darla considered her mother a bright, intelligent, sensible woman. But when it came to men, she seemed to lose her brain function.

"You're seeing my father?"

Her mother's silence confirmed it.

Chapter 10

"**M**om, when did you see him? Recently?" After dropping the hot wing she'd been holding onto her plate, she picked it up and stabbed it into the sauce on her plate.

"He doesn't have a job, Darla. He can't find people to hire him. I just give him money from time to time."

She "just" gives him money. Darla tried not to fume outwardly. "When was the last time?"

"I don't know. A few days ago. At night. I don't keep track of the days much anymore."

"Try to think. What night?" She fought to keep her voice from becoming shrill.

"It was that night...I called you the next day. I thought I ought to tell you about Todd stalking me after our divorce."

"So, he was at your place the same day my house got broken into."

"That's what made me think of calling you."

"Yes, and thank you for that. But I wish I'd known he was here in town that day."

"But Darla, how would he get inside your house?"

"Oh, I don't know. Steal the key you have? Borrow it and get a copy made?" She wasn't succeeding in keeping the shrill out of her words. Good God. Could she trust anyone she'd given her keys to? Gin with the mystery boyfriend. Her mother with the deadbeat, abusive ex-husband. Maybe she should keep all her keys to herself.

"He wouldn't do that. He couldn't. Go look. It's in my desk."

Darla wiped her greasy fingers, got up, and looked in the center drawer of her mother's large, ornate desk in the living room. The living and dining room flowed together, so she was still in sight of her mother. "This drawer?" she asked, pointing to the middle drawer above the kneehole.

"No, no. The bottom one on the right."

Darla opened that one and found an insert tray above the papers below. There it was. Her key lay there on top. In plain sight. It was there, but could have been taken and returned easily enough.

"How often does he come here?"

"Not often. Not more than once a month."

Yeah, right. Not often. Every month, was all. "How long has this been going on? Do you tell him to not be here when I come over? Does he ever come when the aides are here?"

"No, he comes at night. When no one else is here. He doesn't want anyone to see him."

"And he comes inside. In here." Darla closed her eyes, then looked to the heavens, asking for patience.

"Darla, dear, he's never alone here. I'm always here. He never opens the desk."

"But, Mom, *you're* alone with him. You shouldn't be. Please promise me you won't do that again."

"But he's having such a hard time."

Or he tells her he is. And she, of course, believes him. "How much money are you giving him?" There, she had regained control. Her voice sounded almost normal.

"Just, maybe a hundred dollars, here and there."

Darla suspected it was a lot more from the offhand way her mother told her the amount. Maybe she should think about getting her into a facility where people couldn't steal her drugs and her money. And borrow her daughter's house key long enough to make a copy.

"Please promise me you'll have him come here only when someone else is here. Not when you're all alone. It's more important you're safe than that nobody see him. Can you at least do that? For me? Please? So, I won't worry about you?"

Her mother thought she could do that. Darla thought she damn well better. She could think those words. But she didn't talk to her mother like that.

"Just don't get a court order for him." Her mother's eyes pleaded. "I don't want you to do that to him."

Darla drove home, hoping she had made her mother see sense. Hoping she would make sure an aide was with her for the next handout session. But most of all, hoping she could get some kind of a court order to keep him away from her mother.

Moose sensed her distress and, from the back seat, where he obediently remained. He stuck he head forward to rest on her shoulder. The slobber made it a bit wet, but she appreciated his doggie concern. What did people without dogs do when they were upset?

She researched how to get protective orders as soon as she got home. She would call the county courthouse in the morning and get that started. It probably wasn't an instantaneous process, since it was run by the government.

Of course, when she called the next morning, a recording told her the courthouse was open Monday through Friday. And it was Saturday. Naturally. Well, at least it didn't seem to be an emergency at the moment.

Steadying herself, she took up her archery kit, went outside, and walked, slowly and deliberately, to the spot where she always stood, about twenty yards from her target. Her trusty foam bullseye target was in place. She had chosen that kind of target because those stood up well to Ohio weather. She went through her ritual, putting on all of her gear, strapping the quiver belt around her waist, and calmly taking up the bow. The ritual itself was a comfort. It got into a steady frame of mind for the activity. Her first shot wasn't too bad. On the second shot, she was able to hit near the center. After that, she had her groove back.

Archery was superior to axe throwing, she thought. You simply hit the bullseye in archery. No nonsense about where you stuck the blade on which turn. What a ridiculous sport it was.

Things were starting to make sense, she told herself, after she put her gear away and let Moose out to romp around the yard. The situation was better in hand. She had a solution, a plan. So, naturally, she was shooting well.

Her mother's second husband, her own father, was probably the culprit and she would make sure the authorities knew that. She knew firsthand how mean he was and figured it would be just like him to stalk his own daughter in order to get back at his ex-wife. That didn't really make sense, when she thought about it, but nothing that man had done had ever made sense to her. He was just plain angry. Vicious. After she convinced the authorities, then she could get the orders to prevent him from approaching her and her mother. If he couldn't get money from her mother any more, he would move on, she hoped. He was probably only sticking around for his monthly dole. As far as Darla knew, he hadn't been in this area all along. With him out of the picture, her torment would stop and her life would go back to normal. Maybe it would be that simple.

She called Detective Coleman and left a message. He called back within half an hour, interrupting her loading of the dishwasher. She didn't regret leaving that task at all. She would always rather cook than clean up.

"You didn't have another incident, did you?" he said.

"No, thank God. But I talked to my mother last night and I know who's doing all of this. I'm going to get a restraining order against him on Monday."

"We call it a protective order."

"Right. Protective order. That's what I'll get."

"Who is it?"

"It's her ex-husband. My father. He's been hanging around, taking money from her."

"Stealing?"

"No, she's giving it to him."

"But what makes you so sure he's your stalker? Aside from her willingly giving him money, is he bothering her?"

"No, just getting handouts once a month or so. That's how I know he's in town. He was at her place the same day as one of my break-ins."

"Okay, he was in town. But he isn't bothering her? Do you know why he would do these things to you?"

"Not really. But he was abusive to her in the past. He did some stalking of her, too. He even keyed her car once. Two long lines, just like mine."

"How would he have gotten into your house? It wasn't broken into."

"My mother has a key she keeps in a desk drawer, right there in plain sight. It's very easy to find. And she probably doesn't check to see if it's there or not every time he visits. He could have taken it and gotten it copied."

"We could bring him in and question him. What's his address?"

Darla squeezed her eyes shut, angry at herself for not getting that information. "Can you get that from my mother?" Did she want her mother to know she was going ahead with the orders? Probably not. "Never mind. I'll find out."

"What's his name? Maybe we can find him."

"Todd. Todd Taylor."

"I'll call you back if we can't locate him."

Good. She didn't want to ask her mother. What good reason would Darla have for getting his address? Her mother knew she never wanted to see him again. She would think Darla was just trying to get him into trouble. Darla felt guilty going behind her mother's back with the orders, but her mother had been keeping things from her, too.

Chapter 11

Darla mostly fidgeted aimlessly around the house and the yard all day Sunday. Even though she didn't think the detective would call her back, she couldn't quit checking her phone. After all, he had called her back on Saturday and that was his day off, too. But he had probably called only because he thought she might have had more trouble from her bad guy.

Part of her wanted to stay home, guarding her house, to keep her father from trying anything else. Surely, he wouldn't, with her there. Another part of her was going stir crazy. She was worn out from doing archery. She had done it for an hour and her arms and back were both tired and achy. It took a lot of strength to pull the bow. She had the strength, built up over years of pulling the bowstring, and a regular session never bothered her. But she couldn't do it forever. Plus, Moose got impatient when she was out and he was in the house for too long. He tended to start unraveling the toilet paper after what he considered a decent interval. He never misbehaved when she went to work, just when she was in the yard too long and he wasn't. He knew the difference and didn't appreciate deviations from their set routine.

After watching some reruns she had recorded from television, she leashed Moose and took him for a walk. She never watched the crime and judge shows her mother did. Her speed was more comedies and dramas. Even some daytime soaps once in a while. Maybe she and her mother had switched generations, TV-watching-wise.

Moose tugged her along until she insisted he heel, and they made good time down the sidewalk. The neighbors on the other side of the Silversons were in the front yard planting flowers around their gaslight pole. These were Mr. and Mrs. Carlson. They were older, too, but not as much, she thought. Their two toddler granddaughters were tumbling about on the lawn. Darla didn't see the parents of the little girls. She knew the whole family often came over on weekends and holidays. Darla shortened up the leash and held Moose close to her to keep him from bothering their gardening work. He would love to get in there and help them dig up the dirt. Wanting to ask if they had seen anyone around, she stopped to chat when they looked up to greet her.

"Are you babysitting today?" she asked Mr. Carlson, by way of small talk conversational preamble.

He beamed at the two towheads, looking up from his seat on grass. "We sure are. Every chance we get. They won't stay this size very long."

The girl who was about an inch taller than her almost identical sister looked up and noticed Moose. "Goggie!" She shrieked and ran at him.

Moose ducked behind Darla for protection. Darla held out her palms and managed to get the girl to approach more calmly and, after the child had patted Moose on the back two or three times, she returned to wrestle with her sister. The smaller one didn't seem interested in the dog. Darla asked the little sister if she wanted to pet the doggie, but got no response.

"She's afraid of dogs," Mrs. Carlson said. "She was bitten a few months ago."

"That's too bad," Darla said. "Maybe I can come by regularly and she can get used to him."

"Oh, I wouldn't bother," Mr. Carlson said. "They're moving out of state in a few weeks." He stopped puttering with the plants and gazed fondly at the girls. "We'll sure miss them."

His wife agreed.

It was time to broach her subject. "Say, you didn't happen to notice anyone hanging around my place while I was gone, in the last few days, did you?"

"I don't know when you're gone," Mrs. Carlson said. "Your hours aren't regular, every day."

"That's true," Darla said.

"Why?" Mr. Carlson asked. "Did something happen?"

"I've had some...vandalism." Darla didn't want tell them the extent of her harassment. That would be complicated and take time. She just wanted to see if they had spotted the harasser.

"Oh dear. Did someone break in?" asked Mrs. Carlson, dusting off his hands and standing.

Okay, she didn't want to out and out lie. "Well, yes. Either I left something unlocked or someone had a key."

"You don't know who it was? No idea?"

"I'm not sure. That's why I'm asking around. You don't have a security camera, do you?"

Mr. Carlson looked at his wife, then back to Darla. "Yes, as a matter of fact, we do." He pointed to an unobtrusive metal tube high on the porch, near the front door. "I don't think it would get a shot of anyone at your house, though."

Darla eyed the distance. The Silverson house and the tall box elder bushes were all in the way. "I don't think so either."

"You should look, Arthur," his wife said. She was standing now, too. Darla got the idea they both wanted to comfort her. If they didn't have dirt all over their hands, they might have given her a hug.

He promised he would go through the recordings later in the day and call her if he saw anything, but Darla didn't think it would be any use. Although he did say he kept the recordings for a month.

"Was anything stolen?" Mrs. Carlson asked. "You weren't hurt, were you? Or Moose?"

"No, just minor things, really. Some things were disturbed. Moved around. Just annoying." The slashed tire and car door damage weren't minor, but nothing had been stolen, and she hadn't been hurt. Yet.

She crossed the street and knocked on the doors of the three houses on that side of the street, but no one had seen anything and none of them had outside cameras. That was too bad, because they could probably have gotten better angles on her house and driveway from across the street.

She trudged home, discouraged, even though she had known this would be a long shot. Restless and still fretting, she had a snack and went to bed early, but she tossed and turned for at least two hours. After she fell asleep, her dreams were infiltrated by bizarre visions of her father shoving her down a flight of stairs, raking a sharp key down her arm and drawing blood, and other unlikely horrors. Her alarm, waking her to her Monday work shift, seemed to come awfully early. She was glad to escape the nightmares, but the sleep she'd gotten hadn't refreshed her.

Getting washed up and dressed for work, she fleetingly wondered again if Bobby really was her stalker. No one had better access to her than he did. He had never had a key, but he'd been in her house enough times for the period they were dating. He could have made a copy back then, somehow. However people did these things, she thought. Swipe the key? Take an impression in...gum? Wax? Had she seen it on television or in a movie? It didn't sound likely.

Telling Moose to be good and guard the house, she made her way to work. Her tired eyes were having a tendency to close, so she drove slowly and carefully and parked as close to the door as she could. She dashed to the cafeteria for a quick cup of strong coffee as soon as she entered the hospital.

In spite of the coffee, and reinfusions throughout the morning, she was going through the motions that day. Darla cared for her patients, doled out meds, avoided coming into much contact with Bobby Abbot, and somehow made it to lunchtime. It was then she saw she had missed a call from Detective Coleman. She called him back and, of course, he was unavailable. She left her phone ringer on all afternoon, in violation of policy. But it didn't ring.

It wasn't until she was preparing to leave for the day that he called her back.

"We were able to find out where Mr. Taylor is living," Coleman said.

"He's living here in Charity? Or just staying somewhere?"

"He has a lease on an apartment in town.

Darla fumed. "How long has he been living here?"

"At that address, about two years."

"Two years?" Darla realized she had shouted. "Sorry, I'm just...my mother never told me. She's hiding him. Or he's hiding. I would have run into him, I would think, if they weren't trying to hide from me. He's obviously been avoiding me. Hasn't been letting me see him." Not that she wanted to. "So did you question him?"

"I'm on my way to bring him in right now."

"Should I be there?"

"No, you should not. Definitely not."

She wanted to, though, so much. She wanted to confront the man and unleash her rage on him. For mooching money from her mother as well as for tormenting her. "Could you ask him why he's doing this?"

"If he is, I will."

"What's his address? Is it near my mom's place?"

"You know I can't tell you that. I've already told you more than I should. Please don't act on anything I've told you. And don't let anyone know I've told you."

She didn't answer, so he continued.

"I mean it, Ms. Taylor."

"You can call me Darla."

"Whatever I call you, do not let on you know he's renting in town. I'll get into trouble if you do."

"Okay. I won't tell anyone."

"And don't try to find him. We'll handle everything."

She did so hope that was true. She so was ready to be rid of this awful torment.

Chapter 12

Darla drove straight to the county courthouse as soon as she hung up with the detective. They were open today, so she was determined to get court orders to protect her and her mother, whether her mother wanted one for herself or not. She turned into the police station lot just as a car backed out of a parking space near the door of the courthouse. She pulled in, taking that as a good omen. It was about time things started going right for her.

She slowed as she approached the front door, remembering how much she liked this place. The building was old and graceful, with a tall, slim clock tower, a relic from another century. She pushed open the massive wooden double doors and walked through. The high ceilings and smooth, dark woodwork inside gave her a feeling of peace and wellbeing she hadn't had recently. Someone must have polished the wood recently because a faint lemony smell lingered in the cool, still air. She walked to the glassed in enclosure near the front and asked the friendly looking woman there how she would go about getting her orders.

"Orders?"

"Protective orders. For me and for my mother. Online, it says to apply here."

"Yes, you do. First, you need to make an appointment," the woman said. "Let me see when we could get you in." The woman keyed some strokes on her keyboard and peered at her monitor, putting her finger on the screen and tracing down through, Darla assumed, dates that were already taken. "Here's one. We can get you in next Monday. That's just a week. Would that be okay?"

Darla couldn't hide her disappointment. "That's the soonest?"

"Are you in physical danger?" She held her hands above the keyboard, maybe, Darla thought, to type a magic code that would move her up in the queue if she was.

"I don't really know. I just need to keep this guy away from us. The police have been out to my house." Wouldn't everyone who needed protection be in danger, to some degree?

"Can you tell me what has gone on?" She dropped her hands back down to get to work.

Darla told the woman about the other incidents and she looked them up.

"If anything else happens before then, you call nine-one-one," she said, her hands leaving the keyboard and resting in her lap until they were called upon again.

"I've called the police every time," Darla said, getting exasperated.

"These incidents haven't involved abuse, right?"

"Well, not really, I guess." Was it abuse, could it be called that? She didn't know.

"Okay, we'll schedule you Monday at ten. Is that okay? The appointment will take about two hours." With a couple of clicks, Darla seemed to be on the schedule.

Two hours? What would she be doing for two hours? "Why does it take that long?"

"The Domestic Violence Coordinator has to do a thorough interview. There will need to be a hearing the same day. I can give you the paperwork for you to get started on beforehand."

"This sounds like it'll take all day."

"I'd say half a day anyway."

Darla took the papers the woman handed her and looked at her schedule on her phone. She wasn't working that Monday since it would be part of her three days off that week. "I guess it would be okay. Does my mother need to come also?"

"Oh, you want orders for both of you?"

Darla turned that over quickly in her mind. "No, just the one." She would see how the first one went, since she was the only one of them with damages, then she would work on keeping him away from her mother later, after she knew the process better. She didn't want to put her mother through anything if it wasn't going to help.

She waited until late into the night for a call back from the detective, hoping he had cracked her father, made him admit he was tormenting her and her mother. Her mother didn't consider herself tormented, but he was getting her money every month. *How much he had really received?* Probably a lot more than her mother was letting on. And how long had this been going on? Maybe even for two years, the amount of time he had lived here, from what Detective Coleman said

The next day at noon she took a lunch break and checked her phone just as a call came in from the detective. Maybe, she thought, he had grilled Todd Taylor all night and had taken the morning off.

"Yes?" she answered eagerly. "What did he say? Did he admit anything?"

"Not to any of the mischief that's happened to you. I'm not sure he knows where you live, but it's hard to tell. He didn't want to talk and didn't say much."

"But did you make him confess? You can do that, can't you?"

Did the detective chuckle? Was he laughing at her? "If someone doesn't want to tell us something, then no. We can't make them do that. We don't waterboard anymore." He paused. "That's a joke, Ms. Taylor. We can't torture people to get confessions. We can keep them a long time until they get tired of being here, but if they don't talk, they don't talk."

"Well, what *did* he say? Did he act suspicious?"

"I'm always suspicious of everyone, no matter how they act. But right now, I don't believe he's the one doing any of this."

"Did you tell him not to bother my mother again?"

"I can't do that unless she asks me to."

Darla knew her mother would never do that. It would have to be up to her to protect both of them. How would she do that? How do you protect a person who doesn't know they need protection? Her mother was so stubborn! Darla stomped her foot in frustration.

Chapter 13

Darla made a phone call to set up a date to see Gin for a quick drink after work—she at least had to give her a copy of the new key, at most, try to pump her for info on the new guy again—then went back to tending her patients until it was time to go.

Approaching her car slowly after work, and strolling around it, making sure no one was lurking there, she ascertained the tires were all intact and there were no new scratches anywhere. Nor were there any notes under the wipers on the windshield. Her scalp and her stomach loosened up a little as some of the tension drained away, from the relief of not having any new car damage.

She drove to a small corner bar to have one drink with Gin before her friend went to dinner with the new beau. Once again, Darla wanted to find out what she could about this mysterious guy. She had suggested the three of them meet, but Gin had said Ned needed to work right up until their dinner reservations. Darla didn't see why he couldn't squeeze in some time to meet her, since she was Gin's oldest friend. "How much time do we have?" Darla asked, as they carried a couple of glasses of craft-brewed beer to a small table near the front windows.

"We're meeting in an hour, and it's close to here."

"Maybe Ned could whip in for a quick chat, or a quick drink." Darla took a sip of the tangy coolness through the foam.

"I'm afraid not. He's got some business in Dayton today and has to drive here from there."

"I thought he worked for OTB, with you."

"He does, but it's his day off today. He's just in Dayton today. Some kind of part time thing, or something. He goes there pretty often."

"Does he live there?"

Gin hesitated, taking a long swig of her drink. "I'm not exactly sure where he lives."

Darla set her mug down with a thump. "You don't know where he lives? He's keeping that a secret from you?"

"Not deliberately. A few things have come up. We keep making plans to have a cookout or something at his place, but then... Well, he had some plumbing problems, then a few boards on his deck were rotten. It's taking quite a while to get it repaired."

"You can't come over to his place because the deck is being fixed? What about the rest of the house? You could see that."

"I think it's a condo, or maybe an apartment."

"With a deck?" This wasn't really making sense. The guy didn't want her to know where he lived. Maybe it was squalid, or something. Or maybe he was hiding a wife.

Gin shrugged. "I'm not sure. By the way, your mom is doing fine. I was at her place for work today."

"Sorry, I should have asked. Did anyone come by today?"

"Like who?"

"Like my dad."

Now Gin thumped her mug down onto the table. The beer sloshed over the rim a bit. "What?"

Darla told Gin about learning so recently her father was coming around to her place for money regularly and that she had begged her mother to have him come when someone was there in the future.

"He didn't show up today. No men came around while I was there. I'm not sure I'd recognize him. It's been a long time since I've seen him. What's it been? Ten years?"

"Probably. He pushed my mom down the stairs ten years ago. They got divorced right away after and I thought he moved away when his so-called sentence was up."

"I thought he didn't go to jail."

Darla frowned, remembering her anger at his hearing. "He didn't. It wasn't a real sentence. He just had to wear an ankle bracelet and make sure they knew where he was all the time. He also had to pay for her medical bills and take anger management classes. I wonder if he's still taking them. Detective Coleman didn't say."

"The detective? What's he got to do with it now? Did you tell me and I forgot?"

"No, I just spoke to him. I told him I think it's my father who has been stalking me."

"Do you really think that? What would he gain? Do you think he wants to push you down some stairs, too? Why would he stalk you?"

When she put it that way, Darla had to rethink. *Why would he stalk her? What would be the object?*

He had been a stern, distant father to her, although they had spent some good times together when she was younger. Sometimes she forgot all about those now, but they had happened. He had coached her third and fourth grade soccer teams, and had helped her with school science projects. He used to work as a real estate sales representative, which was a good job for concealing his overuse of alcohol. Being able to set his own hours, being out on his own, scouting and showing houses, wining and dining clients, all of that gave him ample opportunity to get well-oiled almost every day. As is sometimes the case with heavy drinkers, he functioned well in spite of all the liquor he put away and was able to hide his condition most of the time. Not at home, though. And less and less as the years went by.

"Is he working here, in town?" Gin asked.

"I don't think he's working anywhere. That's why he's getting his funds from my mom. It would be just like him to want to recoup everything he had to pay for her medical bills and for the settlement."

Gin blew out an angry breath through her teeth. "I hope he shows up when I'm there." She started to gather her things to leave. "I'll make sure he never does that again."

"Wait, I have to give you this." Darla fished the key out of her purse and handed it to Gin.

"Oh, a new one? For your changed locks, right?"

"Right. Please don't tell Ned you have it, okay?"

"Why not?"

"Just...I don't know who was breaking in."

"Well, it wasn't Ned. Or do you think everyone is stalking you now? That's a little paranoid, Darla."

"I know. I am paranoid, more than a little."

"Sorry. I guess I would be, too."

After Gin left, Darla realized she hadn't finished her interrogation. She wanted to ask Gin if she was sure the guy wasn't married. That was the all-important question when a guy was hiding things from you. Gin wouldn't date him if she knew he was, but Darla wanted to plant that seed and for Gin to find out for sure. Somehow.

The next day, Darla got a call from Gin early in the morning, before she left for work, but after she'd been out with her bow and arrows. She was just putting away her target shooting equipment and letting Moose into the back yard. He burst out the door, as usual, his body wriggling with doggy delight, before galloping across the yard.

"Do you want dinner tonight?" Gin asked.

Darla laughed. "I'm in favor of having dinner every night."

Gin ignored her attempt at humor. "Ned wants to meet you and suggested you join us at Charity China."

That was something! Ned wanted to meet her? She sure wanted to meet him.

The name of the restaurant always reminded Darla of a table full of dishes at a church rummage sale, but their Chinese food was decent. "I finally get to meet him? For real? Sure. What time?"

She agreed to meet them at eight and immediately began to formulate ways to interrogate the guy. She needed to make sure he was the right one for Gin. At least for dating. At least for now. The big question she had was, why did he have no online history? And why was he hiding most of his present existence, also? Was he who he said he was?

Darla, having run quite a few searches for Ned Farley, with different guesses at alternative first names, couldn't find any information going back more than three years, even when she paid for one of the personal search companies. The online sites had two addresses for him, both in Charity, but no family information. None at all. That's where she would start her questions, with family.

Having dithered extra-long about what to wear, Darla showed up a few minutes after eight. The two of them were already seated at the bar, drinks in hand, waiting for their table. Even seated, Darla could tell Ned was tall, dark, and handsome. She joined them and, as soon as she climbed onto the stool, Ned's name was called.

"Go ahead. I'll order something and be right there." She got herself a glass of wine and carried it with her to the table.

Gin did the introductions when they were all seated at a booth near the back of the dining room. It was a nice, quiet, rather dark location. It would be easy for them to chat and to hear each other.

"Hi Ned." Darla smiled and extended her hand. "I'm so glad to finally meet you."

He smiled back, not very broadly and touched her hand for a brief moment. "Same here."

Darla was immediately taken by him. No wonder Gin was keeping this guy for herself.

"I've heard so much about you." He showed a hint of a dimple with his killer smile. He had a medium-sized mustache, black, the color of his hair. The man had panache, Darla had to admit. A real lady-killer.

"How nice." Darla threw a glance and a grin at Gin. "I really haven't heard too much about you. Except how great you are." She added that last to soften the interrogation she was about to launch into. "Gin hasn't told me anything about your family. Are they local?"

Ned shook his head with a sad downward look. "No, I don't really know any of them. I was adopted."

Was that why no online info? No, something should still be there, even without any family info. He's been alive his whole life. "Ah, well, how about your adoptive family? Are they from here?" Darla could see Gin frowning at her, but she had to find out. "Where did you go to high school?"

Ned looked her sharply in the eye. "I'm not in touch with them. I don't like to talk about family. They're out of my life, for good, I hope." He took a deep swig of his beer, keeping one steely eye on her while he tipped up the stein.

That look turned her cold inside. It wasn't so much sad and regretful as...threatening? He seemed to be ordering her to back off. She did a quick reassessment of his attractiveness.

Darla was glad the server arrived just then. She knew the menu, so, without looking at it, ordered sweet and sour chicken, as she usually did. Gin got the hot and sour soup, her usual. Ned ordered Mongolian Beef, pronouncing it with comical exaggeration, like he thought of that as a real man's dish.

"How was your day?" Gin asked as soon as the menus were handed back.

Darla knew Gin was trying to deflect her inquisition of Ned. "Not bad. We have two new recovering heart surgery patients and they're both doing well. I'm always glad when that happens."

"Oh, were they bypasses?" Gin said brightly, as if she was intensely interested in Darla's patients.

"One double, one triple." She turned to Ned. "Are you in medicine?"

"Only very recently."

"What did you used to do?"

"I was in finance." He had softened his manner for now, his flash of annoyance gone, as if it hadn't been there.

That was all she could get out of him for the rest of the night, though. She and Gin didn't discuss Darla's mother or Darla's stalker, or anyone in either of their families. Ned and Gin took turns steering the conversation through local events, weather, new movies, anything but what Darla wanted to talk about. The meal was exhausting for Darla.

When they were finished eating, waiting for the check, Ned turned his attention to Darla. "How about you?" he asked, an interested look in his eyes. "Is your family all in Charity?"

"Yes, we've always lived here."

"Do you have pets? Hobbies?" This time he smiled.

Darla thought she might be winning him over. But she wasn't going to fall into that smile, knowing how quickly he could turn. "Yes, a dog. And I like archery." She babbled a bit about Moose and about how her mother was an archery champion, but she, herself, just liked to do it for fun.

All in all, in spite of the one brief flash of annoyance, or something, from Ned, Darla was left with a favorable impression. She didn't know enough yet to approve of Ned as a long-term partner for Gin, but he was appealing, when he wanted to be. And not half bad looking.

The two of them took off together in Ned's truck, an old, battered, black pickup. It would be easy to tell from every other black pickup on the road because it was so grimy. *Had it ever been washed?*

Driving home, Darla knew what she should have asked. She should have brought up the axe club, at the very least. How could she have forgotten to do that? After all, she had visited it just so she should mention it, as a way to try to learn how Ned knew Gin's ex-con father. Were they fellow ex-con embezzlers? He did say he'd been in finance. She could have kicked herself for not asking how he knew Gin and Keith's father. Although it might have gotten her another one of those scary, dark, stabbing looks from Ned. He had a good side and a bad side and the good side was better. That was for sure.

Chapter 14

Wednesday evening, after the dinner with Gin and Ned, Darla couldn't get Ned Farley out of her mind. Watching a TV drama with Moose's warm head in her lap, she tried to figure it out. She was attracted to him. No, no, no. She didn't want to be attracted to the guy her best friend was dating. What kind of a friend would that be? At moments, he had seemed hostile, at other moments, truly interested in her. And pretty darn good-looking. That was just a fact.

Deep in guilty thoughts, she jumped when something heavy crashed through her front window. She flinched, startled, and Moose dashed to the front door, barking. She dropped to the floor, confused, and frightened. Had someone shot her house? No, not a bullet.

A brick sat on the floor amid scattered piles of broken glass. Someone had launched it through her front window.

Whoever had thrown it might still be out there. If only she could let Moose loose on him, let Moose take him down, bite him, do some damage. She didn't dare, though. What if the unknown person was waiting just outside for her to do that? What if he had a gun and shot Moose?

As soon as her hands quit shaking enough, she dipped her phone out of her pocket and called 911. When they promised someone was on the way, warning her, unnecessarily, to stay inside, she crawled toward the brick.

Moose was still barking at the door. Glass splinters littered much of the carpeting, so it was slow going avoiding getting cut. Before she picked up the brick, though, she had a thought. Maybe she should avoid touching it, in case the police could get some evidence from it. She studied it. The missile was a plain red brick, standard size, and had a folded piece of paper wrapped around it with a rubber band. She couldn't see any writing on it. If she had to bet, she would put money on the words *knock knock* being written on the inside.

Moose left the door and started toward her. No!

"Stay!" she shouted, not wanting him to cut his feet on the glass. He whined, but obeyed and sat back on his haunches on the tile floor near the front door. The shards hadn't reached that far and the floor there looked clean and free of glass.

She crawled back to the couch, then made her way to the front hall, crouching to avoid being seen through the broken window, to join Moose so she would be able to let the officers in when they got there. The wailing sirens were approaching. When the whine died down in front of her house, she threw the door open and stepped outside, looking up and down the street. No one was still there, of course. Maybe if the police car had approached silently, the guy would have hung around to see her reaction.

She was questioned by the patrol officer, though she didn't have much to say. The only thing she had seen was the brick, itself. She still didn't have any cameras.

A Crime Scene unit arrived soon. Darla let herself smile, relieved and happy to see them. She wanted to know what was on the paper. The team first took photos and measurements. *Could they tell where he was standing when he threw it?* Then one of them picked up the brick, with gloves, and dropped it into an evidence bag.

"Can you tell me what's written on that?" She pointed to the evidence bag.

"We'll take this in and process it," the technician said. "We probably won't get anything from the brick, but we might from the paper. I'll make sure someone lets you know."

One of the other techs said to his partner, "This is the knock, knock woman?"

The first tech nodded.

Was she famous in the Crime Scene lab? Given the size of Charity, the lab probably wasn't huge. These same people may have worked on her previous onslaughts. She hadn't noticed what they looked like, being so distraught when they were there in their white coveralls, hairnets, and blue booties.

"Do you want us to secure that?" The man pointed to the shattered window.

"Could you?" *Yes, she would like that very much.*

"We'll put some extra patrols on your street and hope we catch this guy." She thought they already had done that, for some reason, but maybe there would be more now.

Two of them nailed a piece of plywood over the broken window. CSI seemed to carry all kinds of equipment. That, and the idea police cars would be driving by, made her feel safer.

At least this latest attack didn't result in keeping her up all night. The police team even cleaned up some of the glass and was out of her house while it was still fairly early. There were enough tiny shards, even after that, to cause harm to Moose—and to her—but she vacuumed after they left and she thought she got it all. If only this whole mess could be cleaned up as easily and neatly.

What did her tormentor want? She fell asleep wondering if this was ever going to stop. But at least she was able to fall asleep.

Darla left her phone ringer on at work Thursday, hoping to hear from Detective Coleman, or maybe someone else at the police department. She was burning with curiosity to find out what was on the note. She also wondered why Detective Coleman hadn't shown up last night. His presence was a bulwark against the evil. He made her feel safe.

When she thought about it, she realized he probably had others cases he had to work on. Her troubles weren't the only thing happening in Charity.

The call didn't come until she was finishing a short lunch break and getting ready to head back out to the floor. She could tell from the number the call was from the police station.

"Ms. Taylor?" an unknown soothing female voice asked. So not Detective Coleman. "We have the information you were asking about last night."

"Oh, the note? Does it say *knock knock*?"

"It does. It says that, then it follows up with: *Are you enjoying this?*"

"Damn. The nerve of that guy." She knew she should feel frightened, like all the other times, but all she could feel right now was anger at the audacity. It was a welcome change.

"Do you have any idea who this could be?" the calm woman asked.

Darla took a slow breath before answering. "If I did, you would be the first to know. No, I have no idea." She was growing angry at the woman on the phone for being so unruffled, which was stupid. "I'm sorry. I didn't mean to snap at you. But no. At first, I thought it was my ex, but it's probably not. Then my mother and I, well, mostly me, thought it was my father. We've been estranged for a long time. Detective Coleman knows all of this. In fact, he questioned my father."

"Yes, I see from the notes those two were suspected at first. So, no one else?"

"I've never thought there was anyone in the world who could hate me enough to do all of these things. What kind of person is this?"

"I'd say there's anger involved."

"Why? Why is he angry?"

"That's hard for me to say."

Of course it was. This woman didn't know her at all. But Darla didn't think she could have enemies. Actual enemies. People who wanted to frighten her out of her wits.

"I have to say," the woman went on, "it sounds like this is coming from someone who knows you. It doesn't have to be a male."

She was right. It did seem like it was someone she knew! Darla had to admit that. She felt tears coming. "I just don't know why anyone wants to be so ugly to me. I would never do anything like this to someone else."

"No, of course not." The woman was using a calm, comforting tone, which served to infuriate Darla even more. "If you think of anything at all, please give us a call. I see we do have some extra patrols going down your street."

"I'll call you when the next disaster happens. For sure," Darla snapped. And cut off the call just before she burst into angry, aggrieved sobs. Her tear-fest lasted a couple of long minutes. But she was at work. She couldn't do this right now. She had to straighten up and get back on the job.

In the employees' restroom off the break room, she splashed water on her face, avoiding the mirror, patted herself dry, and got back to work, going to check on the post-op burst appendix in bay five.

That evening, she took Moose to the front yard on his leash, ready to go for a short walk. She spotted a car driving slowly down the block, almost at a snail's pace. Was she standing out here in the yard as a sitting duck, an obvious target for her tormentor?

Darla froze. She couldn't move. Her mind raced, though. Would he throw a brick at her head this time? What if he had a gun? She wouldn't be able to get back inside her house before the car reached her, even at the pace it was going. It was two houses away. Moose gave her a curious look. She realized his leash was quaking from her trembling hands.

The car passed under a streetlamp and she saw the light bar on top. And the lettering on the door. It was a police car. When it got even with her, the police officer stopped, rolled down the passenger window, and ducked her head toward Darla. "Everything okay?" the officer asked.

"Yes, just taking the dog for a walk. Are you...driving here for me?"

"We're going to keep a presence in your neighborhood for a few nights." She pressed a button on the dash and a spotlight suddenly shone from the car into the bushes nearby.

"That's great. I really appreciate it. Should I be taking my dog out? Or should I stay home?"

"No, go ahead." The officer gestured forward. "I'll be back around to check on you and make sure you get home okay."

Darla's tension flowed away. Her step was lighter as she followed Moose down a few blocks, crossed to the other side of the street, then turned back toward home. The car cruised by as she was about to cross back over to her house. The vehicle stopped and waited for her to walk in front of it. The silly thought occurred to her that, technically, she was jaywalking, by crossing in the middle of the block. But the policewoman gave her a smile and a nod and waited until Darla was safely inside before driving away.

After checking everything in her house thoroughly, all the windows and doors, and the bathroom mirror, she decided no one had been inside in the short time while she was gone, and she relaxed with a book and lemonade for the evening. The new locks had done the trick.

She picked out another cozy mystery and read late into the night, since she wasn't working the next day, and relaxed so thoroughly she fell asleep right there on the couch, the book splayed open on her tummy.

Unfortunately, she had slept through the regular time for Moose's last backyard outing. She opened her eyes near midnight to find his eyes staring into hers from inches away. Disoriented, she laughed when she realized where she was, what time it was, and what Moose wanted.

Slipping her shoes on, she let him out the back door and slowly followed.

As soon as he ran to the back fence, however, he started barking.

The fence was only four feet high. It wouldn't be hard for anyone to climb over it, even with the gate locked.

She tried to call her dog, keeping her voice soft. It was much too late for him to be making all this racket, disturbing the neighbors. He didn't hear her over his own noise, so she dashed the length of the yard to grab his collar and shush him. He quieted as soon as she touched him. His head swiveled away from her, though. His ears pricked toward the trees and undergrowth beyond her fence. She heard it too. The rustling of the dense growth. Someone was out there.

Chapter 15

Darla stood utterly still, listening to the rustling in the bushes that grew among the trees. Moose had quit barking and seemed like he was on high alert. As she had when she thought the police car was coming for her earlier, she was paralyzed. Moose peered into the woods, but didn't act like he wanted to go there. The noise stopped. She listened as hard as she could, breathing through her mouth, not making a sound.

Nothing moved. Including Moose and herself.

She took Moose to the middle of the yard to do his business, though his customary spot was near the back fence. He circled four times and eventually got it done. As soon as he finished, she tugged at his collar, taking him—and herself—inside. She didn't run, but she walked quickly.

The relaxed, peaceful feeling she had just achieved—the feeling of being safe on her walk as well as in her house—was gone. She lay awake in her bed, wondering if Moose had heard a rabbit, or a possum. Or a human predator. Wouldn't he have wanted to chase a varmint? She wished she could ask him. Well, she could, but she wished he could answer.

When Moose whined to go out, Darla opened her eyes, not surprised it was morning already. She must have slept for all of two or three hours. After letting him out and filling his food and water bowls, however, she went back to bed. She had read somewhere, once, a person should take a day off once a month and spent it in bed. The logistics of that were difficult, she thought. How would she eat? Go to the bathroom? Take care of her dog? That Friday, though, she came close. She didn't even get her bow and arrows out.

A call to the local glass company resulted in getting her window fixed in record time. After they left, she didn't stir much at all. Until late afternoon. Her mother called to ask her to their usual Friday dinner.

"Are you feeling good, Mom?" Darla asked.

"I guess so. As well as I ever do. Why?"

"Are you up for something different? Do you want to go out to dinner?"

"Oh my. What would I wear? My hair isn't fixed."

Her mother had an extensive wardrobe and got her hair fixed every Wednesday. "I'll help you get ready. I just want to do something different."

"I haven't been outside for ages."

Her mother had become something of a recluse. Admittedly, it was hard for her to get around, being mostly confined to her wheelchair. But tonight, Darla would get her out of her rut, would push her chair, help her in and out of her car, and her mother could get a change of scenery. Darla didn't know how she could stand being in her house, staring at the same walls, rolling over the same floors, every single day. Maybe it was different when you were older, Darla thought. But going out to eat might do them both a lot of good. Moose would be fine at home alone for the amount of time it took to eat out.

She changed into nice slacks and a pastel blouse, then went out the front door—to discover a large box that had been left by UPS. With trepidation, she leaned over and read the return address. It was from Nabbem. Oh yes, she thought, relieved. That was the security system company. She had ordered this a week ago. Darla was glad the cameras and the system were here, but now she would have to get everything installed and working. She hefted the box up and stuck it inside her front door. She would deal with this later. Maybe it would be easy enough for her to do.

Ha. She pictured herself on a ladder attaching cameras to her eaves, not being fond of being more than three steps up off the ground. She should probably get some help.

Putting this out of her mind for tonight, she drove over to help her mom get ready for their evening. She had fun picking out a long, navy-blue dress with pearl buttons on the bodice. In spite of being partially paralyzed, her mom could stand on her own for a few moments, so it wasn't especially hard to help her dress. Her limitation was walking for more than a few steps. And getting up if she was on the floor, of course. Darla combed her mother's hair and pinned it up with a pearl hair comb, to match the buttons on her dress.

"Take me over there." Her mother pointed to the floor length mirror on the other side of her bed. Darla pushed her chair over there. Amy pushed herself out of her chair and struck a pose, turning to admire both sides. "My, I look pretty decent. You did a good job, Darla."

Darla thought so, too. She needed this evening as much as, maybe more than, her mother, to take her mind off everything. "I'm working with good material."

Her mother gave her a smile and returned to the chair.

"Where are we going?" her mother asked, as Darla steered the wheelchair out the front door. The front steps had been covered on one side with a ramp when Mrs. Taylor became unable to walk. They went down the incline, then followed the sidewalk to the driveway.

"Do you have someplace you'd like to go?" Darla asked.

Her mother brightened, cocked her head, and said, "Yes. Gin was talking about a brand-new Italian place today."

"Luigi's?" Darla had heard an ad for it on television and thought it was mostly a pizza place, but if Gin recommended it, they could try it.

"Gin says they have good calzones. You know I love those."

Maybe it was more than pizzas. She would love to find a new Italian place. She and her mother did their customary dance, getting Amy up from the chair and swiveling her into the front passenger seat. Then Darla folded and stowed the wheelchair in her trunk. She estimated she had probably put an inch on her biceps lifting this thing. And from lifting her mother, too, although she never bore her full weight. Darla's car was fairly new and one of the requirements, when she had bought it, was that it would comfortably hold her mother's wheelchair. She had even taken the measurements to the car dealer and inspected each trunk of every car she looked at.

When they entered the restaurant, Darla was surprised and impressed by the muted lighting, the cloth-covered tables, and the general ambiance of genteel dining. They did, indeed, serve calzones, and a mushroom rigatoni dish Darla had loved at her first bite.

The service had been so prompt they hadn't had much chance to chat, but Darla took a break half way through her entrée, noticing her mother had quit eating.

"I'll take the rest of this home." Her mother fiddled with her fork, not scooping up any food. "I can't eat all of that."

Darla thought maybe she would do the same. But before she left the restaurant, she had to talk to her mother about what the detective had told her. This was a nice atmosphere and there was no place for her mother to escape, to avoid answering her questions.

"Mom, do you know where my father is living?"

"I've told you I don't. I did ask him to stop bothering me. I don't think he'll come around anymore." Her mother looked at her hands, folded in her lap, while she told Darla this.

She was obviously lying. Not only did her body language tell Darla that, but the detective had indicated that she knew. When her mother didn't meet her eyes, it usually meant she wasn't being honest with her. She'd known her mother for a long, long time. This behavior predated the wheelchair.

"But you told him to stay away?"

"I just said that. Why don't you believe me?"

That would be good news. If it was true. If she really did tell him to stay away. But she was lying about not knowing where he lived, for certain. She wanted to confront her mother on this, but maybe she should leave it alone. If her mother had, indeed, told him to stop bothering her, that would be a big step. She would hope she had.

Gin called as Darla got home. "Darla, I have to tell you this. Your mother made me promise not to, but this is affecting her health. Her blood pressure was sky high this afternoon. If it's that way the next time I'm there, I'll have to call her doctor."

"What are you talking about?" *What now?* She had just gotten the issue of her father begging and borrowing from her settled. Maybe.

"It's her ex. Your father."

"What about him? She just told me, minutes ago, she told him to stay away." Which Darla didn't quite believe, however.

"I thought he was supposed to show up when one of us aides are here."

"Well, yes, that's what I asked her to do. But she said she actually told him not to come around anymore."

"I don't think that's what she told him. After I left today, I stayed in my car to make a few phone calls and send some texts. About half an hour after I left the house, he showed up."

Darla wondered if steam was pluming from the top of her head. It felt like it. For sure, she was gnashing her teeth and balling up the fist not holding the phone. Her mother had totally deceived her! Had lied to her! Again! And probably felt she'd gotten away with it, too. The deception was affecting her blood pressure. It was probably affecting Darla's, too.

Chapter 16

Saturday morning, Detective Coleman called her. Again. She was impressed he called on a Saturday, but maybe they didn't strictly work Monday through Friday. After all, she didn't.

"I have some information for you, but I want to caution you against acting on it." His authoritative voice was reassuring.

"You found out who's after me?"

"We're going to try to find out. Your father was observed approaching your mother, against the orders of his probation."

"He's still on probation?" Maybe she wouldn't need protective orders if he was violating probation.

"It gets extended each time he violates it. We can probably bring him in for questioning."

That was good. "Do you really think you can find out if it's him?"

"All we can do is try to get him to talk. I need to urge you not to confront him. It might be dangerous. We are keeping an eye on him and his residence, as well as you."

"Can you put him back in prison for violating parole? That would solve all of our problems."

"It's not that simple. But, like I said, we'll talk to him."

Could she find out where he was living? He was in Charity. The town wasn't that big. "Okay. I'm just glad you found him. Is it near my mother's house? What's his address?"

He grunted. "No, like I keep saying, I'm not going to tell you that. I want you to stay away from him."

"Is that an order? It's not, is it?"

Before she heard the complete exasperation that would soon come to his voice, she ended the call. She didn't want him angry with her. But she had to do something. It looked like he wasn't allowed to give her orders. Or maybe he was and was exasperated she didn't know that. She was going to go on the assumption he could not tell her what to do and what not to do.

Now, could she even figure out where Todd was living? It was a possibility. The cheapest apartments were near downtown. She would start her search there, just south of the business district.

"Come on, Moose, let's go for a ride." It was time to deal with this.

The dog dashed to the door and they set out. She started by crisscrossing the area she thought would be most likely, driving up and down the residential streets, slowly. It wasn't long before she spotted a man who was about the height she thought her father was, as nearly as she could remember. He walked along the sidewalk, then turned into a large apartment complex.

In spite of being called Oak Tree Apartments, there wasn't a tree in sight, oak or otherwise. Moose was in the back seat, intensely interested in this part of town, new to him and probably steeped in smells that were foreign to him. For instance, the occasional used condom and discarded drug needle near the curb were probably awfully intriguing to him. So, he wouldn't be tempted to jump out, Darla kept the window cracked only a couple of inches, so he could poke his nose out, but not get his mouth on any of the filth in the streets.

At the corners of the two-story buildings grew a few scraggly bushes. It looked like the apartments were built four-plex style, two up and two down in each building. Air conditioning units poked through the walls, most turned off, but one or two running with a low hum and dripping onto the sparse grass below. The sign in front proclaimed "Air Cond" and "TV" were available, like an old motel. At least it didn't post hourly rates.

She peered as far down the drive as she could. There must have been twenty or thirty units. How was she going to locate him? The walking man was no longer in sight.

She started to drive farther into the complex, but spotted a police car several driveways away. Were they here because they were keeping track of her father? That would mean he did live in this complex. On the other hand, the car could be here because of a call. Domestic violence, burglary, whatever else the police did all day long.

Taking note of the location, she resolved to return to try to find out if Todd Taylor lived here, and to confront him later, whenever, finally. No one could keep her away from her own father.

At home, she searched her own place to see if anyone had gotten in while she was gone, her new habit. The boxed cameras sat exactly where she had left them. They hadn't installed themselves. She called the handyman service she had used the last time her sinks backed up. They said they could send someone late that afternoon to install the security system. She would stay home until then. Soon, she could quit doing those searches every time she came home. That would be so nice!

On her inside prowl today, it seemed that nothing had been disturbed in the living room and kitchen. The bedroom looked fine. The cap was off her toothpaste. Had she left it off? She never did that. But, in her present distracted state, maybe she had today. None of it had been squirted out. No messages were anywhere to be found.

She settled down with the last book she had started to wait for the service to show up.

The handyman, when he finally got there, as the day was waning, worked quickly and efficiently. He put a camera over her front door, then asked where she wanted the other three. She had considered it and had him put one in the back, aimed at the fence, at the far end of the yard. The other two went on the two front corners of her house. Nothing would be able to penetrate the box elder bushes between her property and the next-door neighbor, but they would capture someone going into them, hiding there, and coming out.

After he left, she made a few forays around her property so she could be filmed, to see how the system worked. She had sprung for the Bluetooth that sent reports to her phone, so was able to look at her movements when she came in. It was dark, so the night vision of the system was tested, too. The camera in the back of the yard, though the light was pretty good, was disappointing because it didn't reach very far. But it would catch someone as they approached the house, anyway. And it would, she presumed, record more during the day, beyond the reach of the lights, if she should be assaulted in the daytime.

She erased what she had done and set the system up to capture whatever happened next, going forward.

Next task. How could she find out exactly where her father was living? She called her mother. She had an idea. Might as well try it. "Mom, I bought myself a cherry pie and have a lot leftover. Can I bring you a piece?"

"That would be lovely, dear. I was just looking for something to eat before I go to bed."

"I'll be over in a few minutes. Half an hour, okay?"

"It will take you that long?"

"I just have something I have to do first. I'll be right there."

What she had to do first was go to a bakery and buy a cherry pie, then zip home, cut three pieces, and wrap them. Then she would be ready to take them to her mother's place. She felt a little bad about her sneaky plan, but couldn't figure out anything better. Cherry pie was a sure-fire draw for her mother.

She let herself into her mother's place with her own key this time, since no one was with her mother right now and she didn't want to make her come to the door.

"I'm in the bathroom," Mrs. Taylor called, in answer to Darla's *yoo-hoo*. "I'll be out in two or three minutes."

Things were going right for her. This gave Darla the chance she had wanted to paw through the drawers in her mother's desk. She came upon a piece of buried treasure very quickly. A paper on which her mother had written:

Todd...Oak Tree...317

Oak Tree! Those were the apartments she had been trying to scout.

She put a piece of pie on a plate for her mother, watched her finish it, then left, feeling only slightly deceptive.

In bed that night, Darla tossed and turned. With her new locks and keys, and with the new security system, she should have felt secure. But the toothpaste tube with the lid off loomed large in her thoughts, keeping her awake for hours. Did she leave it off? No, she never left it off. But she was so distracted lately. She might have left it off. Yes, no, yes, no, rocketed through her thoughts for a few hours.

Moose stood beside her bed and growled in the wee hours of the morning. Darla made herself stay in bed. She told herself no one could get in. No one could harm her. No one could harass her. She was safe. Even if she couldn't sleep.

In the morning, she checked all the recordings and they showed nothing but two raccoons (or the same one twice), a neighboring cat, and a possum. A small rodent was being carried by the cat. The raccoon stopped to look through the grass a few times. There was a busy nightlife in her backyard. Who knew? It was kind of fun to watch all the little creatures. An extra bonus of the cameras that she hadn't thought about.

Darla lazed around in the morning, doing laundry, and cooking a few meals for the week. She shot a few arrows, being out of practice, since she had neglected it for a few days. When she loaded the dishwasher and started to run it, she discovered she was nearly out of dishwashing detergent. There was enough for this load, but she wasn't doing anything else, so might as well run out and get some. The ice cream situation was not very good, either. There was plenty of vanilla, but rocky road was low. Maybe it was decadent, but she liked to have two ice cream flavors on hand. She didn't always want the same kind.

Leaving Moose at home this time, she walked out to her driveway. The driver's side of her vehicle was at the edge of her property, away from the front door, and, when she rounded the front of her car, she saw there was another flat tire. She leaned down. There were those same parallel lines cutting the sidewall. It was deliberate again.

Gin and Bobby weren't around this time. She would have to figure it out herself. She had used her spare tire the last time, so she couldn't change it until she got a new one.

When she called the garage where she usually got her oil changed, they said they could get there within an hour or two with a new tire, so she waited by the front window, getting more furious by the minute. Was there a way her camera could have caught that? The angle was all wrong, she realized, but she might as well look to see what could be changed. When she reviewed the recordings again, there wasn't a thing on them that showed this happening. The man—her dad—whoever, must have noticed the cameras and avoided them. No wonder she hadn't slept easy. This was what had made Moose growl during the night, most likely. Was she ever going to be safe?

There was no note this time, but the jerk would have had to expose himself to her new camera, at the corner of the house, to put a note on the windshield. That was, no doubt, why there was not a note this time. It had to be the same jerk, though, the Knock Knock Guy. Who else would it be?

In the process of aiming bad thoughts at her father, Zeke flitted through her mind. Then Bobby. Should she mention Zeke to the police? She had never given Detective Coleman his name. No, it was too long ago. He didn't even live in Charity.

While she waited, she called the security company to see if they could help her to tell whether or not appropriate adjustments could be made. No one could come out until Monday.

That was great. Just great. At least she was off Monday.

At least she had gotten the tire fixed. They had come out exactly as promised and hadn't even charged much.

Now she had to wait for the security company people on Monday before she could leave long enough to scout out her father's apartment and try to talk to him without the police noticing. If that was even possible.

Chapter 17

Monday morning, however, a glance at the calendar on Darla's phone reminded her she had a much more pressing issue. How could she have forgotten that? Was she losing her mind from all this stress? She called the security company and told them they would have to come later to adjust the cameras. She would let them know. They seemed okay with this, but vague about the possibility of being able to improve the positions and what they could catch for her.

This morning, her popup message from herself on her phone said she had to go to the county courthouse to get the protective order for herself. She would inquire about one for her mother, too. Would she need that, in addition to the probation order? If only they knew who the stalker was.

She was glad she didn't have to drive to another town, since Charity was the county seat of Faire County. Even better, since she was in a hurry to get this done, she got a parking spot on the square, close to the front door of the county building. That would never happen in a big city. She went to the same counter she'd gone to before. After letting the woman behind the window know she had an appointment, she was told to wait in one of the plastic chairs lined up against the wall. They were incongruous and ugly in the graceful old building, but were surely cheap and also easy to clean. There had to be a reason someone bought them. They were uncomfortable, though.

Her wait went on for nearly twenty minutes before she was called to the window and directed down the hallway. She was glad to leave the hard plastic.

The room she entered was high-ceilinged, like the rest of the first floor, but the surfaces were crowded with stacks of papers, binders, and books. She almost missed seeing the small, harried-looking man, dwarfed by the huge oak desk he sat behind.

"First thing," he said, without introducing himself, "is to get you to fill out this form." He held a piece of paper out to her without meeting her eyes. Darla took it from him, thinking she probably could have been doing this form over the weekend, or maybe in the waiting room, rather than wasting her appointment time now. Bureaucracy earned its reputation for inefficient red tape.

"Thanks, Mr..."

He looked up from his papers and frowned. She could almost hear him thinking, *Oh, she wants my name.*

"I'm Peter Hawk.".

That would make a good name for a handsome actor. Darla was amused. Not such a good name for the rather shriveled, sparrow-like man in this room.

She sat down and started to fill out the form. She was barely started when she was stumped by the space to name the person she wanted protection from.

"Sir? The person I want this for? Against? From? I'm not quite sure who is after me, but I have a good guess."

He frowned again. "You don't know who you need protection from?"

"That's right. I think it's my father, my mother's ex. He's in town and he's been bothering her."

"And you don't know if he's bothering you or not?"

Darla shook her head. "Someone is bothering me. I just haven't caught them in the act."

He stood and reached over the desk, snatching the paper back from her. "Come back when you know who you need to file against. We can't give you an order against nobody."

Darla looked at the high white ceiling, carved in ornate, flowery squares. "I guess that makes sense. Can I get an order to protect my mother from him?"

"You say he has been bothering her. What, exactly is he doing?"

"He's asking her for money."

"Is he threatening her? Hurting her?"

Darla's spirits fell. "He's demanding money." That wasn't true, as far as she knew. Her mother seemed to be giving him the money willingly. But she wanted to keep him away from her. She could stretch the facts to do that. She didn't mention the parole violation. Maybe he could be socked with two separate violations. "He's hurt her in the past. I'm afraid he will again."

"Then she'll have to come in to get an order against him. She has to sign it, not you."

He returned his attention to the paper pile on the desk, dismissing her.

Oh well, there was the other order he was violating. The parole. That was a good safety net. She hoped he would be picked up soon for that. She could breathe more easily after that was done.

It looked like she would have plenty of time to get the security people back to her house to readjust the camera, or maybe the cameras, plural. Maybe she would even have to buy another one. She hoped not. Before she started her car, she phoned them again. She was glad they agreed to be at her house in an hour or two. After the phone call, Darla started home.

On the way, she thought about her mother, and how she could protect her. Once more, Darla considered putting her mother into some sort of facility, some sort of home. There was a place not far from her house, a fairly new complex, which offered graduated levels of care. From what Darla could tell, looking at their site online, a person ideally started out in Independent Living. When they needed more help, they could be moved to Assisted Living. The highest level of care was the Nursing Home.

Would Amy be able to live in the Independent Living section? Maybe not. She might have to skip a step and go directly to Assisted Living. Some people probably did that. Darla knew her mother would never discuss any of this with her. She'd tried more than a few times. All Amy Taylor would ever say was, "I'm not going to a home."

If the place was nice, and if Darla could somehow get her to visit there, maybe her mind could be changed, though. Her mother would be more protected in a facility than in her home. She knew she would have to visit it herself before mentioning it to her.

Her mother's house was on the way home, so Darla swung by. She didn't want to go in, just to drive past—she couldn't say why. She knew Gin wasn't working at her mother's today. One of the other workers, an older woman named Joyce was there today from OTB, Only The Best home healthcare.

She slowed, approaching the house, but braked when a man walked out the front door. Yes, this was why she had wanted to swing by. She was still a block away and couldn't quite tell who he was. Her first thought, of course, was it was her father, but the man didn't quite look like him. It had been years since she'd seen her father so she couldn't be sure. This man was about the same height and build she remembered. And he might be bald now, but the last time she laid eyes on him, he had the same hair she did, straight and brown. This man's head was covered in dark, glossy wavy hair. Definitely not him. Surely, he wouldn't be wearing a wig. Would he?

The man turned away from her at the public sidewalk and she didn't get a look at his face. At least her father hadn't been there. That was a relief. Maybe he was a salesman who had been turned away.

Chapter 18

I t was midday by the time Darla got home from her aborted protective-order mission. Within fifteen minutes, the person from the handy-man service knocked on her front door. She had cut it close. But the timing was working out perfectly.

She led him to her driveway, on the left side of her property as you faced it from the street. They ducked under the low boughs of the small tree in the yard. She could see the larger tree, next to the carport would have blocked any useful view.

"Someone tampered with my car yesterday, slashed my left tire. The cameras didn't film it, though. He was on the other side of the car, away from the house. Is there some way I could get this side of my car covered by a camera?"

The man rubbed his chin and stared at her new tire, then peered up at the camera hanging from the eave at the corner. "Well, no, you see. This angle...it just won't do it. There's no way. It can't shoot around a corner and the tree is blocking the view."

"There's nowhere else you could put another camera to get this spot? Maybe you could put one on a pole, out here, or something?" She gestured, vaguely to an area of the yard on the other side of her car. She had briefly considered asking for one on the carport, but she knew that camera there would not be able to see what was beneath its roof. Unless it hung down?

She suggested that.

He shook his head, looking so sad. "It has to be attached to a house."

"Are you sure you can't?"

"How do you think we would do that?" His sad expression gave way to a wounded one, with maybe a hint of belligerence behind it. "Where would a camera go that would film this side of your car?"

Darla looked from her car to the corner, repeating the man's motions. She had to admit he was right. A camera would have to be put onto her next-door neighbor's house to catch this. The car itself was in the way and would shield anyone on the driver's side.

"I guess I need a camera on my car."

He gave her a pained look. "We don't do those. Nobody does that."

Maybe she needed a car alarm. That would have to wait for her next paycheck. She hoped her money would stretch for rent and groceries until then, actually.

After the man left, she took her archery gear to the backyard, leaving a morose Moose behind in the house, and shot a few ends, missing wildly, then settling down a bit. But never hitting the center of the target. She felt only slightly less jangled and frustrated as she let Moose bound across the yard. Again, he stared through the chain link in to the woods for a moment, then went about his business. The dog's behavior didn't calm her nerves at all. She wished he would completely ignore the area outside her fence.

At this moment, she wanted to throw an axe. Really hard. But it would probably go wild, too, in her present state. After all, she hadn't been able to hit the target all that much at Axe Me.

As twilight fell, around six-thirty, she decided to see if she could get past the police sentinel, if that's what it was, the car she had spotted earlier at Oak Tree, the place she now knew to be her father's apartment complex. On the one hand, she was glad they were keeping track of him and not letting him out of their sight. On the other hand, if he was getting out of their sight anyway, this made it hard for her to keep track of him.

She made steeled herself and dressed for the occasion.

It was beginning to be her custom to walk around her car and inspect it every time she used it, which she now did before she got into it and began to drive. All was well. This time. Something was going right.

She parked two blocks away from the street and started walking. She had worn a jacket with a hood, which she pulled up as she turned the corner and started down the internal road into the complex. That had been how she dressed for the occasion, to avoid her face being seen by cameras and people. The unmarked car was still parked in a driveway one building away from where she thought Todd Taylor's was located. She was careful, even with the hood up to keep her head down as she walked past the vehicle.

She kept going, walking, she hoped, with purpose—not ambling along and not rushing, trying to look as if she knew where she was going and walked here all the time. It was surprising how hard it was to make herself walk naturally when she was concentrating on trying to do just that, while keeping her head down and her face hidden. Her body was fighting her. It seemed hesitant to do what her mind wanted it to. "Nonchalant," she told herself. "Be nonchalant. This is no big deal." Her body knew that was a lie.

She had to look up to see the apartment numbers as she passed each building so she would approach the right one. They each held four apartments, and one was labeled 317-320. That one had to be his, if the address at her mother's was correct.

Oak Tree...317

As soon as she started up the sidewalk toward the correct one, a car door slammed. She didn't look around at the surveillance car she knew was there, but quickened her pace just a tad.

It wasn't enough. A large hand tapped her shoulder and she turned around to face a burly man whose light jacket bulged under his left arm. She let herself glance at the patrol car. It was empty.

"Where are you going?" His voice was gruff and unfriendly. A smoker's voice.

"I'm headed toward apartment three-twenty. My friend is staying there." There had to be a 320, the sign said so. 317-320.

He narrowed his eyes at her. Pinning her in place with those steely eyes, he drew his phone out of his pocket. "What's your name?"

"Andrea. Andrea Martin. Who are you?"

He spoke into the phone. "Yeah, she matches the description. Says her name is Andrea Martin." Aiming the phone at her, he snapped her picture, then spoke to the person on the other end again, listening, then saying, "Yeah, that's what I thought." Then he spoke to her again. "Are you lying to the police? Are you sure you want to do that?" His voice was even harsher and more gruff as he flashed a badge in a holder for her see.

Darla's breathing and her heartrate both sped up. "I didn't know you were the police. I'm sorry. I'm Darla Taylor. I just want to speak to my father."

"My orders are to keep you away from him. Go home. Forget about him."

"Who did you call just now?"

There was no answer to that, but she knew Detective Coleman was behind this. He had to be. He was kind of overstepping his job, protecting her like this. Damn him.

Chapter 19

It had been another unsuccessful trip. Darla pounded on her steering wheel a few times before driving to her mother's. Maybe she could talk to her some more about Todd. Or maybe he would be there. What would she do then? It occurred to her she hadn't even planned what to do or say if she had found him in his apartment. Maybe it was good she had been prevented from going to his door. What if he had known who she was when he saw her? And what if he had been angry about her confronting him? He had a terrible temper. What if he had lost it right there? She knew he was capable of harming people. His own family.

For years after he had injured her mother and disappeared from their lives ten years ago when she was eighteen, she had been torn between missing him and being glad she would never see him again. Wishing she could hug him and hoping she and her mother were rid of him for good. A series of brief counselling sessions had helped her to sort out her feelings somewhat and recognize what they were, but she had never adequately dealt with those feelings, never understood just what they were. She had buried them deep within herself. That's what helped her cope. Some of what she had buried was fear. Fear paralyzed her at times. She hadn't been able to function that way, so she had shoved it down. It was what she had to do. And it had worked for a long time.

But those deeply buried feelings had started to surface when she dated Bobby, who sometimes acted so much like her father had, when he was drunk anyway. Those had been frightening times. Dating Bobby, she had once again started having the dreams that had darkened her nights after her mother was injured and while she recovered enough to leave the hospital.

In those terrible dreams, that dark shape loomed at the foot of her bed, projecting malice, danger, and somehow making her know he could see all of her innermost thoughts. And he sneered at them. Even after she had had the dream so many times that the figure was familiar, she never got over the cold knot of breathless dread that remained in her chest when she awoke from the dream.

What if she could confront her father and talk to him, and quit having those dreams? She had wanted to try. She still wanted to, but maybe not alone.

While she was stopped at a light, she called her mother, who told her to go ahead and come over. When she got there, she was both relieved and disappointed her father wasn't there. It was seven-thirty in the evening, after the aide had gone home, so there was a possibility he would try to sneak in.

"Hi Mom, how was your day?" Darla breezed in, trying not to show how uptight she was feeling. She stuck her hands in her jacket pocket so they wouldn't shake.

"Very good. You know Joyce was here today and she brought me some of her homemade blueberry muffins."

"Did you save any for me?"

"Oh goodness, yes. She brings too many. I had as much as I could. Go ahead and have some."

Darla went to the kitchen and found a plate with five muffins on it. She suspected Joyce had brought half a dozen and her mother had eaten a total of one. She bent over them to get a whiff. They gave off a comforting aroma of baked dough and sweet berries. Peeling the paper off one and taking a delicious bite, holding a plate beneath to catch the crumbs, she joined her mother in the living room.

"Joyce hasn't lost her touch, has she? These are so good." In spite of the plate, some crumbs escaped to the couch seat. She picked them up and put them back onto the plate.

"It's so sad. She's pulling back and semi-retiring. She'll just be doing fill-in and substitute work, she says. I'll miss her."

"I will, too. Well, I'll miss her muffins." Darla never saw much of her. She didn't see much of any of her mother's caretakers, except for Gin, and rarely saw her when she was at her mother's, only outside her working hours. The aides worked roughly the same hours Darla often did, so their paths didn't cross much. "I guess they'll send someone new, right?"

"They say they already have a replacement, to start on Gin's next day off."

Gin's days weren't always regular, so Darla asked when that was.

"You'll have to look on the schedule, dear."

Darla wandered to the desk, feeling a tiny bit guilty for having snooped there for her father's address last time she was there, but only a tiny bit. "Gin is working tomorrow and the next two days. Tuesday through Thursday. That's a short week for her."

"I believe she has plans next weekend with that new boyfriend."

"She never said anything about that to me." Gin was being way too secretive with this guy. Darla didn't like that. Was she jealous? Maybe. "I hope you like the new aide."

"Oh, I hope so too. Remember the one we had such a problem with a few months ago?"

Darla nodded. How could she forget? One very young woman had flaunted all the rules and precautions. She got there late, left early, and, in spite of the rules against it, and in spite of both Darla and Amy scolding her about it, kept sneaking cigarettes in the bathroom. It was obvious when she did it. The smoke wafted throughout the entire house. Amy's lungs weren't too healthy due to her inaction since her fall, and she couldn't tolerate the smoke. Eventually they had to call the service and ask for a replacement for her.

"If there's a problem with this one, we'll know, this time, to complain right away and demand a switch," Darla noted, around the muffin she was still devouring. It was almost gone.

"Yes, we will. I should tell you about something that happened."

She was going to admit her father was still coming around?

"I got a phone call from the prison."

"Prison? Oh, from your first husband?" The one who was sent to prison for raping her as well as a few other women, too. Darla was glad that man wasn't her father, anyway. He sounded worse than Ted.

"He hasn't called for a long time. Maybe two years or so."

"He called you two years ago?" So, he knew her number. And probably where she lived.

"I was on the list of people he could call."

"You consented to receiving calls from him from prison?"

"Yes. There weren't many people he could call."

She wasn't making sense. She should not have been in touch with him. "Are you okay?"

"Yes, just a little shaken by hearing his voice again."

Darla put her empty plate on the coffee table and pulled a chair over next to her mother's wheelchair to put her arms around her.

"Thank you, darling. You're such a good daughter. At least Todd didn't make me give you up."

Give her up? What a strange thing to say. An intake of her mother's breath told Darla she had said something she shouldn't have. "What do you mean? Why would you give me up?"

"Just...the other one. Something else. But not you."

Darla tried to make sense of what her mother was telling her. *The other one? Another baby?*

"Mother, you gave up a baby?"

Chapter 20

"My first husband forced me to give up the baby," Darla's mother said. She looked over Darla's shoulder, not meeting her eyes. "I didn't fight him too hard, since I'm sure I got pregnant with the baby the night Elliot raped me. The baby would have reminded me of that night forever." She clenched her hands in her lap and took some short breaths.

"He raped you only once?" She had always thought he had probably done it more than once. Maybe her mother only defined the worst one as rape. She dropped her arms from her mother's shoulders as Amy pulled away.

Amy Taylor wheeled her chair to the window and stared out at the raindrops that had begun to splatter on the window. They made a sound Darla had always found unpleasant, for some reason. Had it been raining that night? The one of her dreams? Her nightmares?

"I suppose many of our…sessions…could be loosely called that. This one time, though, it was more violent than the others. I was sore from the day before when he'd demanded sex four times."

"In one day?" Her mother was in denial, but maybe that's what she had had to do, living with that man. After all, Darla had denied her memories, too. Or had tried to.

Her mother nodded, still facing the window. "I was raw. I tried to push him away. That made him so mad. And, of course, he was drunk. Very drunk. It was the weekend and he'd been drinking for two days."

"You would think that would make it hard for him to...you know."

"Not that man. The more he drank, the randier he got, and the more often he wanted it."

She had never heard her mother speak this way. Using these words, talking about these subjects. She had undergone therapy too, but Darla didn't know how much she had done, or if any of it had helped her. "Mom, that's so awful. I'm so sorry there was no one to help you."

Her mother turned her head. There were tears in her eyes. Then she turned to stare out the window again. "It wouldn't have mattered. I wouldn't have gotten help. He would have found out and I'd have been in worse trouble." She remained silent for a few moments, lost in the past. "That was the last time, though. He was positively brutal. He threw me onto the floor and my head banged on the edge of a table going down. Afterward, I was bleeding from my head and from...down there. When he saw all the blood—there was quite a bit—it sobered him. He apologized for an hour, then he left for a few days."

"Where did he go?"

"I didn't know at the time. But now I think he was out raping other women."

"Mom, I wonder if he was afraid you were badly hurt, or would die. He might have been afraid to come home and see what shape you were in." Of course he wouldn't have stayed to make sure she was okay. Darla gritted her teeth with hatred for the man.

"Yes, that was my thought, too." Amy turned to her daughter. "You and I think alike so much of the time, don't we? We have the same thoughts."

Darla didn't actually think that was true very often. Right now, she was sure her mother wasn't thinking the same thing she was. Other than coming up with the same reason for Elliot Ryan to stay away, Darla was also appalled that her mother had put up with the abuse, hadn't sought help, had let the man almost kill her. "And you got pregnant."

"Yes. We didn't have sex again for months. He had used protection the times before. That's how I know it was that night. Darla, I didn't even want the baby. Ever. When he said he was going to make me get rid of it, that's when I finally wanted to leave him for good. I wanted to have the baby, but not to keep it. It was selfish of me, really. I couldn't bear to keep it, but I didn't want to have the death of it on my conscience. What if it's held against me?"

"What do you mean? Who would hold it against you?"

"God. God would. Well, God might. Who knows?"

Darla realized her mother was talking about Judgment Day. They hadn't been religious, had rarely gone to church, but the Heaven and Hell stuff was on her mother's mind, for sure. With the tears streaming from her mother's eyes, Darla had to hug her. As angry as she was about how her mother had let herself be treated, right now she needed a hug. Darla bent over and wrapped her arms around her mother's thin frame. It was an awkward exercise, while standing, but one she had perfected soon after her mother had been confined to a wheelchair. It was their special way of hugging.

"When did you leave him, Mom? Was that when you did it?"

"Leave him? I didn't leave him. I wanted to, but I didn't dare. He was arrested and put into prison for those other rapes."

At least all women weren't as docile as her mother, Darla was glad to know. They had to have testified against him.

"Do you know what happened to the baby?" Darla asked.

"I never wanted to know. Never asked."

That was another big way Darla's thinking was different from her mother's. She would have had to find out.

"I'm afraid, now that Elliot is…"

"Is what, Mom?"

"Nothing. Nothing at all." Her mother looked away, then wheeled herself to the table next to the sofa where she kept her cup of tea, her glasses, the television remote, and some reading material. Was she being evasive?

The rain increased its tempo. It beat faster and harder against the glass. Darla's anxiety went up a notch. Why was that sound so uncomfortable? It was just sad to her and…just sad. Filling her with sorrow. Rain on a window had always been that way for her.

"Is he getting out? Is that what he called to tell you?"

"Well…" She looked away again, avoiding Darla's eyes again.

"Mother, has he contacted you? Have you seen him?" Again, she wasn't sure if her mother was being truthful. Why did she not want to tell Darla anything about these men? These awful men she had been married to? Was she trying to protect her daughter from them? Darla was old enough she didn't need protecting that way.

"No, no, dear. I haven't seen him."

Darla came back to the topic a couple more times, but her mother wouldn't admit to knowing when Elliot Ryan was being released, or if he already *was* released.

Darla drove home through a driving rain wondering if she could believe what her mother had said. How could she find out if he had actually been released? It was frustrating she was being so evasive. That was a sign she was lying, sometimes, too. Why couldn't she tell her own daughter the truth?

Tuesday morning, before work, she called the station for Detective Coleman and was put through to him right away. He spoke before she could bring up the subject of Elliot Ryan.

"We are bringing Todd Taylor in for questioning soon. Is that what you're calling about?"

"No, but that's good to know. When are you bringing him in?" Maybe she could waylay him after that.

"I can't tell you." Did that mean he knew and wouldn't tell her? She moved on to the subject she had called about. "The reason I called is because I've been talking to my mother about her first husband, Elliot Ryan." She spelled the name for him. "I think he might have been released from prison, or might be released soon. Can you tell me if he has been?"

"Do you know where he was incarcerated?"

Why hadn't she thought to ask her mother that? "I guess I don't. Can you find out?"

The clicking of his keyboard came over the line. Surely, he could locate a prisoner. Surely, he was in Ohio.

"Here he is," the detective said. "Okay. Looks like...looks like he got of Marion about a week ago."

After a moment of stunned silence, Darla shouted, "A week ago? She knew and didn't tell me. I know she knew that."

"Who knew? Your mother?"

Darla clamped her lips together, too angry to speak. "Um hm."

"Ms. Taylor, if your mother was listed as his contact, she would have been notified by the facility when he was released. Yes, she almost surely knew."

"So, he got out last Tuesday?"

"A little over a week, then. Last Monday."

"So, he could have thrown the brick through my window?"

"Ms. Taylor, that's unlikely."

"Why is it unlikely?" There went her voice, up half an octave. It was so annoying when it did that.

"The note with the brick."

Oh yes, the note. "You mean because it matched the other notes. The ones before that. And the phone calls."

"Yes. If he had made the calls from prison, before he was out, they would have been noticed. And he was still inside for the other incidents."

"Okay. Thanks, Detective." That was a bit of relief. Frustrating, because it didn't answer anything, but a tiny relief.

Back to square one. Unless Elliot Ryan had someone outside the prison doing his dirty work. But why would he want to harass her? Did he even know she existed? She wouldn't keep him on her mental list of suspects. It was a short list. Only one person was on it, again. Todd Taylor.

Chapter 21

Later, after work, Darla gave contacting her father another try. An idea had occurred to her while she was at work. She would tail him *from* his apartment, since, even though she had just about located it, she couldn't follow him *to* it. After going home and changing her clothes, and, of course, tending to Moose, she parked around the corner, where the guardian police car couldn't see her. And waited. And waited. And waited.

She was finally rewarded when, soon after 8:30, he came walking around the corner and headed down the street, going away from her. Quickly, she slid out of her car, locking it with the button so it wouldn't beep, and started after him. With him on foot, it made more sense for her to tail him that way, rather than in the car.

He hadn't gone far before he walked into a small neighborhood diner. It looked rather dingy, but maybe that's what he could afford. On her mother's money. Through the large, streaked windows, she could see him take a seat at the counter. After a half a minute or so, she pushed the door open and took a seat on a stool covered with cracked plastic, leaving one in between them.

The counter server approached him first, taking a pad and pen from her apron pocket, and got his order for coffee and a ham sandwich with chips, then moved to Darla.

"I'll have the same," Darla told the young woman, not really wanting to eat anything and not wanting to waste time looking at the menu. It was too late at night for her to drink coffee, but she knew she would nibble at a few of the chips, at least.

Her father looked over at her when she said that. He squinted. "Do I know you?"

Her heart was pounding, but she didn't think he could hear that. "You might."

"Where do I know you from?"

"Where do you think?" She tried to remain calm, but she knew she was upsetting him. Did she want to do that?

He gave her an ugly look and picked up the newspaper on the counter, opened it, and buried his face in it. She may have changed, growing up, becoming an adult, but he had not. She would know him anywhere.

Her ambivalent feelings toward him bubbled over to ferocious rage.

The memory of that night came flooding back. She had been cowering in her bedroom with the covers over her head to muffle the shouting when it happened.

Before it got to that, her father had come home drunk. Again. That's how Darla had first known it would be a bad night. Darla was sitting at the kitchen table doing homework when he stomped into the kitchen and glared at his wife, soundlessly demanding his supper. Her mother dished up the chili that she had been keeping warm for several hours and set it in front of him with a spoon, then filled a glass with ice and water and set it by the plate. Her hands shook and a few drops of water spilled into the chili.

Darla's dad snarled softly, but picked up his spoon and took a sloppy bite of chili. Darla and her mother were both holding their breath, hoping the meal would please him.

"What the hell! Can't I get a hot meal when I get home after a long day?"

"Is it not warm enough?" Her mother's voice broke. "I can heat it up some more. I didn't want it to burn."

Darla knew she had been trying to keep it warm for at least two hours.

"No, it is *not* goddam warm enough. Here, you taste it." He scooped up a spoonful, stood and crammed it into his wife's mouth, spilling most of it on her and the floor. "Now look what a mess you made. Clean it up!"

Darla fumed, angry at him for humiliating her mother. Also angry at her mother for letting it happen.

He loomed over her while she swiped at the mess on the floor with the closest thing, one of her good dishtowels, chili dripping down the front of her clothing.

"What's wrong with you? Why are you so slow and clumsy?"

Darla shrank in her chair from the toxic atmosphere. She was angry, but also frightened. This wasn't going to end well. It never did. When he got started, he never stopped. She slipped from her seat and sneaked away to her bedroom. Stuffing her fist into her mouth so no one could hear her sobs, she tried to remember the good times, her antidote for these times.

The circus her dad had taken her to, to see trapeze performers, a beautiful spangly lady on a prancing horse, a lion tamer in a cage with the snarling beasts. The baseball game with cotton candy and all the soda she wanted. Watching the fireworks on the Fourth of July from a blanket spread in the hot, crowded park, after a picnic of fried chicken and coleslaw, followed by her mother's homemade pecan pie.

The shouting from the kitchen grew louder. She pressed her pillow over her head. She could still hear. Her father was cussing at her mother non-stop and she heard her mother's soft whimpering, trying to tell him she was going to...whatever. To do whatever he was demanding.

Darla clearly heard him bellow his last insult. "You're nothing but a useless whore. You're good for nothing."

There came a terrible bumping, thumping sound that seemed to go on forever.

Then there was complete silence.

She crept out of her bed and cracked open the bedroom door. It was a small house. She could see into the kitchen from her room.

Her father stood at the head of the stairs to the basement, shaking from head to toe. He turned toward her with a wild look in his eyes.

"Get back in your room!" he shouted.

She closed the door. When she heard him falter down the wooden basement steps, she opened it again and crawled to the top of the stairs.

The man who was with her now, in the diner, wasn't the loving father who took her to ballgames and circuses. She could only see the man at the foot of the basement stairs, kicking her mother and telling her to stand up, getting her blood on his shoes while he kept kicking and kicking and kicking. Darla had run to the bathroom to throw up, being careful to do it as quietly as she could.

She had harbored ambivalent feelings for him all these years. Now, with that vivid flashback searing her brain, she left behind any wavering. There was no longer any ambivalence. There was no more love for him. She hated him through and through. Her grip tightened on the fork beside her plate. Then she made herself take a breath and let go of the utensil.

"I'm your daughter." She looked at him through hostile narrowed lids with steel in her eyes.

He jerked his head up and drew back, nearly falling off the stool. "Darla?"

"Darla. And I'm here to tell you to stay the hell away from my mother."

He narrowed his own eyes. She knew that look. But he wasn't going to lay hands on her here, in public. He was only abusive in his own house, where no one could see his cowardly bullying. He was not a brave man.

"She can't give you any more money. Don't go to her place again."

"You can't tell me not to see my own wife."

"She's not your wife. Stay away from her. I'm getting a protection order so you can be arrested next time you go there. And stay away from me, too. You can't scare me."

Darla didn't wait for another reaction. She threw a twenty down beside her untouched plate of food, hopped off the stool, and walked out, feeling the daggers of his enraged stare between her shoulder blades.

She didn't start shaking until she was inside her car, trying without success, several times, to start it before her key finally went into the slot and she was able to turn it.

Chapter 22

Darla stumbled into her house, still trembling from the adrenaline aftereffects of her boldness with a man she used to be terrified of. Somehow making it to her bedroom, she pulled the covers over her head, still shaking.

It was probably a few minutes before she noticed Moose pawing at the spread and whining softly.

"Oh, Moosie!" She threw off the covers and buried her tear-wet face in the fur on his nape. He strained to turn his head and lick her. When she lifted her head, he succeeded and consumed her tears with his sweet, soft, slobbery tongue. It felt so good.

On Wednesday, Gin called Darla when she was driving home from work to suggest they meet up for a quick drink.

"I guess I don't have anything else to do. Where do you want to meet?"

"Let's go to Left Field," Gin said.

"Left Field? That's a sports bar. We'll be the only women there. Why do you want to go there?"

"I'll tell you when you get here." Her voice lilted. She sounded thrilled with some sort of secret she was obviously keeping from her. That was kind of annoying.

Darla got home, let the dog out, fed him, and changed her clothes, pondering why Gin had wanted to meet at a place like that. Gin had never made a secret of hating sports bars. She made fun of them all the time and, to Darla's knowledge, hadn't been inside one for years. She had dated a minor league baseball player years ago and that was his preferred watering hole. The liaison had been brief, mostly because of the sports bar thing. Why on earth would she want to meet Darla there?

Still wondering, and bit uneasy, Darla drove to the place and went inside. She really did not like unknowns.

It was dark and loud. Banks of televisions hung near the ceiling on three of the walls, all but one silent, with closed captioning turned on. The live one was playing the NFL draft. Men were shouting at the screen so constantly, Darla wondered how they could tell what was going on. The set was playing sound and had closed captioning also turned on, but the letters were small, since the screen was so far away. She wondered why they didn't have a big-screen TV for whatever was most interesting that night. Left Field wasn't even the best sports bar around, obviously.

Gin touched her arm.

"Oh, there you are," Darla said, turning at her sudden approach. "My eyes haven't adjusted."

"Yeah, it's pretty dark. Come on over here."

She led the way to a booth against the wall opposite the bar.

Darla stopped short.

Ned Farley sat in the booth, grinning like he'd just played a big joke on her or something.

"What's the idea?" Darla said, standing while Gin slipped in next to Ned. *This* was Gin's surprise?

"Come on, sit down," Gin urged her. "You want a beer?"

"No. I do not want a beer." When they met for a drink, it was usually something girly. A Cosmo or a strawberry Daiquiri. "I want a Daiquiri. Can I even get a Daiquiri here?"

"Darla, sit down."

"Why did you haul me into a sports bar?" Darla didn't like the leering look on Ned's face. "What's going on?" Against her huge, growing desire to run out the door, she sat.

"Ned just wanted to meet you again," Gin said.

"Hi, Darla. Surprise," he said, losing the smirk.

"Yes, I'm surprised. Okay, why is this a secret?"

"Hey, it's not a secret," Ned said. "Sorry. It was a last-minute thing and this was convenient."

That didn't even make sense to Darla. "I didn't see your truck out there," she said to Ned.

He shrugged. Had he hidden it? He wasn't about to explain anything to her.

"Okay, so why am I here?"

"Just wanted to talk. Get to know you a little better."

Darla shot a questioning look at Gin, who was looking another direction.

A draft pick was announced and the room erupted in shouts, some joyous, some angry, some very drunk.

"And you think this is a good place to talk?" shouted Darla.

He gave her a charming, lop-sided smile. "Maybe not, right?"

Trouble was, Darla had the feeling he knew his smile was charming. However, it felt calculating right now. Not all that charming. As before, she was drawn by his good looks, but put off, at the same time, by something she couldn't quite name. Anyway, here she was. She should put this time to good use and find out something about this enigmatic guy.

"You know, I think I want to talk to you, too," Darla said. "I was wondering about how you know Gin's father."

A flicker of confusion ran over his face. "Gin's father?"

"Yes, Gary. Gary Holland. Gin's father."

"We're on the same throwing team," he said, after a short pause. "Axes. We throw axes. I thought you knew that," he added, throwing a smile at her. The attractive one, not the ugly one he'd had when she first arrived tonight.

"I thought you might have known him before that."

"Darla," Gin said, warning in her tone. "What do you mean?"

"Oh nothing. Just wondered. Your dad is a generation older than Ned is. It's an unlikely friendship."

"Hey, he's a great guy," Ned said. "I like him."

"Where did you live before you moved here?" Darla was determined she was going to try to pry into that opaque background, the one which didn't exist in cyber space.

"Here and there. I've moved around a lot."

"Yes, you said you were in finance. I wondered if you knew Mr. Holland then."

"No, I didn't know him until recently." His eyes narrowed ever so slightly.

Did he know of Mr. Holland's prison term? Did he think she was implying they knew each other from prison? She was, but did he suspect that?

"Never mind." Darla made a dismissive gesture. "You're in medicine now, you said. You work for OTB?"

"Yes, with my company," Gin said. "I told you that." Gin sounded as peeved as Darla felt. Good. That served her right.

"Yes, you did." Darla glared at both of them. "How did that happen?"

Gin shrugged. "Just a happy coincidence. He's even on some of the same jobs."

Had Gin gotten him the job? Where had she gotten that impression?

"I'll go get some drinks at the bar," Ned said. "It looks like nobody's coming over here to take our orders."

They worked the same jobs? Darla had to process that.

When he was at the bar, Darla spoke softly to Gin. "Is he going to be coming to my mother's place?"

"I'm not sure. I can check the schedule."

There was another outburst from another draft announcement.

Darla's unease built. She had to get out of there. There was no way she was going to drink anything this guy brought over to her, either. She didn't trust him one bit.

When the racket had died down, Darla turned to Gin and lied. "You know what? I completely forgot to let Moose out. I'd better be going."

"You haven't even had anything to drink."

"And Ned has no idea what I want, so I don't know how he'll get my order. I'll talk to you later. Just have a good time with him, okay? I'm really tired tonight."

Darla really was tired. She wasn't just saying that. The disturbance she felt in Ned's presence made her tense, wore her out.

Chapter 23

Darla hadn't been home more than half an hour when Gin called her.

"Are you done with your date already?" Darla asked, surprised. Did she dare hope they had broken up?

"It wasn't really a date. He just talked me into getting you there because he wanted to, I guess, know more about you."

"Why would he want to do that?"

"I think because you're my best friend, silly." Gin gave a little laugh.

He hadn't asked her any questions about herself, though. Was he just socially inept? "Where are you now?"

"On my way home. I wanted to call and make sure you're okay. Something seemed wrong when you left."

How could she tell her best friend she didn't like to be around her boyfriend? Didn't trust him? She didn't think Gin should trust him either, but she couldn't tell her that. Darla knew how she would react. "I'm just really tired, Gin."

"I'm sorry. Hope you get to rest up tonight. I know you work long shifts."

She did, but she was—mostly—used to that. "Where did Ned take off to?"

"I'm not sure. He said he had something he had to do."

"Still being secretive, huh?"

Gin sighed and Darla could imagine her shrug. "He doesn't tell me everything, that's for sure."

"You're working tomorrow and not Friday, right?" Darla said. "Could you possibly come over after work tomorrow and take care of Moose?" Darla was thinking of doing a big grocery shopping on her way home from work and didn't want Moose to wait for that. She could come home first, then tend to him, but it was convenient for Gin to do it, too.

"Oh drat, I can't. I've lost your dang key again."

Chills crawled up Darla's back. "You've lost it? Again?"

"I don't know how I'm losing all these keys."

Darla didn't know how either, since Gin hadn't lost her house key in all the years she'd lived here. Ned took it. She knew Ned took it.

"You know he has it," she said.

"Who? Ned? Don't be silly. What would he want with your house key?"

He might want to terrorize me, she wanted to say. He might want to squirt out my toothpaste. He might want to mess with my mind. She knew some men were jealous of their women's friends. Abusive men. The kind who wanted the woman to cut off communication with everyone they knew. Everyone who would encourage them to leave the abuser.

"Gin, I'm getting a very bad feeling about this guy. There's just too much...stuff. You don't know his background. He knows your dad, probably from prison. That's probably why there's no record of him. He was in prison, so he wouldn't have any addresses to find online for a few years. Probably changed his name when he came out. He's weaseling his way into your life and you know nothing about him."

"You're just like Keith. My own brother and my own best friend—neither of you want me to be happy."

"Gin, I *do* want you to be happy. But I want you to be safe, too. I don't think you're safe with him. He makes my skin crawl. Makes me feel sick."

"That's a fine thing to say to me. My lover makes you sick to your stomach?"

"Let me know if you find my—"

Gin had hung up. The connection dot on her phone was gone. Darla was going to have to change her locks again.

Darla was getting wearier by the minute. She plopped down on her couch and flicked the TV on. Before she even decided on a channel, her phone rang. It was her mother's number.

"Mom? How you doing?"

"Darla...Darla...help me."

Her voice was frail. She sounded fragile and scared. "Where are you?"

"Help...help me."

Darla's first thought was to call 911. But maybe she should check out the situation herself first. She rushed to her car and sped to her mother's house. At least she hadn't lost her mother's house key.

"Mom! Mom!" She shouted as she ran through the house. Living room, kitchen, bedro—

Oh no! There she was. On the bedroom floor. Her wheelchair was tipped over and her mother lay on the ground next to it, twisted and bleeding. Darla knelt next to her. She was barely conscious, but breathing. Darla whipped out her phone. Now it was time to call.

"911? My mother has had a fall. She's hurt." Darla gave name and the address, and soon heard the ambulance siren outside.

Darla ran to let them in and lead them to the bedroom.

Two young people entered, name badges identifying them as John and Susan. They hauled their equipment quickly into the room and started tending Mrs. Taylor with calm efficiency, first asking her name, the year, if she knew who the president was. She passed those with flying colors, but in a feeble, strained voice.

One of the EMTs, John, looked up from tending her mother and asked Darla, "Do you know how this happened?"

Darla knelt behind the EMT and tried to ask her mother. "Mom? How did you tip your chair over? Do you remember?"

Her mother's eyes were filled with agony. Blood from her head wound, from where she must have hit it on something on the way down, streamed down her face as the medic mopped it and pressed on the wound to stop the flow. Maybe she had banged her head on the nightstand.

"Darla. It was..."

Her mother looked so weak.

Darla rocked back and almost fell herself from the powerful flashback that seized her mind in a sudden flash.

Her mother at the foot of the basement stairs.

Bleeding.

Her father standing over her.

Kicking her.

Darla's vision started to gray out. Her ears rang. She grabbed for...something to hold onto.

She felt a hand on her shoulder. The other medic, Susan, was talking to her. "Ms. Taylor. Ms. Taylor. Stay with me."

Darla opened her eyes to see the EMT, Susan, bending over her and calling her name. Darla's sight and hearing started to clear up in a few seconds. She was lying on the bedroom floor near her mother, seeing tiny dancing spots and hearing ringing in her ears. Those both faded soon, to her relief.

After she was ready to sit up, the medic helped Darla into the living room and guided her over to the sofa.

"You need to rest a bit," Susan said. "I'll be back in a minute to check on you."

Darla felt horrible she was adding to their job. She expressed her feeble thanks and waited.

A few minutes later, Susan poked her head out of the bedroom door and beckoned Darla back to her mother's room.

A wave of panic hit Darla again. She realized she smelled alcohol. Just a quick whiff. She told herself it was from the EMTs cleaning her mother's wound. But a vivid picture of her drunk father flitted before her, then vanished.

She watched them finish cleaning up her mother, who was now sitting upright in her chair, her head bandaged, and a splint on her wrist. She must have twisted her wrist in the fall.

After they packed up their things, Susan walked quietly over to let Darla know what was going on. "She needs to go to the hospital. Can you talk her into it? She's refusing to let us help her out."

"I don't think I can. She's awfully stubborn. But I'll try." For five long minutes she argued with her mother before admitting defeat.

"I'm sorry. I can't convince her."

"We might have to insist on it."

Darla pictured them forcing her mother out of the apartment and her mother screaming. Maybe crying. Maybe trying to scratch them. Then she thought of something. "I'm a registered nurse. Is there anything I can do instead of that?"

"She's not in bad shape, just the cut on her head and a sprained wrist. We'd like to scan her brain, but if you sign the waiver, and take responsibility, we could let her stay with you."

Breathing a sigh of relief, Darla agreed and signed the form saying her mother was declining the ambulance ride "against medical orders."

"You know what to look for. But let me say, if her wrist is still swollen in a day or so, give us a call and we'll x-ray it. I felt it carefully and it doesn't feel broken, but we can't always tell by feeling it." Susan handed her a card with a number to call. "Call me or nine-one-one if you see any signs the head wound is causing internal bleeding, or anything worse."

Darla smiled an apology. "Thanks so much. She's awfully stubborn. I'll go ahead and call her own doctor, if that's okay."

"I was just going to recommend that. Yes, she should at least see her own physician within the next few days. Get her checked out thoroughly. We'll leave her with you. You're staying the night?"

"Oh yes, I definitely am." Well, she was now.

"I'm glad her head wound doesn't need stitches. But be sure to call the number I gave you if anything changes."

Darla promised she would. She knew scalp wounds produced a lot of blood and the bandaged area wasn't large, so she was sure the paramedic was right about the stitches.

"Do you need any help getting her to bed?" Susan asked.

"No, I can manage that. She usually gets herself to bed, but I'll help her tonight." Darla would have to stay with her mother tonight. At least until she was bedded down. Maybe the whole night. Yes, she should stay all night. She had said she would.

After Darla managed to walk the EMTs to the door and lock it behind them, she returned to her mother. Her color was good and she looked less dazed.

"Mom, how on earth did that happen?"

Her mother just shook her head and gazed at her hands, folded in her lap.

"Never mind. I'm staying here tonight."

"Would you?" She raised her eyes to her daughter's face. They still had some of the haunted look they had had when Darla first got there.

She didn't mention she had to, to keep her mother from being carted off against her will. "Sure. I'll run home and get some things, and let Moose out one last time. I'll be back in a few minutes."

She wheeled her mother into the living room and handed her the remote so she could watch television while Darla was gone.

Chapter 24

After Darla's rushed trip back home from her mother's house to tend to her dog and pack some overnight necessities, she returned, finding her mother right where she had left her, and relieved about that. How on earth had her mother tipped over her chair? That had never happened before. It hadn't been time for her to get into bed. So why was she even in the bedroom? Would her mother tell her anything if she asked her?

She tried a few tentative questions. "Mom, what were you doing when you tipped your chair over?"

"Oh, you know." She waved her unbandaged hand.

"No, I don't."

"I wasn't aware I had to clear my every movement with you, dear." Her mother was getting peeved, so Darla let it drop and ended up watching television with her mother for another hour or so. After the ten o'clock news, which was the early news in their Eastern Time zone, Darla asked if her mother wanted to go to bed yet.

"Yes, I think I do."

She didn't seem ruffled any more, from the questions Darla had asked earlier. That was good. Darla didn't want to rile her mother any more tonight, so she would desist from trying to find out what had happened.

"Can you manage on your own? I can help you if you need anything."

Her mother prided herself on being as independent as she could be, in her dependent state, and had always insisted on putting herself to bed, since she had recovered from her injuries all those years ago. But there were new injuries now, so Darla thought she had to ask. She wished her mother would unbend and let people do more for her.

"Let me see what I can do, dear. I'll call you if I need you. Will you be okay on the couch?"

It wasn't Darla's first night on the couch. She didn't love it, but she was used to sleeping there occasionally. "I'll be fine, Mom."

"Don't you have to work tomorrow?"

"I do. I might leave before you wake up, unless you want me to stay longer." She would have to dash home, tend to Moose, get dressed for work, and maybe sneak a shower in while she was there, if she could.

"No, no, you need to do what's best for you."

"And for you, Mom." Darla leaned down and kissed her mother's soft cheek. Amy Taylor stroked her daughter's hair.

"Love you, sugar." Her mother gave her shoulder a squeeze.

"Love you, spice." That had been their customary exchange when she was a child and she'd almost forgotten about it. Darla blinked back tears watching her mother wheel herself into the bedroom one-handed.

She didn't hear anything else, so assumed her mother had gotten herself into bed. One tiny peek before she bedded down told her she was sound asleep, and safely in her own bed.

After setting an alarm on her phone for very early the next morning, Darla slept lightly, hearing her mother's soft snoring and rain pattering on the roof. It seemed the wind was picking up, too. Maybe she shouldn't have left the living room to get a drink of water in the kitchen, earlier, when the weather portion of the news program had been on.

When Darla heard her mother speaking, she woke up completely, realizing she had fallen into a deeper sleep. She couldn't make out what she was saying, but her mother sounded alarmed, frightened. A nightmare? Maybe Darla should wake her from her bad dream.

Making her way to the doorway, a wave of horror hit Darla. It was the smell of alcohol again. This was not antiseptic rubbing alcohol, cleansing hospital alcohol. This was whiskey. He had been here. She steeled herself to enter the room.

"Todd. Todd. No. No, Todd," her mother was mumbling in her sleep, shaking her head from side to side.

Darla hurried to the bedside. "Mom, wake up. You're having a bad dream." Did her mother still dream about that day? No doubt she did. Darla did, too. In a rush that almost took her breath away, Darla remembered again it had been raining that night. The night her father crippled her mother. She completely lost her breath for a moment and had to sit on the edge of her mother's mattress.

Her mother opened her eyes and her frightened words tumbled out. "Darla, it was Todd. I didn't fall. He pushed my chair over. It was Todd."

Darla jumped up and started hyperventilating. She was going to have an attack. Another flashback. She had to comfort her mother. "He's gone, Mom. He's not here now. I'll make sure he doesn't come back."

Her mother relaxed. Then she smiled, closed her eyes, and drifted back to sleep.

Darla stumbled back to the couch and curled into a tight, tense ball, pulling the blanket over her head, as she had when she was a child. She shook violently, clenching her teeth to stop herself from crying out, breathing too fast, on her way to passing out.

After a couple of minutes, she willed her breathing to slow, as she had been taught to do in her PTSD classes.

In through the nose to a slow count of four.

Hold the breath for a count to four.

Out through the mouth to a slow count of eight.

After four or five deep breaths, her pulse slowed, her equilibrium returning.

She knew this attack had been triggered by the smell of whiskey. Her father had been in that room. He had left the smell behind. It was the same smell he had carried with him, as a cloud, when he pushed her mother down the basement stairs, years ago. The smell had also made her remember the rain. Now she knew why she was uneasy whenever it rained. It was part of her trauma from that awful night. A puzzle piece that had been missing until this moment.

What her mother had said was, no doubt, true. He had pushed her over. Maybe even injured her, intentionally. Had she refused to give him money this time? Maybe now she could convince her mother to take out an order of protection against him. Darla had the next Friday off. She would visit the courthouse again, this time with the name, finally, of the person they both needed protection from. Now they could fill out the forms.

Chapter 25

Before Friday could come and Darla could visit the courthouse again, she had to get through Thursday. She couldn't take off work to do it. Also, she had to make sure her mother got through Thursday in safety. Darla got up very early, checked on her mom, who was sleeping, breathing evenly. Darla tried to leave quietly, but when she opened the door, a burst of thunder startled her. She ran back to see if the noise had awakened her mother, but it hadn't. She barely made it to her car before the rain started. At home, however, she had to run through a pelting to her front door. For the umpteenth time, she told herself she should keep an umbrella in the car. The problem was, she never thought about it when it wasn't raining. At least this one was a warm rain.

After rushing through the ritual of letting Moose out, toweling him off when he came back in, feeding him, showering, and dressing, she picked up her one umbrella and ran back to the car.

After she slammed the door shut, and before she started the engine, she noticed her heart wasn't racing. She wasn't even hyperventilating. Was she cured of her fear of the rain? Did knowing what it stemmed from free her or the terror? She hoped so. For now, it did, and she was grateful for that.

On her way to work, she called the police station and was able to get Detective Coleman on the phone.

"My mother was attacked by Todd Taylor last night. Is there any way to rush a protective order for her?"

"Slow down, Darla. When and where was she attacked? And how?"

"At her home. He pushed her wheelchair over, and I think he hit her in the head, too. She had a cut that was bleeding."

"You saw him do this?"

"Well, no."

"How do you know it was him?"

"She told me! She said it was him. Todd Taylor."

"Did you call anyone last night? For help?"

"I called the paramedics. They came and treated her, but said she didn't need the hospital."

"Slow down. You're leaving something out."

She could tell he was restraining himself, being patient with her. Yes, she was jumbling this up. He needed to know everything, and how it all happened. That made sense. "Okay. She called me for help and I drove over there, but I didn't know what had happened until I got there. I found her on the floor and called the paramedics. She was dazed and woozy and could barely talk. She told us, me and the paramedics, that she tipped the chair over accidently, herself. I stayed overnight with her because she seemed so frail, and in the middle of the night, she started calling out for him to stop. She said his name, Todd. Well, she shouted it. When I woke her up, she said he had been there. She let him into her home, and he pushed her over.

Tipped her out of the wheelchair, onto the floor. And left her there bleeding."

"And you're sure you believe her?"

"Detective, I smelled him. I smelled the whiskey. I know he was there. He came there drunk. That smell lingers for hours." Long enough for her to detect it much later and have an attack of fear and trembling. "At first, I thought it was something the medics were using on her, but then I realized it wasn't."

"It would have been easier if she had called 911 herself."

"She couldn't. She was unconscious, then dazed. When she came to, she called me and she could barely speak." It was only a stroke of luck her mother had her phone with her when it happened. And Todd didn't take it away from her.

"I understand. There's something I need to tell you."

"I'll go get the protective order tomorrow. I'm off work."

"You know you'll have to take her in. She has to file the paperwork."

Darla stewed about that for a moment. Her mother had grounds for the order, but did she, herself?

"Listen to me, Darla. About the incidents that have been happening to you—"

"Yes, how do I file for protection from those?"

He let out a breath. "You don't. Not against him. He's not the one who's been bothering you."

How could he say that? Of course it was him.

He continued before she could object. "For the incidents on Thursday the eleventh, the toothpaste writing on your mirror and the excrement on your porch, Mr. Taylor was in an anger management class for an hour, then with others from the class during the rest of the relevant time."

"The excrement, as you call it, happened in the middle of the night."

"Yes, they were out drinking until very late."

"So, he's still a drunk." He was managing his anger, but not his drinking. That wouldn't work. "What about the night the brick came through my window?"

"Another anger management class."

"That was a Wednesday. They have them on different days?"

"Days, nights, different hours. They're scheduled often so there's no excuse to miss them."

"You're sure he was there?"

"Positive. There are cameras at the entrance. We've gone through the footage."

He was on camera. Not at her place, at the useless classes weren't teaching him not to beat up his ex-wife. "Okay. Thanks." They were taking this seriously, looking at the camera footage.

So, she, herself, still couldn't get an official order against anyone, since she didn't know who to get it against. How frustrating. The second tire slashing had been the most recent act of terrorism against her. Would it be the last? They had slowed. Had they stopped? Or were the attacks building? Her tires, the poop, the toothpaste, the brick. Was she safe now or not? Who on earth was her tormentor?

At least her mother could get protection now, beyond the caretakers, but would Darla be able to talk her into doing it? The stubborn woman might, would probably, deem the caretakers enough protection for her.

Her windshield wipers started squeaking. The rain was letting up and her window was dry. She barely remembered driving to the hospital. She flicked the switch off, parked, and went inside the to begin her workday.

The next day, her day off, she called her mother and told her she would be over soon.

"Of course, dear, but you don't need to come right now. The new aide started today, so he's here. We're doing fine."

He? Her mother didn't usually allow male aides to take care of her.

She didn't want to tell her mother why she was coming, to pick her up to file the protective order. She stood a better chance of talking her into it face to face. Maybe. She hoped.

It was a gloomy day, cloudy and drizzling on and off. The weather matched her mood. She was dreading what might turn out to be a confrontation with her mother. This was important, though. She would stand her ground. She could be just as stubborn as her mother. They were related, after all.

Maybe the new aide could help her, could convince her mother her wellbeing depended on that man staying away from her. Even if she'd been mistaken about him being there and pushing her over, and Darla thought there was very little chance of that, her mom would be better off without ever seeing her ex again. Would it be better to have a male there, to guard her against Todd Taylor?

These thoughts all ran through her head as she drove to her mother's place. She knocked on her mother's front door to warn the aide, then let herself in with her key.

"Mom, I'm here."

Her mother rolled into the living room from the kitchen. "Darla, that was quick. You have to meet my new aide."

"Where is he?"

"He might be in the bedroom, putting clothes away."

Darla went to the doorway of the bedroom. Yes, the new aide was folding clean clothes on her mother's bed. He looked up at her.

He was Ned Farley.

"Don't look so happy to see me," he said, with a smirk.

Revulsion settled in her stomach and made her grit her teeth. "What are you doing here?"

"My job. Why?"

She turned and walked back to the living room. She was going to ignore him.

"Mom, we have to go run an errand this morning." Her mom was dressed and looked ready to go out, to all appearances. "Do you want a jacket? It's a little cool out." Her mother got cold easily.

"Where? What do we need to do? Gin did a lot of shopping last time she was here."

"It's something at the court house. I'll tell you when we get there." For some reason, she was reluctant to have Ned Farley know their business. It would make sense to tell him Todd Taylor should not come around, but it made her weary to think of explaining everything to him. Her conflicting feelings about him exhausted her. Above all, she didn't quite trust him, though he must have been cleared by the company.

"You'd better tell me what this is about." Her mother looked annoyed.

"Mom, I'll have to explain it to you in the car."

Darla grabbed a light jacket from the coat closet, stepped behind her mother's chair, and started pushing it toward the front door.

"Are you sure, darling?" Her mother now looked apprehensive.

"Mom, don't worry. This is just something we need to do. It's some official business. Ned," she called, before going out the door, "we'll be gone for a while. Be back in an hour or so." Or several hours. This could take a long time.

He popped out of the bedroom and frowned after them. "Where you going? What's the deal?"

"Be back soon." Darla flashed him a broad fake smile and slammed the door after them.

Chapter 26

To her pleasant surprise, Darla didn't have any trouble getting her mother to sign the form that would keep Todd Taylor away from her. Being attacked and injured by him, again, had done the trick. Darla was grateful her injuries had been minor...this time. Even the cut on her head didn't look so bad today. But nothing like this must ever happen again. They were told someone would be by for her mother to fill out an affidavit, as they called it, for the police report. She also learned a court date would be set for his hearing. A hearing—that sounded good. Everyone was taking this seriously. Maybe he would be locked up.

When they were finished, Darla started to leave, then decided to do some more business there. "Mom, can you wait over here while I see about something else?" She wheeled her to the seating area in the lobby.

"What is it, dear?"

"Another matter."

Darla suspected Ned had been stealing her house keys from Gin. She returned and talked to the official who had just helped them. She tried to get a protective order for herself against Ned. Being suspicious he had stolen keys, however, was nowhere near enough grounds for that, she was told. Now she would have to take her mother back and place her in his care. That was disappointing. If only she had a tangible reason for asking the agency to replace him.

"What did you do, Darla?" her mother asked when she returned to her.

"Nothing. I tried to get something else done, but I can't do it." Yet.

She drove her mother home without voicing any of her suspicions, so as not to make her any more upset than she already was. The woman talked all the way back about how awful it felt to sign the form.

"Imagine, asking the authorities to keep away the man I married."

"Um hm," Darla answered, not knowing what to say to that. She couldn't imagine it either. Of course, she'd never been married, so that had something to do with it.

"Just think, he's your own father. And we have to be protected from him. That's just not right, is it?"

And more in the same vein. More which Darla had no good responses for, no good thoughts about. As they pulled up at her mother's place, Darla thought maybe she should have been trying to convince her mother she didn't want a male, and should ask for a female. That had been her feeling in the past.

After Darla helped her mother take off her jacket, she settled her in front of the television screen and sat beside her wheelchair, on the couch.

"If you have something you need to do," her mother said, "I'll be fine with Ned."

He appeared behind them, silently. "I'll take good care of her. You can go."

Darla gave him a sweet smile. Sweetish. "When is your shift over, Ned? I'll stay until then."

"I leave at four. We'll be fine. Mrs. Taylor, I have some mint tea ready for you."

"Oh, you dear boy," her mother said. "My favorite. It's just what I need right now." She handed the remote to Darla and wheeled herself to follow Ned into the kitchen to have her tea. She wished she had thought of making her mother's favorite tea for her.

Darla, she told herself, *this isn't a competition. She's your mother. She loves you and you know that.*

But that man is not a relative. She doesn't need to like him, she argued.

She watched him from the other room as Ned made sure her mother was comfortable, brought her a cloth napkin and asked if she wanted a cookie, or anything else. His gaze seemed fond. As for her mother, she certainly acted like she was fond of him.

Maybe she was wrong about Ned. The voices still warred in her head. One of them won.

"Mom," she called from the living room. "I think I'll go, after all."

"Yes, dear. I'm in good hands." Her mother sounded cheerful and happy.

Darla left, kicking herself for being rude to Ned. They would have to get along if he was to be her mother's caretaker.

She target shot for about an hour in the back yard, wading through the wet grass to retrieve her arrows. At least the rain had quit for now. When she let Moose out, he loped to the back fence again, as he'd done a week or so ago. It was daytime now, so she followed him and peered into the woods. They were so much scarier at night. In the daylight, they looked like trees and bushes and undergrowth.

"Wait here, buddy. I'll let you out to explore in a minute." She put away her shooting gear and got Moose's leash. Then, with him pulling ahead, on the scent trail of something or other, she followed him through the back gate.

They didn't have far to go. Moose soon whimpered and started pawing at a pile of wet leaves.

"What's in there?" Darla whispered. She pulled him back and saw, nestled in the bed of leaves, a damp sausage, of all things. Gingerly, she picked it up, over Moose's objections. It wasn't very old, not visibly rotten, still plump, and fresh looking. It even smelled good. She glanced down. There was something else, something that had been beneath it. It was a piece of paper in a small plastic bag.

She almost knew what it would say before she drew it out, unfolded it, and read it.

Knock knock

She gritted her teeth so hard it hurt.

By the time she got through to the detective, after five or six minutes on hold, she had calmed down enough to be glad this note wasn't inside her house. Maybe it was because her tormenter didn't have her key any more. Whoever left dog bait, Moose bait, out here must not be able to get inside her house. Maybe they'd noticed her new security system. That was good because she hadn't had the locks rekeyed, as she had intended. She'd been pretty distracted.

She stayed right where she was, per Detective Coleman's instructions, and he arrived shortly.

"Show me exactly where it was." He motioned the crime scene techs forward.

Darla showed him the leaf pile, still looking like a nest.

"I guess you've handled this, right?"

She nodded and one of the techs took the note, the plastic bag, and the sausage and officially bagged and labelled them.

Moose sat obediently, but whined when the sausage disappeared. She would be sure he got extra treats when they returned to the house.

The crime scene team fanned out and explored the woods and her yard, front and back, after she was told to return inside the house. Moose was happy about that, since he got treats inside. Darla and Moose both kept track of them sweeping for clues.

As they were leaving, the detective knocked on her front door to tell her they were done. "If we find anything on the note or the bag, we'll let you know."

"Or the sausage?"

"Or the sausage. We mainly want to make sure it isn't poisoned."

Darla gasped. She hadn't considered that. Moose could have eaten poison? What if that had happened? "I don't think it had been there very long. There are a lot of other animals, wild animals, in those woods, that would have eaten it if it had been there very long."

He agreed with her, but didn't think they would have any luck finding the person who left the bag there. "After he dumped it, he could take off and be long gone by now. I'm sure he is."

At least Moose hadn't eaten any poison.

Her phone pinged with an incoming text from Gin. It was short. Not sweet.

WTF

Darla replied: *What do you mean?*

If that's the way you're going to treat Ned, don't bother acting like you're my friend.

Gin, I am your friend. I always will be. What do you mean???

It was five o'clock. Ned had gotten off work already, she knew, and had probably talked to Gin about Darla not trusting him—wanting to stay for the end of his shift. But she hadn't. She *had* trusted him. Why was he stirring up trouble between her and Gin? What a jerk.

Darla texted Gin twice more with no response:

Talk to me.

Tell me what's wrong.

She called and got sent to voicemail. Had Gin blocked her?

Darla checked social media and Gin was gone, not visible. She had blocked Darla everywhere. She was stunned. What kind of hold did this guy have on her?

She couldn't sit still, had to do something. In spite of the late hour, she took her archery gear outside and began to shoot some ends. After the first two, which, for her, was twelve arrows, her mind started to clear. She gathered her arrows and loosed another end. Walking to pick up the arrows, she gave some thought to Gin and Ned. Was it possible they were teaming up to make her life miserable? Was she that poor a judge of character? Did she not know Gin at all?

Most importantly, could she trust her? After trusting her for years? Nothing made any sense. How could she abandon Darla after so long? They were best friends. Did all those years mean nothing?

Another round of six.

If there was any doubt, any question about trusting either one of them, she didn't want them near her mother.

One more round of six shots and her mind was made up.

She released Moose for a short romp, then stomped inside, her pulse racing with what she was contemplating.

Keeping her voice as calm and reasonable as she could, she called the company that provided the caretakers for her mother. Due to the nature of their business, someone handled the phones 24/7. She told them there had been some problems with both Gin and Ned and she would prefer not to have either of them at her mother's house again. She offered to help her own mother out if they couldn't find anyone for tomorrow, since she was off work on Saturday. They assured her they could cover the shift and were sorry for any problems she had encountered with them.

It took her awhile to sit and recover, for her pulse to slow and her breathing become smooth. Her stomach didn't quit roiling, however. She had mint tea in her own kitchen and made some for herself to calm her nerves. It didn't work all that well. *Had she done the right thing? Yes, she had to do it. Maybe she didn't have to. Maybe she should have gone to Gin and talked it out. No, Gin made it clear she was not communicating with the friend who had gone through everything with her. Gin's father going to prison, Darla's father injuring her mother. They had gotten each other through those things, and everything else, big and small.*

But now her friendship was dying, and she was mourning its death. She had depended on it for so long. She would miss it. Nothing could replace Gin.

Chapter 27

Saturday morning, Darla awoke very late, still sick about breaking up with her best friend. She tried to call Gin again, but, once again, her call didn't go through. This would not do. She couldn't leave it this way. Her stomach ached so bad. She would have to go over to Gin's place later. But what would she say? If she could say anything. Would Gin slam the door in her face? Shoving the thought as far down as she could, she quit pacing the kitchen floor. Took some deep breaths.

Right now, it was Saturday and she was going to try to have a leisurely day.

She shot three ends, then let Moose out. This time he ignored the woods beyond the back yard fence, she was happy to see. It was the meat he had been drawn to, not a villain crouching in the bushes. She threw tennis balls for him until his tongue was hanging out. They both went inside, exercised and feeling good. Mostly.

Darla puttered around doing laundry and housecleaning and watching TV before she settled down with the novel she was half-way through.

Her phone was on the end table beside her. Toward the end of the day, it buzzed with a call from her mother.

"Hi Mom. Are you having a good time with the new person today?"

"Oh, she's not new. They sent Joyce. I know her."

"Great." That was good. Joyce didn't work full time, so there would have to actually be someone new eventually, but not yet.

"Darla, I have to tell you something." Her mother's voice broke. It sounded almost like a sob.

"What is it, Mom? Are you okay?"

"The warden called me."

"Warden?"

"Yes, from Elliot's prison."

Oh yes, Elliot, her first husband, the one raped her, and others. "What happened?"

"He's out.

The detective had already told her this. "He's just calling you now, to say he's out of prison?"

"He was released a while ago."

"He was released a few weeks ago. Detective Coleman told me." She made her way into her bedroom to get ready for bed.

"You didn't say anything," her mother replied.

"I know. I didn't want you to worry. I hoped he wouldn't bother you. Or me." The prison, in Marion, Ohio, wasn't very far away, though. "Someone should scold that warden. He didn't notify you when he was supposed to."

"Please don't do that. He did call. I just didn't want you to worry."

What? Darla huffed out an angry breath. Her mother had known and hadn't told her.

"I had crossed him off my list but should I wonder if he's the one doing all this mischief to you?"

"What made you change your mind about that, Mom?" She stripped down and pulled on her nightgown. She would shower in the morning.

"My memories have been resurfacing. They're not good. Also, I heard from a woman."

There was a pause. "Yes?" Her mother must have been reluctant to go on. "A woman? What woman?"

"She testified at his trial, also. We became friends for a short time, then lost track of each other. Well, we didn't lose track, we just quit getting together. We don't have anything in common. She owns a gift shop in Columbus. It's so cute. I bought some things there once."

Darla needed to rein in the reminiscences if she was going to learn anything useful. "Mom." She interrupted her mother to get her back on track. "She called you, yes?"

"Yes. She called a few minutes ago. She heard from him today."

"From Elliot Ryan." Darla plopped onto her bed and Moose laid his warm head on her knee. That must be what prompted her mother finally say the warden just called her, even though she'd been lying before.

"Yes." Her mother stalled again.

"What did he say to her?"

"It's not that he said anything. He mailed her a note. Stuck it in her mailbox, rather. There wasn't any postage on it."

Darla took in a deep breath and turned cold inside. "What...did it say?"

"It said he would be in touch."

"That's all?" What a letdown. Not *knock knock*. Or *I know where you live.*

"She took that as a threat. She's decided to leave town for a few days."

"Does Detective Coleman know about this?"

"I suppose I should tell him. I'll call him tomorrow."

"Make sure you're all locked up, Mom. Do you want me to stay with you tonight?"

"Oh no. I'll be fine. Everything is secure."

"Okay. I'll check on you in the morning."

"Thanks, dear. You're such a good child. You are the best one. I'm glad I got to keep you."

Darla's phone vibrated with a call from the detective. "Gotta go, Mom. Be careful."

"Ms. Taylor." He sounded grim and official. *Now what?*

"I need to advise you Todd Taylor was picked up half an hour ago."

She glanced at the clock on her nightstand. It was midnight.

The detective continued. "He was caught lurking beneath a window at your mother's house."

"Oh no." Had he been around there all day? "Do you know if he...did anything?"

"He's been under surveillance since this morning when the caretaker saw him approach the house, then leave."

The caretaker. Good old Joyce. Darla was so happy she had been on duty today. She was also glad she had made sure the company knew about the restraining order. Joyce had actually noticed her father and had reported it. How lucky Ned wasn't there today. She didn't know what he would have done.

"Do you know why he left? This morning? Did he talk to Joyce? The caretaker?"

"No, they had no contact. He might have seen the shadow we had on him, at least that's what we think. He didn't approach, he was just seen near, and heading in the direction of her house. We decided to continue to keep an eye on him the rest of the day. Sure enough, he returned tonight and came too close for the protective order."

"What happens now?'

"We're holding him until he appears before a judge. He'll get a fine and some jail time."

"How much?"

"Don't know yet. Maximum is six months and a thousand dollars."

"Well, he'll be out of our way for a while anyway. That's good."

"Have a nice night. I'll call your mother in the morning. I didn't want to disturb her this time of night."

"But you wanted to disturb me."

He chuckled. "I knew you were up. Your lights are on."

What? He hung up before she had a chance to ask him if she was still being watched. And if he was the one watching her. She smiled at the thought. It made her feel safe if he *was* the one. The more she thought about the detective, the warmer she felt. Maybe she should check that attraction before it got started. Maybe it was too late.

Chapter 28

Darla felt pretty good Sunday morning. Nothing was hanging over her head, lurking, threatening.

Todd was locked up. It was such a relief she and her mother were safe from him. Even though the detective had convinced her Todd hadn't done some of the mischief. She wasn't sure she was staying convinced, though. He could have had an accomplice. Someone could have done some of the damage at his bidding when her father was sure to have an alibi, like being at an anger management class. Those classes were at random, odd times. Wouldn't a person normally go to them at a set time? On a regular schedule? Unless he was deliberately creating an alibi? Darla had no idea. But she had many, many suspicions.

She forced herself to stick to her usual routine and not worry about all her problems. She tended Moose, ate breakfast, shot some arrows, took the dog for a walk around the neighborhood. Although she looked for a police car keeping track of her, she didn't see one. Maybe she was being protected by someone so skillful they couldn't be detected. But the detective said he thought her father spotted his tail yesterday. They couldn't all be good, right? Some were probably better than others. Or maybe she wasn't being protected any more, since her father was in jail. It would be better if she didn't drive herself crazy going back and forth thinking about this. That much was for sure.

Later in the day, when her mother called, she remembered she hadn't checked on her yet, as she'd promised. She also remembered Detective Coleman had said he would be calling her this morning. She was on her couch with a glass of iced tea when her phone trilled. Moose's ears pricked up. It was as if he could tell who was calling. That dog loved her mother, and vice versa.

"Darla, you'll never guess what happened last night." She sounded breathless.

So, the detective had called her.

"Mom, who is with you today?"

"Joyce is here again. She spotted Todd and didn't even tell me. She called the police without letting me know."

It was good Joyce was there again. Maybe Gin and Ned were already fired, or replaced, or whatever the agency was going to do with them. "Joyce probably didn't want to alarm you, Mom. Anyway, he didn't do anything when she saw him. He just went away, right?" Darla was glad Joyce knew about the restraining order and she had made sure the company knew.

"Yes, he did, that time. But the detective says he came back. Wait, how do you know about this?"

"He called me last night, around midnight. He didn't want to wake you up because everything was all over by then. There was no point in worrying you. He's locked up for now."

Her mother let out a breath. "I'm glad he didn't call, I guess. It would have made me worry all night. I don't think I would have slept very well."

"Probably not."

"I'm shocked Todd would do that. He was notified about the stay-away paper. Why would he risk it? Do you think I should try to talk to him?"

"No, Mom. I am positive you should not do that. Very positive. Absolutely one hundred percent."

"If you think so. We didn't have dinner on Friday, dear. Do you want to do it today?"

"We could do that. I don't have any big plans." Friday had been the day Darla had planned to stay all night to guard her mother against Ned, just in case it would be needed. Friday had been all messed up. "I'll bring something in, if you like."

"Don't go to any trouble. I'm not hungry for anything special today."

"I'll surprise you, okay?"

"Yes, dear. That would be lovely. You *are* the best one." Her mother hung up with those words echoing in Darla's mind. She had said much the same thing last night.

You are the best one. I'm glad I got to keep you.

What did that mean? Those statements made her uneasy. There was something behind them. Something Darla didn't know anything about. She was certain. Did her mother have lots of other children she hadn't kept? How many more secrets did the woman have?

Darla made an overdue trip to the grocery store soon after the call. Walking across the parking lot to the store from her car, she enjoyed moving through the air, so warm and still. It had been windy and semi-stormy for a few days, but now the sun had broken out and turned it out to be a gorgeous summer day. Taking advantage of the change in the weather, Darla took her time strolling into the store.

When she pushed her cart out to the car after shopping, the weather still held. Birdsong trilled from the trees that dotted the lane dividers and provided welcome shade for parking beneath on hot days. They also provided perches for birds who did their business on cars below, so it was always a dilemma for Darla, whether or not to park under one of them, if a space was even available there. There were always spots in the full sun, naturally.

She brought a big chicken pot pie to her mother's house and warmed it in the oven. She had gotten it fully baked from the grocery store. It was a specialty of the local store, one of many that made Darla shop there almost exclusively. Her mother watched the six o'clock news while the pot pie heated and Darla busied herself by setting the table in the kitchen.

"Darla, come see this," she called, and Darla trotted in from the kitchen.

They both watched the weatherman indicate they were under a tornado watch. Oh great. She'd been so wrapped up in her problems, but she should have thought of that. Stormy, followed by warm, still weather. Living in Ohio, one learned about conditions that created tornadoes at a young age. These were those conditions. Cold, followed by sudden warmth.

"I always forget, dear, which is the watch and which is the warning?"

"The watch means there might possibly be a tornado and we should watch for one, in case one forms. The warning means one is coming." The change in the weather had swirled the Ohio air around, riling it up as it often did this time of year.

"Oh good. We don't need to worry about this."

Darla looked out the window. The air didn't have the pre-tornado yellowish-green quality and the clouds didn't look loopy and looming, like they did when conditions were right for a funnel cloud to imminently form. "You're probably right. Nothing to worry about." There were a lot of tornado watches.

As they ate the chicken pot pie, with a salad Darla put together from fixings in her mother's refrigerator, Darla tried to draw her out on the subject of her first husband. "I take it you still haven't heard from Elliot Ryan?"

"No, dear. I don't expect to. I'm not his favorite person, nor he mine."

It was time for her to delve into those statements her mother had been making in the last few days. "But I'm your favorite child."

"Yes, dear. You're my only child."

"You know, Mom, I've never even seen a picture of him, Elliot."

"I got rid of them."

"All of them?"

"Almost all of them. I kept one. I don't know why."

"Where is it?" Darla had to know more about this guy. Was he a danger to her? To both of them?

"In my bottom dresser drawer. In the back, underneath everything. If you must, you can get it and look at it."

"I guess I don't 'must,' but I'd like to."

Darla had finished eating, so she left the table and went to her mother's bedroom while Amy finished eating. She pawed through her mother's bottom drawer on her knees to retrieve it. She seemed to keep old, torn, and stained clothing in the drawer.

Someday, Darla should probably clean it out. At last, her fingers touched something more solid than cloth.

The picture was small, and framed. That was surprising. She had expected to find a bare photograph. She switched on the light on her mother's nightstand to see it better. He was handsome, with strong features, his head was crowned with thick, glossy black waves.

"He's Black Irish. That's what his family called themselves. The Ryans." Her mother had wheeled up behind her, noiselessly. "Strange term, isn't it?"

Darla almost dropped the photo. She was speechless. She couldn't answer her mother for a moment. This was the man she had seen leaving her mother's place when Darla had been on the lookout for her own father. He had been here. She had seen him walking out the front door. She had almost forgotten seeing him that night and hadn't asked her mother who he was. Until now.

"And he hasn't been here? At all? He didn't come inside here?"

"No, no. Definitely not."

Was her mother telling the truth? How could he have been coming out the door and hadn't been in touch? She realized she couldn't trust her any more. Her own mother.

But there was more to her mission tonight. More information she wanted.

Darla replaced the picture and pushed her mother back to the dining room. "I saw some ice cream in there. Do you want some?"

Darla dished up a couple of scoops for each of them and festooned the dessert with pastel mini marshmallows. Her mother's cupboard was always eclectic.

"Mom, I have to ask you what you meant. You said I'm the best child and you're glad you got to keep me. You've said that a couple of times lately. It's been bothering me."

Her mother sucked some ice cream off her spoon before answering, shaking her head dismissively. "I only have one child. You're it, Darla. I don't need any more children."

"But Mother, you did have a child, a baby you didn't keep."

Her mother dropped her spoon into the bowl with a clang. Had she forgotten she'd told Darla about that? Her mom bit her bottom lip, which kept trembling in spite of that. When a solitary tear rolled down her wrinkled cheek, Darla jumped up and got a tissue for her. "Mom. What is it? You can tell me."

"I don't like to talk about that time in my life. I don't even like to think about it."

"You had a baby with him...and gave it up."

Her mother bowed her head. "I told you that?"

"Yes, you did. And you're not in touch with the child? Or the father?"

"Elliot. He's the father." She denied being in touch with either one.

Darla couldn't believe her mother, though. She knew that now.

Chapter 29

"O kay, I'll tell you..."

Her mom took a breath. Then the details tumbled out like a torrent, once she started telling the story, her history. The dirty dishes sat congealing, ignored by both women. Amy Ryan, as she was then, had gotten pregnant after one of their infrequent, but very rough sex sessions, as she'd told her before. Darla bit her tongue to keep from correcting her mother and calling it what it was, rape. Her mother knew very well what it was, but didn't want to say it. Darla couldn't blame her. Her mother had lived through hell with that guy. With both of her husbands. No need to make this worse.

Elliot hadn't wanted a child and insisted she give it up when it was only a few days old.

"I admit, I didn't want to keep it. I didn't want anything to do with a person who was half Elliot."

By this time, her bitter tears were flowing and Darla was handing Amy tissue after tissue.

"Mom, you've told me this once. You don't have to talk about this anymore. I'm not going to run out and have a DNA test to find the child." As soon as she said it, though, she wondered if it would be a good idea.

Her mother gave her a grateful look and squeezed her hand. "Darla, I think I want to go to bed now. Let's not ever talk about this again."

"Sure, Mom. Do you want any help?"

"I don't need it. You go on home now."

Her mother was a proud person and wanted to do all of the things she could, only accepting help for what was too difficult. Darla knew this, but her mother's life might be easier if she would accept more assistance. Sometimes she wondered if the aides were bored with not having enough to do, because her mother wouldn't let them do anything, wouldn't let them help her.

Darla headed for the kitchen sink which was full of dirty dishes.

"Leave those for my aide tomorrow," her mother said.

"Do you know who's coming?"

"I'm not sure. Maybe Joyce, or maybe someone new." She smiled for the first time since they began talking about Elliot Ryan. "That will be nice, meeting someone new."

She had never mentioned the absence of Gin and Ned. Maybe she was glad they were gone, for her own reasons.

Darla kissed her mother goodnight and drove home, thinking about how she might have a sister out there in the world, somewhere. She had always wanted a sister. Maybe she would try to find her sibling. But she wouldn't tell her mother. Unless, maybe later, if she turned out to be...

Fantasizing about what a half-sister would look like, she unlocked the side door and entered her house, hoping it was safe and secure. The car parked two doors away might be her guardian. She didn't want to give them away, so hadn't looked too closely.

Moose was curled up in front of the kitchen sink. She let him out one last time for the day. No more barking at the back fence, to Darla's relief. Breathing in the cool night air, she wondered if she could find out exactly where Elliot Ryan was. Maybe he had only approached her mother's door—no, she definitely saw him coming out of the door. The door was closing as he left. Maybe he had talked to the aide and left without seeing her mother. Highly unlikely. Her mother kept track of everyone who came around. There weren't that many.

She sat on the back porch swing and listened to the tree frogs and locusts blasting out their cacophonous choruses, accompanied by the rhythm of the squeaky swing chain. Those creatures must have exceptional eardrums, she thought, not for the first time. They were so small and made such a racket.

When she came back inside with the dog, he went straight back to the cabinet under the kitchen sink, pawing and whining.

"What's in there that you want? You know you can't have the garbage, silly boy."

Darla opened the cupboard door and found a yellow sticky note stuck to the inside of the door. An icy chill ran through her. She almost didn't have to read it.

Knock knock

Hours later, after her whole house had been gone over for fingerprints and they had collected fibers, DNA, and hair, including lots of dog hair Darla was sure, Detective Coleman stayed and talked with her.

"This is someone who is not bothered by your dog," he said.

"Someone my dog doesn't bother, too," Darla added. "He's usually friendly to everyone. When I got him, I was told he wouldn't guard against intruders unless they were attacking me. That's just his nature. His breed. The nature of a lab. But he did show me where the guy had left the note. Do you know how he got in?"

"He appears to have another key, unless the lock was picked. There's no forced entry we can find. That's odd, isn't it? For your dog to zero in on that place? Maybe there's something else in the area he's interested in."

Together, they looked at the space under the sink. The wastebasket was there, the note was gone, taken to the lab. There were some cleaning supplies, rags, and sponges. Everything toxic was where Moose couldn't reach.

Darla pulled out the wastebasket and Moose came running, nosing past her legs, and acting intensely interested in the contents of the trash.

"Something's in there," the detective said. "Do you have a large piece of plastic? A trash bag? Crime Scene took all of their equipment with them. They went through this, I saw them, but I think they must have missed something. Something that is attracting Moose. I need to go through this myself."

She cut a couple of trash bags open and laid them on the kitchen table.

"Why don't you take the dog into the other room and I'll call you if I have any questions."

As she left, she saw him taking the contents out, one item at a time, wearing his latex gloves to handle the garbage. Moose stayed in the room with her, sitting at her side obediently, as he was ordered to, but whined pitifully, his eyes not leaving those gloved hands through the doorway.

It didn't seem like it had been a minute before he called her back. "I found this beneath the top layer." He held up a half-eaten hot dog. "Have you had hot dogs recently?" he asked.

Moose squirmed, all his attention riveted on it.

"I never have hot dogs. How did that get there?"

"That is how your intruder made friends with your dog, and it's also how he made sure your dog would lead you to the message."

"He fed half of it to Moose?"

"And buried the other half in your wastebasket. I guess Crime Scene wasn't taking Moose into account. Hot dogs aren't unusual in trash bins."

Darla had to admit, it was a good plan. And it had worked. "Do you think it's poisoned?"

Detective Coleman studied Moose. "He seems okay. But we'll have it tested."

Moose certainly didn't seem to be poisoned. His eyes were bright and he was alert, eager to get at the other half of the hotdog.

Who on earth was this fiend? How could they ever catch him? How did he get inside?

"Let's look at your security cameras," the detective suggested.

That took another hour. It was after midnight when they finished going through the recordings for the time she'd been at her mother's. There seemed to be some motion in the very corner of a couple of the frames a few times, but they couldn't tell whether it was an animal or a person.

"You should have cameras at all your doors."

"I think you're right. We can't see enough. And I need to know where Elliot Ryan is," Darla said. "I'm positive I saw him coming out of my mother's house on Monday. I was hanging around, trying to see if my dad was there so I could talk to him."

"Which I wish you wouldn't try to do."

"I can't now. He's locked up, at least. But could this be the work on my mom's first husband? He really hates her, she says."

"I would imagine so. It was before my time, but I remember hearing about the case. But why take it out on you?"

Darla shook her head. She didn't know. There was no answer to that. There were no answers to anything.

After the detective left, Darla couldn't sleep. And she had to go to work in the morning. She sat, fidgeted, paced, ate, transitioning from scared and perplexed to angry and back to perplexed. She was furious and the only thing she had to aim her fury at was a shadow.

Chapter 30

She slept on the couch for two or three hours—it didn't make any sense getting ready for bed at that point. The pattering of light rain on the roof lulled her to sleep, though she didn't need anything to lull her. She was so tired she could have slept on a cement floor.

When she woke up and let Moose out, there was no rain. Had she dreamed it? Was her fear of rain actually, completely gone? She wasn't quite convinced a terror that old—she'd been afraid of storms for so many years—would disappear in an instant. She put it out of her mind as she showered and got ready for work.

When she called her mother before work, she seemed pleased with the new health care worker, Lillian Chang.

"She has the most gorgeous, thick hair, Darla. You'll have to come over and meet her."

Darla promised she would, but maybe not today. She intended to crash after her shift. It was fortunate she was so good at her job because she performed it on autopilot that Monday.

However, as soon as she stumbled through the house after work on her way to let the dog out back, a loud knock sounded on her front door. She ran to it and cracked it open. It was her neighbor, Arthur Carlson, from two doors down.

"Hi Mr. Carlson. Can I help you?"

"I might be able to help you. I'm sorry it took so long. Been busy at work. But I finally looked through all the recordings and found something that night your car was damaged."

Her mood lifted instantly, her weariness forgotten. "You saw it? You can see the person?"

"I can, but the picture isn't that good. You probably need to look at it. Do you know when you can come over to do that? You can see it at my house."

"Right now. I have to get the dog taken care of. Ten minutes?"

"Sure. Bring Moose over. The granddaughters are here again. They'd love to see him."

One would love to see him, she was sure. The other, she remembered, had been bitten by a dog and was afraid of Moose. Anyway, he would love to see them.

Once there, Moose was let into their back yard to play with the older girl, while Mr. Carlson led Darla to his study. The younger one, the one who was not a fan of large dogs, toddled into the room after them and sat on the floor, looking at them with huge, inquisitive eyes. Darla couldn't blame her. She hoped she would someday get over her fear.

Mr. Carlson had a nice big screen to view the security footage and, once he found the place, he gave his seat to Darla so she could see it clearly.

Well, not clearly, she realized. The image was fuzzy, grainy. There was positively a person keying her car, ducking down to avoid being seen from her house. Beyond that, she was almost certain it was a male, but couldn't make out any facial features. He had a good head of hair that looked black in the gray-tone broadcast. *Was it Elliot?* He had hair like that. But that didn't make sense.

The older granddaughter shrieked in the backyard, probably chasing Moose, and scaring him out of a year's growth. The younger one, in the room with them, giggled and ran to the window to watch the activity in the back yard.

"Can I show this to the police?" Darla asked. On television crime shows they could enhance everything and make all of the fuzzy pictures crystal clear.

"Sure, go ahead. I've copied it over for you." He handed her a USB stick. "I figured they might want to see it. I hope it helps. Sorry, again, I took so long to get around to it. I really didn't think it would catch anything from so far away."

"I can't thank you enough. They're still looking for the person, so this might help. Can't hurt. The more evidence they have the better, right?"

He nodded.

She took the flash stick from him and rescued Moose, who might have had enough of the screaming girl, then hurried home to call Detective Coleman.

"Can you bring it to the station?"

"When?"

"Now? We need to see it right away."

Her mood was lifting even higher. Maybe something would come of this. She had the urge to call Gin to report developments, then remembered Gin wasn't speaking to her.

"Guard the house," she called to Moose, knowing he wouldn't if an intruder had treats, and drove to the police station. She tried not to worry about him, with her house being watched by passing patrol cars.

Detective Coleman guided her to a large room in the back filled with what looked like scientific equipment. That's probably what it was, she told herself. Stuff to examine evidence with. She hoped it was all state of the art. As good as the stuff on television.

She watched a lab technician load the video and run through it, waiting for the magic moment when she cleared up the grainy images.

After the tech had viewed it, with the Detective and Darla looking over her shoulders, she stopped it and sat back.

"That's it?" Darla asked.

"That's all that's copied on here," she said.

"I mean, can you make the picture better? Can you enlarge it, or, I don't know, clear it up somehow."

She saw the detective stifling a laugh.

"Too much TV?" Darla asked.

"Yes," the technician said. "Too much TV. If I enlarge it, it'll look worse. We can improve it a bit, but we won't get a portrait. We'll work on it and we'll let you know when it's done. That'll take some time."

"Come on." Detective Coleman beckoned her to his office.

When they were there, he asked if she wanted anything to drink. Why did people always think a drink would help anything? "No, I just want to know who you think it is. Can you tell any better than I can?"

He shook his head. "Probably not until we get it back from the lab. But we could tell that he had on a puffy vest with vertical stripes. Have you seen that article of clothing on anyone?"

He must have more experience deciphering those kinds of videos. She hadn't noted the detail of the vest, but he was right. You couldn't tell the colors, but you could tell it had a couple of wide stripes down the front. The night had been chilly, so it was most likely a down vest.

"Elliot Ryan has hair like that. So, someone with thick, dark hair, and that vest. I don't think I've seen it before, but I've only seen Elliot Ryan once. Just glimpsed him."

"It doesn't look old enough to be him, but it's hard to tell," he said. "Let us know if you spot the vest."

"I sure will." She stood. "I hope nothing has happened while I'm gone. To Moose, I mean, or my house."

"We have a car on your block. I think you'll be okay tonight."

It was late when she got home. She started to sit and watch TV, then realized how hungry she was. She put together a PBJ, and wolfed it down outside while Moose explored the back yard. She tensed up, but relaxed when nothing seemed to bother him, or get his attention.

After she put him inside, she went back out to do some shooting. She usually left her target and the stand in the yard. Zeke had made her a nice wooden stand out of weather-treated wood. He had been as handy at making and fixing things as he'd been at lying to her about his family. In the darkness, she couldn't spot the target. She turned on the back porch light so she could see it.

Oh no! Where was it? Had someone stolen her archery target?

Even though she was done with Zeke, for life, she would be upset if someone had stolen it. Against her will, she often remembered the sight of him making it in her back yard, shirtless, on a hot summer day, grinning at her through floppy blond hair that never stayed out of his face. If only he hadn't been a complete fake. A cheat and a liar. Every woman's nightmare, the perfect guy with a wife and kids in another town.

But the target wasn't there. And she needed it.

She raced the length of the yard and found it tipped over, flat on the ground. Zeke had tied sandbags to the legs so it wouldn't fall over. It hadn't even been windy in the last few days. Not windy enough to do this. Someone must have knocked it over.

Bending to pick it up, she saw red paint on one of the legs.

Knock knock

The words were scrawled. It was either red paint, applied with a fine brush, or maybe fingernail polish. Something to get her attention and scare the wits out of her. Again.

She felt like screaming to rival the tree frogs.

Leaving it on the ground, after being careful not to touch it, she went inside, too worked up to shoot now, even if she could. Her hands shook as she stowed her gear. Moose, sensing her distress, leaned against her legs. She knelt to bury her face in his fur and her tears started. Was this never going to end? How was she, or the police, or anyone on earth, to ever catch this monster?

She looked through the video from her new security cameras, but they hadn't caught anything at the end of the yard. Or on any other side of the house. He had evaded the patrolling police car and her cameras once again. And no neighbors had cameras that would catch anything in her back yard.

Too distressed to call the detective and tell him, for all the good it would do, she took a sleeping pill and went to bed early. If she had recovered her equanimity by then, she would call him in the morning. If she tried to say anything right now, she would start screaming.

Chapter 31

It was hard waking up in the morning. Darla had known it would be when she took the sleeping pill the night before. That was why she rarely took them. They worked well on her, almost too well. After downing two extra cups of coffee, she finally felt she could function. She called the detective to tell him about the target stand. He said he would send someone to fingerprint it. They both knew that wouldn't do any good. This guy had never left a finger print on anything before. He wouldn't begin doing that now. When she asked, he told her the neighbor's video had not been processed yet. It would take longer than this, he said.

She called her mother to tell her good morning, but didn't mention the new harassment.

"Darling, you have to meet Lillian. She's an angel. Can you stop over after work? Just for a minute?"

She said she would. Besides, she wanted to check Lillian out, since she was new. Make sure she wasn't associated with any of what was happening to herself right now. She would ask her if she knew any of her coworkers. Like Gin. Or Ned. Everyone was a potential suspect in her mind. Complicit, guilty, until proven innocent.

Getting dressed, Darla considered calling in sick for a minute. If she did, though, what would she do at home all day? Worry herself into a tightly-wound knot of anxiety, that's what.

Once again, she got through the day at the hospital only because she was so experienced at doing what she did. She was also conscientious and cared about the patients entrusted to her, though. She wasn't exactly on autopilot, because personal interaction was always called for, but she was close. At the end of her shift, she reflected, not for the first time, she was lucky to have this job. Especially now. She so badly needed something worthwhile to concentrate on. And she loved being a nurse. She always had and always would. Yes, she was lucky.

Stopping at home to tend to Moose, she decided to bring him along, since her mother loved seeing him so much and it had been a while. So, they both went to her mother's to meet the new health care worker. Moose, a good judge of character, was there as a partner.

Lillian opened the door at Darla's light rap. She could have walked in, but didn't want to take the new woman by surprise.

"Hi," Lillian said with a huge smile. "You must be Darla, Ms. Taylor's daughter."

It was curious she called her mother Ms. instead of the usual Mrs. *Why was that*? Darla took her hand and greeted her. "We're so glad you're here. Mom has spoken highly of you."

Lillian looked back at Mrs. Taylor parked next to the couch. "She's a joy. It's no trouble helping her out."

"This is Moose," Darla said releasing Moose to bound over to her mother, lick her hand, then warily approach Lillian, and sniff her with his tail wagging.

"Hello, Moose." Lillian bent down and showed him the back of her hand. "You're a pretty boy."

She had passed the Moose test. That was good. Darla decided she liked Lillian, but just needed to clarify a few things for her own peace of mind.

"Have you worked for OTB long?"

"OTB?"

"Sorry. I call it that. Only The Best."

"Oh, yes. I've been with them for about four years, I think. I moved here from California to care for my grandmother, then started working here after she passed away."

"I'm so sorry to hear that," Darla said. She was glad Lillian had been with the company for a while. That meant she was a trusted employee. She hoped.

"That's okay. It was time. She suffered at the end. I like this company. They treat us well."

"It's good to hear that. Do you know many of the other workers?"

"Not really. We don't see each other unless we have shifts at the same place. I know a few by name, but there's no real chance for us to get ever to know each other. We don't have company picnics." She smiled at her last comment.

Darla felt she had to keep going. "Do you know the others from your company who have worked here? Gin? Or Ned?"

"No, I've never run into either of them." A slight frown crossed her smooth brow. She wasn't very old. "Wait, I think I was at a job where Gin also worked once, but never met her. I know the name. Gin Holland, right? I've seen it on the sched-ule."

Satisfied she wasn't a friend of either of them, Darla settled next to her mother and they chatted about the weather and Moose. Lillian, as expected, had already given her mother something to eat.

"They say we might be getting bad storms, Darla. I hope you won't have trouble driving to work tomorrow."

"No, Mom, I'll be fine."

Lillian left the room to tend to the laundry. Darla lowered her voice and scooted closer to her mother.

"Why does Lillian call you Ms. Taylor, Mom? Did you tell her to?"

"I did. I can't shed my name, nor do I want to, since you have it, too. But I can shed the title that tells the world I was married to him."

"Mom, I'm sorry, but I have to ask you. Are you sure you don't know anything else about Elliot? Or if my father has any friends who would be doing things to me for him?"

Her mother shook her head. "Has anything else happened? I've told you and the police everything I know."

Darla didn't want to mention the minor incident of tipping over the target. And, of course, painting the frightening message on it. Running into a dead end once again with her mother and Elliot, Darla started on the other subject that had been on her mind. "How about the baby?"

"Baby? What baby?"

"The one you gave up. I'd like to know more about her."

"Oh, that. Him."

"Him?" Okay, she had a brother, not a sister. But she wanted to know more. "What do you know about him?"

"Why do you want to know about him?"

"I just do. He's my brother. My half-brother. Was he adopted? Did you keep up with him at all?"

"Not really. I didn't ask to be updated. I did, though...I did keep him longer than I led you to believe."

She was lying to Darla again. Darla kept a straight face, not wanting to show her mother how exasperated she was becoming with her. "How long did you keep him?"

"I...couldn't bear to abandon a tiny baby. I kept him longer than I should have. I always knew I wasn't going to keep him. He was three when I gave him up." Her mother gazed past the television, out the window, staring into the dark.

Three years! That was a big difference from a few days.

"Wasn't it harder after you got to know him?" And, Darla assumed, love him. He was a baby. Everyone loves babies.

"It was hard. But he looked more and more like his father every day. I was afraid I wouldn't be a good mother to him." She turned her eyes, full of tears, to Darla. "I really have missed him so much. I wondered, for years, if I'd done the right thing. I guess I'll never know."

"What was his name?"

"Justin. I named him Justin Ryan."

"That's a nice name, Mom."

"I kept one picture." Her mother wheeled herself over to the living room desk and opened a bottom drawer. She reached to the back and drew out an old snapshot.

Darla followed her and took it when she held it up.

"Just put it back there when you're done looking at it."

Darla snapped a picture of it with her phone and put it back. The subject, Justin Ryan, was an adorable curly-headed moppet with baby-fat legs and cheeks, grinning at the photographer, his eyes sparkling.

"Did he keep the name?"

"I don't know anything about him. That was his name when he left me."

Darla could almost feel the ache from giving up a baby who looked like that. So full of life, of joy. After he was given away, had he kept feeling the same joy? Had he kept smiling like that?

It must have been so hard on both of them. She wanted to cry for them both.

At her own home that night, her mother's words kept returning to haunt her. She went over and over them in her mind. How awful it must have been for her, to want and to not want her own baby, at the same time. To have a tug of war going on in her heart. To miss her baby and still not want to ever see him again. Hers and Elliot's baby. The "Elliot" part was the problem. If only he hadn't been the father.

Her poor mother. She had had so much tragedy in her life. Much more than Darla had ever even known about. And she'd known about plenty without all of this!

Darla had stared at the image of the little tyke until the image was burned into her mind. She fell asleep, haunted by the toddler and wondering what had become of him. And wondering how her mother could stand to not know.

Chapter 32

Wednesday was the first day of May, May Day, and the nurse's station, the hallways, and some of the long-term patients' rooms were festooned with artificial flowers. The cheery feeling lifted Darla's spirits, which had still been down in the morning. Her usual morning call to her mother had been brief and they'd said basically nothing. Everything they'd talked about the day before was swept under some sort of emotional, protective rug.

Late in the day, Detective Coleman called to tell her the video was back and the enhancement had worked well. Better than he'd thought it would.

Anxious to go there and see it, the rest of her shift dragged like slogging through Ohio spring mud in heavy shoes. At last, it was time to leave. She raced to the station, leaving Moose for later. He would be okay, she told herself. It wouldn't take long to look at a piece of video.

However, she was kept waiting for twenty minutes before she could see Detective Coleman. At last, he came out to the lobby and rescued her from the hard plastic chair.

"You came straight from work?" he said, looking at her nursing scrubs.

Obviously. She nodded instead of saying she wore these clothes all the time whether she was working or not. She wasn't feeling humorous. "Where is it?"

"Follow me." He led her into the room filled with the complicated-looking equipment. The same woman she'd seen before beckoned them over to her station.

"This turned out really well. That's a good system your neighbor has," she said.

They both looked over her shoulders as she fiddled with the machine. Soon, a clear picture of Darla's car came up. In seconds, a figure appeared at the edge of the screen, bent over, and creeping alongside her car. From the abundance of dark wavy hair, it must be Elliot Ryan, her mother's first ex.

Then he looked around before he defaced her door with his key, and she could see his face clearly for a split second. It wasn't Elliot.

It was Ned Farley.

His hair was so similar. Why had she not thought of him? Well, she tried hard not to.

Darla realized the detective was watching her closely. "Do you know who this is?"

"Yes," she said, her voice hoarse. "I know him. He's dating my best friend."

"We'd better go to my desk so I can get some information from you on this.,"

"Wait. I have to call someone." She took out her phone to call Gin. She was the one Darla always called if she needed someone to take care of Moose, but she put the phone away without completing the call. Anyway, she was blocked now. They weren't talking to each other, after all. She couldn't call

Gin and ask her for a favor. That would be crass. They would somehow have to make up first. Except Gin was dating Darla's tormentor. "I should go home to take care of my dog. He can't go much longer."

"I'll follow you there. I can get your information at your house, just as well as here."

She didn't know if that's what he was supposed to do, but she wasn't about to object.

After she had tended to Moose, she and detective sat at her kitchen table where he drank a cup of coffee she had just brewed and she had a cup of decaf.

The detective took his notebook and a pencil out of his jacket pocket. "Tell me everything you know about him."

"I don't know much. I've tried to find out more about him, but I haven't had any luck. His name is Ned Farley and he says he used to be in finance. I've asked him where he's from, where he's lived, and he is always evasive. Right now, he works for Only The Best, the home health company who sends the people who work for my mom and other home-bound people like her."

"They should have done a background check on him. I can see if I can get any info from them. Anything else?"

"He drives a dirty black pickup truck, but I don't know the license number. He knows Gin and Keith Holland's dad. They are on an axe throwing team together."

"Gary Holland? How do you suppose he knows him?" His voice sharpened.

"Do you know who he is?"

"I know a lot of people who have been in the system."

"Yeah, I wondered. Ned might have been in prison with him. Gin and I have both searched for him online and he doesn't exist very far back."

Detective Coleman narrowed his eyes and bounced the eraser end of his pencil on the notepad. "It would make sense he's been in prison, if you can't find online information. The company isn't supposed to hire people with records of certain crimes. Violence, abuse, or theft. But he must have gotten past whatever check they did on him. He might have been in for financial crimes, like Holland."

"Could he have a fake ID that would fool them?"

"It's possible. Ohio doesn't require an FBI background check. A lot of places do only what they have to." He stood. "I'll look into this, but first, I'll bring him in for vandalism."

Good. Was she a bad person for being glad he was being charged? No, not when the crime was damaging her car. Why would he do that?

Right after she rinsed out her toothbrush and was ready to climb into bed, the detective called back.

"Did you arrest him?"

"I'm afraid not. The address he gave his company is bogus. Doesn't exist."

"Oh no. You can't find him?"

"We'll find him, just not tonight. We know where he works."

"So, they didn't do a very good background check, I guess." That was disappointing. And dangerous for people like her mother.

"These places sometimes get desperate for employees. This one is known for bending rules and looking the other way."

"Do you think I should get someone else to look after Mom? Some other company?"

"I wouldn't use Ned."

"No, I've told them already. He's not working at my mother's house. But the company. Should I trust them?"

"They don't have a bad rep. Just a slack one. His name might not actually be Ned or Farley. If he assumed it recently, it would come up clean on a casual check. It's good he's not working with your mother."

"He was, but I had him taken off." She also had her best friend taken off. What was happening to the world she used to know? She felt the floor tilting beneath her feet and grabbed the edge of the bed she was sitting on. "What now?"

"Sit tight. We'll find him."

Darla knew she would have a hard time sleeping, so she used one of her sleep-inducement methods that wasn't a pill. She padded out to the kitchen and made herself a cup of chamomile tea, watched a mindless rerun on television, then was able to fall asleep.

At three am, however, she woke and sat up, her heart hammering.

She knew exactly who Ned Farley was.

She had to talk to Gin. No, not at three in the morning. But very soon.

When Darla's alarm went off at six, she called Gin. Who didn't answer, of course. She called three times in a row, hoping she would pick up, would realize this was urgent. Even if they weren't speaking to each other. That was temporary. Gin had to know that.

Darla didn't even know Gin's work schedule now that she wasn't coming to her mother's house. She didn't want to text her about this. She couldn't risk "Ned" seeing her message, so she resorted to a voicemail. Would Gin pick it up? She had no idea. Neither she nor Gin used voice mail on the phone much.

Darla tended the dog, showered, and dressed for work. Moose sensed her distress and glued himself to her side, staring at her with his big brown puppy-dog eyes. Literally, his puppy-dog eyes.

Her heart melted. "Oh Moosie, you're such a good friend. I wish people were more like dogs. I wish Gin was more like you. Loyal and kind."

Moose licked her elbow, almost making her spill the tea she held in her right hand as she sat at her breakfast table, gearing up for her day. It made her laugh, and it felt so good. What had her life been like before Moose came to live with her? She could barely remember. Colorless, she was sure. Bland, boring, and colorless. But with a best friend and a mother who, as far as she knew then, didn't lie to her. All those lies lent a darker color to her present world.

Driving in to work, she thought maybe she could call OTB and leave a message for Gin to call her. Would she pay attention to a message left there? Better yet, maybe she could get Gin's schedule. If she knew where she was, she could be waiting for her after work and talk to her. Gin needed to stop seeing Ned. She had to make her see. She finally got a chance to follow through and do it on her mid-morning break, and called the company.

"Only The Best, can I help you?"

"I hope so. It's very important I get a message to Gin Holland. I need to see her today. Can you tell me where she's working?"

There was a slight pause and the voice returned, a little less pleasant, but still cordial. "I'm sorry, we can't give out that information. Would you like to leave word here for her to call you? I can certainly get a message to her."

"I would, but I'm afraid she might not do it. We've been having a quarrel. But it's important. It's for her own safety."

"If you'll give me your name and number, I'll relay the message to her."

Darla gave her the contact information, but no real message. She couldn't chance Ned learning about it. "And you have to make sure she calls me. It's very important."

"You don't want to leave a message to pass on?"

"No, I'd rather not. You can tell her it's private and urgent, please. You can do that, can't you?"

"I'll give this information to her. Thank you." The voice was no longer pleasant. The call cut off.

Darla had hoped they'd share Gin's schedule, though she would have known better. But now, she didn't think the woman on the phone would relay the urgency and she didn't think Gin would call her. She would have to come up with a Plan B.

Chapter 33

Darla drove home from work through a hard, pelting rain. The weather had turned weirdly warm, as opposed to just warm, and the raindrops felt hot on her skin as she ran into her house from the car.

Spring weather, you could never tell what it would do.

All afternoon, she had left her phone on, for the rest of her shift, against hospital policy, hoping Gin would call her back. Driving home, she checked it at least three times, and once again when she got inside. If you could wear out a phone by looking at it, hers would be ready to be replaced.

As soon as she opened the kitchen door, Moose ran into the backyard, loving the rain, jumping, and biting at the almost hot water. The drops seemed huge to Darla. She had no doubt Moose was catching some.

Before she let him back in, she was prepared, holding a large beach towel. She shielded herself with it while he shook off the water, complete with wet-dog smell. Then she used it to dry him off, as best she could. He was so good, the way he stood still while she did that.

Checking her phone once again, it was obvious there was no call from Gin. It was also obvious this wasn't the way to contact her. She would have to think of something else.

Braving the storm, she drove to Gin's, but Ned's battered black pickup was parked in front. She knew she should march into the apartment and pull Gin aside, and was disappointed in herself when she couldn't do that. She drove back home.

The next night she tried again. She was glad it had finally quit raining that morning. It was Friday night and, if Gin and Ned still had the same schedules they had had, neither of them would be working on the weekends, there would be a good chance they would go out together. They could stay out late and sleep in on Saturday. That was what she would have done, had she been dating anyone at the moment—what she had done when she was, in the past.

Just before Gin was due to get home, if, in fact, she had worked that day, Darla parked a block from her apartment building. Sure enough, Gin drove up twenty minutes later and went inside. Darla waited. Half an hour after, Ned's old truck rattled up from the opposite direction and parked near Gin's car. Her timing was good.

Her luck was good, too. Darla breathed a sigh of relief. If he had come from the other direction, he would have seen her.

Within minutes they both came out and got into Ned's truck. Gin's Toyota was so much nicer, Darla wondered why they used his old rattle-trap. Maybe it was a macho thing. She could have given him credit for chivalry, but didn't feel the least bit chartable toward him. No points for the guy who slashed her tire.

She followed them, staying three or four cars behind, to the local movie theater.

Great. Now I will have to wait a few hours. She didn't want to follow them in and confront them in a place where people weren't supposed to be talking. There was a small deli nearby, so she went inside to get a sandwich and use the restroom, then returned to her stake-out an hour and a half later. She would follow them to the next place, probably back to Gin's, then call the detective to come arrest him. Or should she follow him home to see where he lived? If he stayed the night, that wouldn't work.

As she debated, they came out, laughing and finishing the giant movie drinks, their arms around each other's waists.

Darla wanted to shout, "Gin, no!" Her friend had been completely taken in. Why would she trust a stranger and alienate her best friend? How could she do that? Darla didn't think she would ever trust a guy, any guy, over her best friend. As angry as she was getting over this whole situation, watching them at this moment, she couldn't ever get as mad at Gin as she could at him. Damn him. She had to make every effort not to let him poison their friendship. But there Gin was, laughing with him, touching him, ignoring phone calls from her best friend.

Darla blinked back tears at the fresh signs of betrayal and followed them again. It wasn't easy, in such a small town, to put several cars between them, but the fact this was Friday night helped. There was a quite a bit of traffic in this part of downtown, the place where people went to unwind from the week.

Looking around, trying to make sure she was surrounded by enough cars to not be seen, she thought she detected a police car, but didn't see it again. Too bad, she could have let the officer know she had Ned Farley, as he called himself, in her sights.

The distinctive truck pulled up next to a medium-nice restaurant. Darla slowed, her car not reaching the front door until they were inside. She scribbled down the license number, then drove past the truck and parked just beyond it, two spaces away, at the side of the place they'd gone into.

When she climbed out of her car, the air was so heavy she could barely breathe. The sun was setting, shedding a glare across the glistening pavement. Darla glanced up, wondering if they were in for a tornado.

The sky didn't look good. She also sensed an eerie quiet. It was a scary kind of stillness which comes just before something bad happens.

Her phone rang, a call from her mother. Maybe she wanted to warn her about a storm coming? No alert from the weather service had come over her phone. She had to get inside. Darla turned off her ringer, even put her phone in airplane mode so it wouldn't give her away, and went inside the restaurant.

Ned and Gin were at the bar. That was a problem. She would rather they had gone to a table. Then she could have taken one nearby, one she wouldn't have to walk past them to get to. And do what? What was she waiting for? Maybe she should go back out to her car and trail him to wherever he was living so he could be picked up and charged with the vandalism, at the least.

They were at the near end of the bar, close to the front door, where it curved, so that their backs were to her and to the door. Ned's outer vest hung over the back of the barstool. The one with the wide stripes down the front. Those stripes had shown up so well in the video. Darla was glad they hadn't seen her, but couldn't decide what to do next. She hadn't thought this out well enough.

Before she could ponder this, the building shook and the lights blinked. She stood still just inside the door. Heads jerked up and backs straightened as everyone went on alert.

A man at the far end of the bar stood up, waving his cell phone. "Hey, I got a notice. We got a tornado warning," he shouted. "It's heading right for us!"

Pulling out her own phone, she saw it was on hers, too.

A tornado warning. Not a watch. One was approaching.

Knowing that she had better keep up with the weather now, she took her phone out of airplane mode.

Two of the wait staff started pushing the heavy tables together and directing people to crawl underneath them. The indoor noise level rose quickly, up to a roar, as people raised their voices in near panic. If her phone had not already alerted, she wouldn't have been able to hear it now.

Darla had been near many tornados before and some had even touched down close to where she'd been, but she'd never been in the direct path of one. Had never even seen one up close. This was awfully frightening. Her hair pricked up, on her head and her arms, along with her heartbeat, as she scrambled beneath a set of tables near the front. Someone came in the front door and a louder roar could be heard from outside. She bit her lower lip and refrained from whimpering, like she wanted to.

What about Mom. She tried not to panic? *Would she be okay? Would someone protect her?*

There was absolutely nothing she could do now. Except worry.

There was no time to get anywhere. Tornadoes moved fast.

The sound outside grew even louder and chugged in a quick, deadly, steady rhythm. The wind continued to shake the building. Darla hoped the place was sturdy and hoped the tables were heavy enough not to be blown away if the roof came off the restaurant.

Bearing down on them like a train, the chugging grew faster and closer until it was an almost unendurable roar.

Others were screaming, faintly now, their cries coming through beneath the sound of the juggernaut. The other people beneath Darla's set of tables grabbed each other. She took the hand which clutched hers and grabbed the person on her other side. She knew this was a good tactic, making them into a single mass that was, they hoped, too heavy to be lifted by the funnel. It had worked, reportedly, in other storms.

With a whoosh, the room grew lighter.

The roof had blown off.

The tables shifted and rattled, but stayed on the ground. The dim glow from above lent more unease, eeriness. Along with the overlying sense of panic weighing on everyone.

Darla was sure the crisis lasted only a few seconds, but those seconds seemed like ten minutes, at least, maybe more, and then the wind and the storm were gone. The tables quit vibrating, settled down. People started to crawl out from under them, encountering a carpet embedded with glass shards from the bar bottles and glasses that had broken as they had crashed onto the floor from the bar and the tables.

When Darla stood, dazed, she saw some people were bleeding from the flying glass. One woman's face was covered with blood. She must have gotten a bad cut on her face, Darla thought. With a jerk of recognition, Darla realized it was Gin. She rushed to her.

"I'm okay." Gin grabbed her hands. "It's just one cut on my forehead. It's bleeding a lot, but it's not deep." Gin glanced at the table she'd been under. Ned was still there, cowering. "You can come out now, you know," she said.

His eyes looked wild. Darla realized he was still terrified, maybe in shock. She knelt next to him and spoke quietly, gently. "Justin, it's okay. You can get up now."

"You're sure?"

It was her half-brother, the man her mother had given away as a very young child. A man who detested her, for some reason, and was doing a good job at making her life hell.

Chapter 34

"Justin. Justin Ryan?" The voice behind Darla was deep. And so very welcome.

Detective Coleman took two steps around Darla, leaned down, grabbed Justin's wrist, and snapped the first half of the set of handcuffs onto his right wrist. Justin, formerly Ned, twisted away, his eyes even more wild, but the detective snapped the other half on his other wrist, behind him, then lifted him off the floor by one arm.

"Detective," Darla breathed. "What are you doing here?" It seemed like a miracle he had shown up at just the right time. "How did you know...?"

"I've been following you for a few hours. I wondered when you were going to call me."

She couldn't speak. She was so relieved he was here, but also was afraid she was in a lot of trouble. "Just as soon as...as soon as I figured out where he lives."

"Uh huh."

It didn't seem like the detective believed her.

"Really, I was. Then, when I got here, I was just ready to go back to my car and tell you he was here. But I wasn't positive this was Justin Ryan. Pretty sure, but not positive." She hadn't known if Justin would even know that name. It could have been changed when he was given away. His new family, or foster parents, or whoever raised him, must have kept the name Justin. His last name probably wasn't Ryan though.

"We are now, aren't we?" The detective actually smiled at her. "I heard him reply to his name when you said it. Good work."

"Well, when the storm hit, I couldn't go outside." She was babbling. Making too many excuses.

She remembered the gust of noise and air as someone came in just before the twister hit, when she'd already been beneath the table. That had to have been the detective. She was so tightly wired from the danger and from being sure he was her tormentor that she turned to the man cowering beside Detective Coleman and unleashed her anger. "What the hell is wrong with you, Justin Ryan? Why have you been making my life hell all this time?" Her fists were balled and it was all she could do not to pummel him.

"There will be time later," the detective said.

"There's time now." Justin had apparently recovered from his terror during the storm and had found his backbone. He turned to Darla and sneered at her. "You have no idea. You don't know what it's like to be sent from one awful foster home to a worse one. And then to another one even worse than that. Nothing but abuse and neglect. No love, no caring. And you, the golden child, staying with Mommy and Daddy, never a care in the world. No one beating you, giving you rags for clothes, garbage for meals."

For some reason, the detective was letting him rant on. Darla shrank under the onslaught of his hatred and jealousy. "I never even knew you existed. My mother never..."

"*Your* mother? *Our* mother! But maybe you're right. She was no mother to me. She never cared about me. She gave me away and never once tried to track me down, to see what happened to me. I could be dead for all she knew. How would she like it if her golden child was dead? I asked myself that so many times."

Had he meant to kill her, eventually?

"Okay, that's it. Let's go." The detective cut off his vitriol and hauled him through the opening where the front door had been, still gripping him by his upper arm. They both had to step over some of the shattered remains of the door. It had been a heavy one.

Justin screeched at her all the way out. "If you were dead, she'd see. She'd see what it's like to be alone. It would serve both of you right."

His invective was cut off only when the detective folded him into the back seat of the cruiser and slammed the door. Coleman took off without telling her what would happen next. She would probably have to give some sort of statement. Nothing happened in the law enforcement world without paperwork, she had learned during her ordeal.

Gin was standing next to her, dripping blood onto the littered floor.

"What just happened? Who's Justin?" Gin's voice was full of confusion.

Darla explained his real name was Justin Ryan and he was actually her half-brother, and their mother had given him up as a baby.

"It took me a long time to figure it out. And for my mother to finally tell me about him. I never knew she had another child. Ned, Justin, has been the one tormenting me. He's the person

I've been trying to uncover, to identify. I put it together, but I still wasn't quite sure until he answered to his real name, just now. I was afraid for you, Gin, once I figured it out."

Gin gave her a bewildered look, but didn't ask any questions.

"Come on," Darla said. "My car is right outside. If it didn't blow away. Let's get you some attention."

After they got in, Darla reached into the back to grab the old sweatshirt she kept in the car and stuffed it into Gin's lap. She doubted Gin could see through the blood flowing down her face.

"What's that for?" Gin asked.

"You can mop up the blood with it. It's old, it's okay. Go ahead and sop up some of that so you can see."

"Thanks." Gin swiped at her face, wiping the stream out of her eyes and away from her nose and mouth. "I probably don't need to—"

"Hush, we're going to the hospital. I'm pretty sure you need a couple of stitches."

Darla wasn't able to tell how big the cut was, or even where it was. There was still a great deal of blood on her face. She hoped it wouldn't leave an ugly scar on Gin's face.

She had one more pressing concern. As soon as they were on the way to the hospital, she called her mother's number, holding her breath while the phone rang. She almost cried when she answered.

"Darla? Are you all right?"

"Mom, I'm fine. Are you?"

"Yes, we're doing okay. There isn't any power, so it's dark in the basement. Joyce carried me here, can you imagine?"

"Joyce? Is she there?"

"She is. I was so happy to see her when she showed up."

"Did she work today? What was she doing there so late?"

"No, she didn't work today. She heard the storm warnings and came over to make sure I'd be okay. My day shift aide had already left, so I was alone."

Gin whispered, "How is she? How's the house?"

Darla mouthed back "She's fine."

"Mom, tell Joyce how grateful I am to her. How's the rest of the house?"

"Joyce just now went upstairs to check. I don't think there's any damage here."

"I can come over and help her get you upstairs." Darla couldn't imagine how the older woman had been able to carry her mother down the basement stairs.

"I'll ask her if she needs help when she comes back down. I'm relieved you're all right. Is your house okay?"

Her house. Moose! She had to check on him. "I don't know yet. I'm driving Gin to the hospital."

"Oh dear! Is she hurt?"

"Not badly, Mom. Just a cut, I think." Darla had reached the emergency entrance. "I gotta go. I'll be back over here soon." She could leave Gin there at the hospital if there were a lot of people, a backup in the waiting room, and come back later. *Wasn't there bound to be a backup, right after a tornado?*

At some point she and Gin were going to have a lot more to talk about. She was glad the car trip had been taken up with her call to her mom. This wasn't the right time. She didn't want to talk to Gin right now about...everything. Anything.

Her first stop now had to be home. Moose must have been terrified.

Chapter 35

Darla almost collapsed onto the porch floor when she heard Moose greeting her from inside. Her shoulders slumped in relief. She had been so keyed up, she hadn't realized she was carrying her shoulders nearly up to her ears.

The outside of her house seemed to be intact. Her whole block looked like it was. The funnel must have skipped this part of town. She opened the door to be jumped on and licked with much more enthusiasm than she had ever seen from him. And he was an enthusiastic licker.

She knelt and ruffled his fur while he licked her face. "Oh, Moosie, were you so scared? I'm sorry I wasn't here. Poor Moosie."

After their love-fest-greeting, she took the dog out back and looked around. Her target, propped back up on a hay bale, wasn't even disturbed. Those bales wouldn't have kept it firmly in place if the storm had hit her yard. She glanced upward and breathed thanks her small corner of the world had been spared.

After the dog had taken care of his usual business and had given the yard a thorough sniffing, she called him. "We have to go check on Mom, Moosie. Let's get going." He seemed to understand every word she was saying. He ran to the back door, ready for the mission.

Inside, she leashed him and took him out front, where he bounded into the back seat. She swore he at least knew the word "mom" when she said it. At the sound of the word, his ears always pricked and an eager expression overcame his doggie face.

Maybe she should have checked out the rest of the house, but she had to get to her mother's place as soon as she could, had to check on her mother, make sure she was safe. Besides, the storm hadn't done any damage here and she knew exactly where the intruder had been.

It took some time to reach her mother's home. As she drove, she could see the area between their houses had been badly damaged. The tornado had obviously touched down here and there, jumping from spot to spot. There was nothing subtle about a tornado. Some roads were already officially blocked off, others were just plain impassable. She was somehow able to find a route there, involving swinging way out of the way and going down some alleys. Moose stared out at the wreckage from the back window, as impressed by it as she was, it seemed. She wondered what the aftermath of a tornado smelled like to a dog.

When Darla got there, she saw her mother's neighborhood had remained as untouched as her own. She breathed one more sigh of relief.

"Small favors," she muttered, opening the rear car door for Moose and holding him back as he bounded for the front door.

Joyce opened the door just before they got to it. "I thought I heard you coming. She'll be so happy to see you."

Darla wasn't sure if she was referring to her mother being happy to see Moose or to see her daughter. Joyce was a big fan of Moose's, too. Darla dropped Moose's leash and let him run inside.

Darla stopped to thank the woman. "Joyce, I can't tell you how glad I am you came by. I was in a restaurant that got ripped apart when it hit."

"You didn't get any of the messages from your mother?"

"I saw them, I just couldn't respond." Not quite true. She could have answered the first one. How was she to know this would be so devastating? It occurred to her then, she *would* have known if she had responded to her mother. "Is she still downstairs?"

"She is. I've been trying to figure out how to get her up the stairs." She headed for the basement door. "I don't think I can do it by myself."

"How did you get her down?"

"I sat with her in my lap and we scooted down, one step at a time."

Darla tried to picture this. It sounded awfully difficult. "You're a saint, Joyce."

Joyce turned and beamed at her. "Why, thank you. I think we need a saint named Joyce."

"I know some Catholics. I'll put in a good word."

They chuckled at that.

As they started down the stairs, Moose pushed ahead and beat them to the bottom.

"Oh, you darling boy," her mother cooed. "Come give me a kiss."

Moose gave her more than one. Sometimes she objected to being licked, but not today. Her mom sat on the floor, a perfect target for the dog anyway. He couldn't knock her over to the ground as Darla often feared he would.

"You're both all right?" Her mom asked.

"Perfectly. We're fine."

"What happened to Gin? You said she was injured."

"She got hit by some flying glass. I think. She has a cut on her face. I took her to the emergency room and it'll be a while before they can get to her. It's crowded with tornado victims, it looked like."

"You were with her?"

"Not really. We were just in the same place. A restaurant got hit pretty bad. I'll tell you all about it later." Darla didn't want to air the dirty family linen in front of Joyce. She was going to have to tell her mother about Ned. Correction. About Justin. She didn't look forward to that.

She also didn't want to worry her mother by telling her the restaurant's roof had blown off. Even though it was after the fact, her mother would spend a lot of time fretting about what could have happened.

Right now, Darla had to figure out how to get her mother up the stairs. She stared at her, sitting placidly on the floor beside the dog, waiting for someone else to do something. Nothing was occurring to Darla. Joyce, though, had some ideas. Some good ones, at that.

They ended up shifting her with Joyce lifting her under her armpits and Darla grasping her legs. She wasn't heavy and, with both of them sharing her weight, it wasn't difficult to get her to the top of the stairs. The wheelchair was where Joyce had left it, beside the doorway to the staircase. After the two women settled her into her chair, her mom announced she needed to go to bed.

"Aren't you hungry?" Darla asked. "We could get you something, quick."

"No, dear. Joyce brought snacks downstairs. I would like to go to bed now."

Sometimes the woman was downright imperious sounding. Darla could forgive her anything tonight, as long as she was alive and uninjured.

It seemed like her mom was asleep as soon as her head touched her pillow. Maybe before. The ordeal must have been tiring for her. It had been for Darla.

"I'll stay here tonight," Joyce said. "I don't think I can get home, anyway, from the radio reports I've been hearing."

"It's hard to get around in some places." Darla had no idea where Joyce lived, but was relieved she had offered to stay the night. "She's usually alone at night. I guess you know that. But I'm very happy for you to be here for this night. Just to make sure she'll be all right. She might have bad dreams. Nightmares. That happens sometimes, without a tornado."

"I can handle that. I know you have to get your friend from the hospital," Joyce said. Saint Joyce. "You run along now."

"Yes, I will. Thanks." Darla did have to get Gin from the hospital, but she wasn't sure Gin was still her friend. Also, it might be hours before that could happen.

In the car, before setting out, Darla called Gin. She had to try three times to get through. The local airways were full of people checking on each other, she assumed. The fourth try worked. Gin picked up.

"Do you know how soon you'll be able to leave?" Darla asked.

"Now. I can leave now." She sounded cold and stiff.

"Do you want me to drive you?"

"Yes. That would be fine."

Darla thought "please" would have been good. She would take Moose along, since dropping him off would make it a big delay, going home, then back to the hospital, with the roads so erratically blocked. Darla braced herself for a cold reception.

The dog stayed in the car while Darla ran inside, leaving her car parked just past the ambulance entrance. Gin was waiting for her just inside the door, her forehead wrapped in a thick bandage. When she saw Darla approaching, she pushed the door open and walked past her to the car without a word.

"How bad is it?" Darla asked, trailing behind and clicking the door locks open. "Did you have to have stitches?"

Gin got into the car and waited to answer until Darla was in the driver's seat. "No stitches, I'm happy to say. Just butterflies. Oh!" She jumped, then turned, as Moose licked the back of her neck. "You're here." She finally smiled.

"I was at Mom's, helping get her settled, so I brought him along."

"No problem. Hey, Moosie, glad you're okay."

Don't ask how Mom is. Darla started the car. "To your house?"

"I guess so. That's where I live."

So that's the way she was going to be. Smart aleck. Cold, unfriendly smart aleck.

Darla clamped her lips together and drove, determined not to unleash anything upon Gin. After a mile or so, she asked, "Will you have a scar?"

"They don't think so. It's right at my hairline."

"Did they have to shave any of your hair?"

"Just a little. I know I'm going to look weird for a while." Gin turned to Darla and gave a small grin. "I need to thank you for driving me there."

Yes, you do. "You didn't have a car at the restaurant, did you?"

"I guess you would know that."

"What do you mean?"

"I think you followed us to the restaurant."

"I followed you all night. After I figured out who Ned was, I needed to lead the police to him. They were trying to bring him in for questioning, once they knew who he probably was, but they didn't have a good address for him. The one he gave Only The Best is no good. Did you know that? Have you ever been to his place?"

"Let's not talk about him. Let's not talk about anything."

That was fine with Darla.

After threading through back streets and alleyways, in silence, except for the heavy breathing of Moose, who was still excited about Gin being in the car, Darla eventually drew up in front of Gin's apartment building. "Okay. Let's not talk. Not now. But we do have to talk about all of this. Soon. I have a lot to say to you. And there are things you should know." Didn't she even want to know the rest of the story, of Ned/Justin being given away? Being her half-brother? "Aren't you curious?"

"Later. Thanks." Gin opened the car door and fled into the frigid night.

Chapter 36

Darla woke up on Saturday with a bad feeling. When her fog cleared and she remembered what lay ahead for her, she realized why her gut felt the way it did. Not only did she have to talk to her mother about the baby she had given up, the baby who had grown into a man who hated both of them, she also had to talk about the same person with Gin. She hoped their friendship could be restored. Gin hadn't been entirely hostile last night, just...so...cold. So distant.

She decided she should tackle the conversation with her mom first. A glance at the clock told her she had slept in long enough that her mother should be up and ready for the day. Amy Taylor wasn't always an early riser.

For this mission, it was better she leave Moose at home. She wanted her mother's full attention to be on her and what she was saying. No distractions for licking, or petting. If Joyce had left, there would be no aides there, since she didn't have them on Saturdays and Sundays. If Joyce had not left, Darla would suggest she do it. This conversation needed to be private.

The sun and the sky, even the soft breeze, acted like nothing had happened the day before. Business as usual with the weather. You could believe that if you only looked up. If you saw the wreckage on the ground, you would know.

Things worked out in her favor, for once. Joyce was coming out the door as Darla pulled up.

"Oh good, you're here," Joyce said, unlocking her car. "She shooed me out and I don't think she should be alone. That was an awful night we had."

"It was. Did she sleep well?"

"Fairly well. She was a little restless. She kept waking up, but wouldn't let me do anything for her."

"No bad dreams then?"

"I wouldn't say so. Some stirring and mumbling while she slept, but she didn't seem disturbed."

"That's good then. Thanks, Joyce. I'll make sure you get paid for your time."

"Oh, poo." Joyce waved her away. But Darla *would* make sure she was compensated. Even if Joyce didn't report these hours, Darla would tell the company.

"Mom," Darla called as she entered. "Where are you?"

"In here, dear." Her voice came from the bedroom. She was out of the wheelchair, kneeling in front of an open dresser drawer, the bottom one. Large manila envelopes had been extracted and were arrayed around her.

"What are you doing? Can I help?" At least she was on the floor of her own volition this time. Although she would need help getting up.

She looked up at Darla's entrance. "No Moose? Where is he?"

"He's home, this time. I didn't bother bringing him. So, what are you doing down there?"

"Oh well." Her mother shrugged. "I'm getting out my oldest photographs. I'd like to go through them."

"That's great, Mom, but I have to talk to you about something first."

"Let's talk while we gather these up and take them to the dining room."

"No, Mom. We need to sit and talk. This is important."

Her mother looked at her in alarm. "You sound awfully serious."

"I am. Dead serious."

After she helped her mom into the chair, Darla picked up the large manila envelopes and carried them into the dining room. What pictures did her mother want to look at? Her former husbands? Justin, as a baby?

Stacking them into a pile, she sat facing her mother, who had pulled her wheelchair to the table.

She wore a worried frown. "What's this about, dear? Are you in trouble?"

"I've been in trouble for a few weeks now. I've been stalked and harassed and scared out of my wits."

"Well, yes, that. I know you have. It's terrible." She reached to hold her daughter's hand.

"It is. And now I know who's been doing this."

Did her mother look frightened? Maybe. She probably thought it was one of her ex-husbands, as Darla had thought off and on. She spoke quickly to allay her mother's fears for her own safety.

"It's your son, Mom. Your son, Justin."

Her eyes grew enormous. She dropped her hold on Darla's hand and grabbed her own face. "Justin? The baby I gave up?"

"That one. The one you never told me about for all these years. The one you never asked after, never looked for."

"I couldn't, Darla. I thought I explained that to you." Now she clutched her hands together, nearly wringing them.

"You did. You told me your reasons. But I don't think I'll ever completely understand them." She remembered the picture of the absolutely adorable little boy. "But worse, he'll never understand. And he's bitter and hateful because of the way he grew up."

"He has every right to hate me." Her voice was small. It caught and cracked on her words.

"He does. And my problem is he hates me, too."

She frowned. "You? How could he hate you? How does he even know who you are?"

"It's not hard to find out things, Mom. It gets harder and harder to keep secrets like this. The technology we have is working against that."

"How can you be sure he's the one who's been bothering you?"

Darla had to stand up and move around. She had to make her mother understand. Not, specifically, to shame or blame her, but so she would assume some of the responsibility for what had happened.

She walked around the table as she spoke, her mother's eyes never leaving her. "I have him on camera keying my car, for starters. Also, you should have heard him when the detective handcuffed him and took him in for questioning. He spewed out his pent-up hatred of me. He's had years of abuse and neglect in the foster homes he's been in."

"Handcuffed? What are you talking about? He was supposed to be adopted! He wasn't supposed to end up in foster care."

Darla had to look away from her mother. "No one promises kids they will get adopted. Did someone tell you they had a family lined up for him?"

"Well, no, but they promised…"

"Promised what?"

"That they would try, try very hard, that they could find him a home, that they could make that happen for him. I didn't ever want him to suffer."

"Well, if he's telling the truth, he did suffer."

"But he's getting locked up now? He's been doing all this to you?"

"Mother, I have no idea if he's locked up! He was taken in for questioning and he'll probably be held for a while. I don't know if anyone can prove he did all this stuff, if he decides to deny it."

"I hope they can lock him up."

"I thought you didn't want him to suffer."

"Well, not then. He was a baby."

"How about now? Maybe you can see him, if he's being held in jail. I can take you there. You can explain what an awful time you had with his father, and why you felt you shouldn't be raising him. Maybe you can apologize."

"I don't think I can do that, Darla. I don't want to see him."

"Now? Or ever?"

"Ever. I don't want to see Elliot or Todd or him. Ever. I want them all to leave me alone."

"You. You want them to leave *you* alone. It isn't *you* who has been being tormented." Darla was breathing hard in her anger. Her pacing quickened. There was no way not to blame her mother. It was her fault. Even if she had been lied to and thought he would have a good set of parents, she never tried to check on him.

"I'm so sorry, dear.," Her mother said it, but Darla wondered if she really was. She left a few minutes later, stomping out and slamming the door. On the way home, she realized how awfully self-centered her mother was. Maybe she always had been that way and Darla hadn't seen it. Being crippled, as she was, everyone always made everything about her since the accident. They kind of had to.

Darla's life, after the accident, had certainly revolved around her mother's needs. Darla's activities could only happen if her mother was taken into account. She couldn't play soccer or volleyball because her mother couldn't make it across the field or up any steps by herself. Amy Taylor hated to accept help, but her attitude kept Darla from doing the school sports she wanted to. Darla could have used some help.

As the daughter of a disabled person, she had accepted that as just the way it was. The way it should be. *But was it? Should it be? Should a parent's life leave room for the child in the center of the circle of concern? The child? The other child? The children? Or was it fate they were left on the edges? Outside, looking in?*

The tears burning a hot trail down her face were tears of fury.

Chapter 37

To take her mind off her unfamiliar, newly hostile feelings toward her mother, Darla turned her thoughts to Gin. Last night she had let Darla drive her to the hospital and home. Darla's stomach pangs told her it was almost noon. Maybe she and Gin could have lunch. At least start talking to each other. She sure could use a friend.

When she called and suggested they meet at Vicky's Restaurant in half an hour, she was a little surprised Gin said yes with no hesitation. Darla had thrown on jeans and a tee shirt to go to her mom's. Should she change her clothes? Why? It was what she usually wore on her days off. Vicky's was a casual lunch place. No, she'd go like she was. She left right away. In her mind this might turn out to be sort of a special occasion, but it didn't require dressing up.

Darla got a booth near the front so Gin could find her. From where she lived, Gin should be there in ten or fifteen minutes. Darla ordered iced tea for both of them, telling the server to wait until her friend got there.

Ten minutes later Gin came through the door, saw Darla immediately, and slid onto the bench seat. She gave Darla a smile. That was a good first sign.

After the server left the glasses, clinking with ice cubes, and took their orders—both hamburgers—Gin cleared her throat. "I own you an apology. I've had all night to think about this. I think Ned was stealing your keys from me. I didn't want to believe it, but I caught him near my desk twice. Both of them were the times that your keys went missing."

"I don't see why you should apologize. He's the one who did everything."

She shook her head. "I just didn't want to see it. There were so many signs."

"Like what?" Darla wondered if Gin's signs were the same as the ones she had seen.

"Well, that thing about not having a history, a background."

Darla nodded. That was certainly one of her red flags. The biggest one.

"He was so damn nice to me. He was charming. Good looking. He said and did all the right things."

"He is good looking, I agree. Maybe he's been too good to be true?"

"I guess. But I wanted it to be true." Gin toyed with her iced tea glass, tracing her finger through the ice sweat. She looked up at Darla with hopeful eyes. "If you can forgive me, I'd like to work for you mom again. I miss her."

It only took Darla a moment to answer that request. "Sure, I think it would be fine." She would have to talk to her mom, who wasn't feeling friendly toward Gin last time they spoke about her. Since they'd known Gin for so long, Darla thought she'd come around.

They paused while their burgers and fries were delivered, then each took a bite.

"I have to tell you I thought he was charming, too." Darla set her burger down. "I kept getting a bad feeling in my gut when we'd talk about him, but when I was with him, those few times, I was hooked." As she'd said, he was too perfect. Not real. Putting on an act.

Gin nodded her acceptance of Darla's views. "One other thing. The bar, Axe Me. My dad. I should have cross-examined my dad at the beginning. I talked to him last night. They did know each other from Marion."

Darla nodded slowly. That had been a suspicion, certainly. "They were in prison together. Does he know what Justin was in for?"

"Embezzling. He handled finances for a small company in Dayton. Dad didn't know what the company was, or what it did, just that Justin stole money from them when they put him in charge of the books."

Darla shook her head. She wondered if she could have looked up the prison records. Maybe they were public. She just didn't know, but she should have thought of that.

"Dad said Ned had a gambling problem," Gin continued. "He used to bet on everything that moved in prison. He ended up being the main cigarette bookie by the time he was released. Dad said Ned's last foster father had been a gambler. Another thing, my dad always called him Ned. But he had to know he was Justin. That's who he was in prison, Dad told me."

"He never had a chance, did he?"

"What do you mean? Just because he had bad foster parents doesn't mean he has to end up in prison, or do what he did to you. Lots of people overcome stuff like that."

Darla knew Gin was talking about herself and her brother, dealing with their felon of a father. "You're right." She was, kind of. But not entirely. She and Keith had a wonderful mother who did all she could to steer them right. That had made up for a lot.

"So, I don't understand. He's really your brother, you said?"

"Half-brother. He's the son of Mom's first husband. I never even knew he existed, but he found out I did."

"So, what he said was true? About the foster homes?"

"And Mom never looked for him? Yes, it is. I talked to her last night. And this morning."

"Darla, is he going to get away with this?" Her teeth were gritted and her eyes were angry. She had been duped. Darla didn't blame her. She was angry, too. "He can't get away with this, Darla."

"I don't know. He was very careful. Meticulous. He never left any traces behind."

"There must be something."

"There's some video, but it's probably not clear enough to identify him positively."

"Video?"

"Yes, my neighbor caught him on camera keying my car, wearing that striped vest. You know that vest, right? But keying a car isn't a serious crime."

Gin stared into her iced tea glass. "And the rest?"

"Separately, none of it is that bad. I'm not hurt. When the brick came through my window, I could have been. But I wasn't. Just a bunch of little harassments. That scared me half to death. When they kept coming, one after another, they added up to a lot." Once again, she felt herself getting steamed, frazzled.

When they were just about finished, the server brought the check. Darla grabbed it.

"What are you doing?" Gin said. Not with a smile.

"I'll pay." Darla grinned. "I invited you." They usually took turns paying, but it had been a while and Darla had lost track of whose turn it was.

"No, you don't have to. You drove me. I'll pay for my meal. Then we'll be square."

Driving home, Darla fretted. Were they keeping score now? They had never done that before. She wanted their relationship to be exactly how it had always been. Easy and warm. Would that happen?

At home that afternoon, Darla went over everything in her mind. All the tortures she had gone through. The police CIS people had never found any trace evidence, even though they had bagged and taken away some things. She agreed with Gin. He could not get away with this.

The detective called her around five. "I'm sorry, Darla. We had to release him."

No!! She was speechless. "You can't...you can't...hold him? He said he did all those things."

"Yes, he did. But he realized what he'd done. He asked for a lawyer and, as soon as the lawyer got here, he told his lawyer he hadn't said a thing. Then he clammed up and his lawyer denied everything. Just because he's not Ned Farley, well, that's not a crime. That's the only thing he'll admit to."

"He keyed my car. We have the video."

"That's a misdemeanor. Vandalism at most, if we can even prove it's him in the picture."

She already knew that, as she had admitted to Gin. And to herself. "Did you find out where he lives?"

"Can I meet with you in about an hour somewhere? Maybe Gordo's?"

It was a popular local bar and grill. She hadn't been there for a long time. Her old boyfriend, Zeke, used to like to meet there. After she discovered his other family and booted him out of her life, she had stayed away. She didn't ever want to meet him there with his wife or kids. It was a nice place, though.

"Sure, I'll be there. Now what?"

"Do you think your mother can talk to him? Would she have any influence?"

"She might, but she won't do it. I begged her to."

"We'll keep a patrol on your house. He's probably more dangerous now than he was before."

That was right. He was probably furious. "And my mother's house? Can you protect her, too?"

"I've asked for that. I'm pretty sure I'll get it. I'll let you know."

Her period of feeling safe had been awfully short.

Chapter 38

S he drove through signs of clean up, in places. In other places, nothing had been done yet. How long would it take to erase the signs of this destruction? Or could it be completely erased? Some places would need to be extensively repaired, some would probably have to be torn down and rebuilt from the ground up. Again, she breathed a small prayer of thanks that both hers and her mother's houses had been spared.

The restaurant had been spared, too, she saw when she drove up and parked in the front. She hadn't taken into account that it might not even be there anymore.

The detective was sitting at the bar when Darla walked into Gordo's.

She climbed up next to him, a little self-conscious about having a drink with a police officer, even if he was off duty and not armed. Well, maybe he was armed, but at least, not obviously. "Hi, Detective Coleman."

"Wes," he said.

"Wes?"

He laughed. "That's my name. Wesley. But call me Wes."

She hadn't ever thought about him having a first name.

"I'm buying," he said.

She was getting off easy on paying for food and drink today. Gin had insisted on buying her own lunch and now this. She ordered a rum and cola. That wouldn't impede her driving, if she just had one. She had been self-conscious at first. Now she was nervous, drinking with a guy who could arrest her for drunk driving. Not that she ever did that. But there was always a first time.

He leaned his head in close to hers after the drinks came and lowered his voice. "You asked about his address. I can't officially give it to you. Understand?"

She nodded, wondering where this was going.

"I do want you to know we found out where he lives."

"But you won't tell me"

"I can't. I really can't. We're watching him closely, twenty-four seven and we won't let him get near you. In fact, you're not meeting me here now."

Darla started thinking. Hard. She wanted to know where he lived. How could she figure it out?

"I can see your wheels spinning, Darla. Don't. I know you'll try to find out his address and you might even succeed. But I want you to know I do not want you, under any circumstances, to contact him on your own. That might be dangerous."

She blinked.

"Can you promise me that?" She had never seen him look more serious.

"Yes, I won't do it. But—"

"I'm trying to keep track of you, so I hope I'll know if you do. I can't watch you all day, though. I have other things to do. But this is too dangerous for you. He expressed a lot of hostility toward you and your mother, both of you."

"You wanted her to talk to him."

"We do, but not without one of us there. Please. Someone from the department."

"Detective Cole—"

"Wes."

"Wes, I don't know if I can talk my mother into it. Even if I do, I'm not sure it's a good idea. She has a bad attitude toward him. After all, she abandoned him. She never wanted him."

The detective—Wes—shook his head. His eyes looked so sad. "Families get so messed up."

He had probably seen a lot of messed up families. Messed up people create families like that, messed up. "I almost understand Mom's attitude, but not quite. He was the product of a husband who abused her, raped her, and he looks just like his dad."

"That's right. You said you saw his dad."

"I did. I saw him leaving my mom's place. I thought it was Ned. Justin."

"Did you find out what he was doing there?"

"No, she wouldn't talk to me about him at all. Do you know where he is?"

"We're pretty sure he's left town now. He didn't report in to his PO. He'll turn up somewhere."

"You don't think he's in touch with his son, do you? That they're both in on this?"

"It's hard to say, but I don't think so."

"So, about my mother talking to Ned. I mean Justin. If I can convince her, how would it happen?"

"At the station. We'd bring him in."

That should be safe. Could she convince her mother to talk to him? She wanted her to. That might make both of them feel better. Unless it made both of them feel worse. What a mess.

Darla left after one drink, as she had decided to do. She did sometimes have two when she was out, but the detective, Wes, made her nervous. He'd asked her if she wanted dinner, but she had declined. That might seem too much like dating. He was big and strong, and made her feel safe. But she had no inclination to date him.

Then it dawned on her. All this business with fathers, bad fathers. Detective Coleman, Wes, felt a bit like a father to her, but only a bit. He was watching over her, seemed truly concerned about her, not just the way his job required him to. She hoped they could keep in touch after this business was over, if it ever was. He was what was missing in her life, though he was way too young to be her father. More like a...mentor? A comforting presence? But this business sure complicated things.

As she drove home, she looked behind her almost constantly to try to detect a car keeping track of her. She hoped they were there, even though she couldn't see them.

It was eight-thirty when she got home, not too late to call her mom.

She was surprised when Lillian Chang answered the phone.

"Hi, Lillian. It's Saturday. What are you doing there?"

"We had a meeting, and Ms. Taylor agrees with the agency that she should have someone here more often. We're going to cover the weekends for a while."

That was a great idea, but Darla had to check her mother's long-term care insurance policy and see if it would stretch that far. The settlement she had received from Todd Taylor was more than handsome. That settlement had kept him out of prison, but had left him broke. And her mother well off. Darla probably shouldn't worry about her mother's financial situation, but she felt she had to. Her mother was cavalier about money, in general. She hadn't checked her balance in some time and she had been giving money to Todd. Who knows how much? Or for how long? Darla made a mental note to look at her statements very soon.

"Can I talk with her, Lillian?"

"Sure, she's right here."

"Mom, a couple of things. I saw Gin today. She's embarrassed about Justin."

"Embarrassed? How?"

"That she was dating him and she didn't check him out well enough. That he was doing all those things to me. That he turned out to be who he is. She fell for his line. But, after all, so did I. So, I can't blame her."

"Not quite. You're not quite the same as Gin. You were suspicious of him, weren't you?"

"Suspicious, but I didn't know he was my half-brother. Maybe because I didn't know I *had* a half-brother. One who has ample reason to hate me. But, Mom, back to Gin. To her, he was a perfect gentleman, the ideal partner. He did everything right. I met him and could see that. He was treating her well."

"So, he could do everything wrong to you."

That was so true. "Mom, Gin told me she wants to work for you again. Now that you're having more shifts, maybe you could use her."

"Maybe." Her mother drawled the word, hesitant. "Let me think about it. Maybe she could start off working one or two days a week."

"You've always liked her."

"You used to, too, dear. She was your best friend. And now?"

"We're working through it. I don't know if we'll be best friends again, but we've made a start. We had lunch today and we talked. It was good. I think we'll be okay eventually." As she said that, she realized she did hope for that. Maybe they could even get back to where they'd been. Where they'd always been.

"I promise I'll think about it."

"One more thing. I just spoke with the detective. He thinks it might do some good if you talk to Justin."

"Why? What on earth would I say to him? That I'm sorry I couldn't stand the sight of him and had to get him out of my life?"

"Maybe not. Could you apologize to him? That might help him."

"Why do I want to help the person who is harming you?"

"Mom! So, he'll quit doing it!" It was a good thing they were on the phone. She wanted to seize her mother's shoulders to shake some sense into her. Her grip on the phone was like a vice. Consciously, she relaxed her fingers. And her jaw. She was gritting her teeth, too. The woman could be so infuriating.

"I'll think about that, too."

That was that. When she hung up, Darla had no idea if her mother would rehire Gin, or if she would consent to speak to her son. When she thought about him coming to her mother's house, his mother's house, for hours, working as her caretaker, it gave her the creeps. He could so easily have done harm to her also. Had he planned on doing that eventually? On finishing the job Darla's own father had started?

Chapter 39

Except for a short trip to the grocery store, Darla stayed in her shell, her cocoon, and didn't talk to anyone at all on Sunday. She had to pass two different churches, both of which had been destroyed. It gave her a lift to see the congregations of both of them were gathered anyway, next to the piles of rubble that used to be the churches. A robed choir at one of them sent a sweet hymn drifting into the window as she drove past. She didn't have any trouble getting to the store and getting back home. The streets were being cleared rapidly.

She was tired of her mother. Exasperated, really. Frustrated. The woman needed to see things her way, to move on. To rehire Gin and to deal with her past sins. It was a sin, Darla thought, to get rid of your own baby, no matter what else was going on. She could have been a good mother to him and he would not have had such a miserable life. Then he wouldn't have hated both of them like he did now. *Who knows, maybe she would have turned out the same if Elliot Ryan had been her father instead of Todd Taylor.* Both husbands, both of them the abusive bastards that they were, were interchangeable. Her mother had made the same disastrous mistake twice. At least there had never been a third husband. She had heard her mother wonder what man would ever want to take on a woman in a wheelchair. And one who was near her age? One more like those two could have been even more tragic. Much more tragic.

The fleeting feeling she'd had, of regarding the detective as a father figure, she realized, was ridiculous. Yes, she could probably use one. But the feelings growing inside her were not those of a daughter. Not by a long shot. His strong, handsome face kept cropping up in her mind. Also, the whole, tall, dark package of him. He did make her feel safe, and she wouldn't mind exploring just how safe he could make her feel.

Finding herself at loose ends, she remembered that several television series were ending their seasons lately, this month and last month. She had recorded a few of her favorites and was able to spend the day vegged out on her couch, running through a bunch of them. She was so inactive, so lethargic, she didn't even get her archery gear out that day. Not a single phone call came through, so she lazed and idled undisturbed, sipping iced tea, then progressing to rum and cola, as it grew dark outside.

Around ten-thirty, she stood and stretched. She'd been sitting for over an hour without stirring and she was slightly stiff. "Moosie, I'm worn out from doing nothing all day. Let's head to bed."

She had taken him out about an hour ago, so he would be good until morning. She checked her doors, all locked, and got a glass of water to put on her bathroom sink. She sometimes got thirsty in the middle of the night when she'd had a little something to drink. Or more than a little. She used to keep a glass of water on the nightstand, but she'd knocked it over a couple of times and that wasn't fun. Moose padded after her into the bedroom and they both settled in for the night.

A strange noise, a high-pitched one, woke Darla from a sound sleep, and she fumbled for her phone on the nightstand and tilted it up to read it. Two a.m. Her glance caught a glimpse of the dog bed.

Empty. Moose wasn't in his bed. Enough moonlight came in through the window to see that.

She called him, but there was no response. A coldness crept inside her. Something was wrong. Something besides Moose not being there. He sometimes got up and roamed during the night. Maybe he considered it patrolling the house.

But the atmosphere was wrong. Holding herself completely still, barely breathing, she listened for another sound. What had that first one been? Something on a high pitch. A whine? Was Moose hurt?

Her first instinct was to dial 911, but she knew her house was guarded. Did that make it perfectly safe, though? At the moment, the only sound was the wind in the trees outside, drifting in through her bedroom window, which was cracked open an inch. Had she imagined the noise? She could check the security recordings on her phone, but would have to take it off the night setting, the do-not-disturb setting. She thought for a second. Her phone would make a sound if she did that, and the intruder, if there was one, would hear it.

What to do?

She had to check on Moose. She was afraid to call his name, to make a single sound. Shifting the covers off of her body, slowly, noiselessly, she swung her legs to the floor, ready to sneak through the house. Should she be carrying a weapon? Probably. What on earth would she use?

Moose was her protection, the security she counted on, and he wasn't here.

As she stood, a dark figure loomed in her doorway.

She grabbed her bedside lamp.

"You think you can knock me out with that?" It was Justin. In her house. At night. Mocking her. Frightening her out of her wits. Her heart was suddenly pounding in her ears. Sweat sprouted on her palms as she gripped the lamp.

"Where's Moose?"

"He'll be okay when he wakes up. Probably. Unless he has a bad reaction to the meds I gave him."

"What did you give him?" Her words came out between her teeth, gritted in anger, her fear eclipsed now. No one was going to hurt her dog. She held the lamp, her grip tightening.

Justin inched closer. "You can't hurt me with that."

No, she couldn't, but she could call for help. She switched it on and off, on and off, on and off, before he grabbed it from her and smashed it on the floor.

"You know you're gonna die, bitch. Right?" He chuckled. "No one knows I'm here. Your dog is knocked out."

"How did you get in here?"

His laugh was a sharp bark. "I picked up a few skills inside. You know I was inside, right? You've snooped around and found out a lot about me. Too bad you're not more like Gin. She believed what I told her. Anyway, your locks aren't that hard to pick."

"So why did you steal the keys, before?"

He shrugged. "It's easier. Faster. Now shut up. I'm about done with you."

She wouldn't go down without a struggle. Was he holding a weapon? She didn't see one. Was he planning on strangling her? With what?

Then she saw it.

He raised his right arm, holding the biggest knife from the knife block in her kitchen.

He was going to stab her.

No.

He wasn't.

Not if she could help it.

She lunged forward, swiping his legs with hers to knock him over. She grabbed for the knife. Got his arm. It was cold and sweaty.

He caught her forearm with a slash on his way down. He was up in two seconds.

His words came out in an obscene snarl. "Now you did it. I'll be so glad when you're dead. Our mother, cunt that she is, will be so, so sad. I can comfort her." His leer was obscene. He held the knife before him, dripping with her own blood.

The lamp was on the floor beside her, where Justin had thrown it. She seized it and threw it at his head.

A bloody gash opened on his forehead. "Now you've really done it. This is it." The leer was gone. His eyes glinted with hatred in the filtered light from outside.

She crouched, ready to take him down again.

He made a slight movement, then stopped.

The room filled with light.

And uniformed police.

"Freeze. Drop it."

Darla blinked in the sudden brightness, squinting to see who had come in. It wasn't the detective, but the two uniformed figures were just as welcome.

Justin's face lost all expression as he opened his fist and let the knife fall to the floor.

Darla collapsed beside it, her nose nearly touching the weapon. But just for a second. She scrambled up. "I have to find Moose." She ran past them.

One of the officers came to the kitchen with her. Moose raised his head when they came into the room and switched on the overhead light. Darla knelt beside him. "Oh, Moosie. Are you okay?"

He shook his head, like he was clearing cobwebs. He managed to reach over and lick the blood on her arm, then staggered to his feet.

The female officer smiled. "They told me the dog was drugged. I guess the guy in the bedroom didn't get the dosage right to keep this guy down very long."

Darla couldn't smile yet. Her dog had been down long enough for Justin to have killed her.

"Weren't you watching his place? How did he get past you?" Darla asked, trying not to sound accusatory. After all, Justin had outsmarted her, too.

"We didn't see him leave. But I think I know what happened. Just now, upstairs, I noticed a rip in his jeans. I think that's from the window he went through. When Detective Coleman called us to tell us he thought the guy was here, we talked about it on the way here. We think he went to the basement of the apartment building, then climbed out through a back window."

"You weren't watching the back?"

She shook her head. "We should have been doing that, obviously. We didn't think his apartment connected with it. It's only supposed to have outside access. There's a trap door to it, we found out."

Mistakes had been made. They weren't the only ones. But she had another concern now.

"I'd like to take my dog to the emergency vet to get him checked out."

"Sure. We'll have someone take you, right after we get a quick statement."

"What time is it?"

The woman looked at her phone. Darla's phone was still in her bedroom. "Two thirty."

It would be a short night for her after all this. She was slated to work tomorrow, so she'd better call in now to the night shift to tell them she wouldn't make it.

Chapter 40

Darla straightened her back. A few months had passed since the ordeal and she had been bent over her mother's desk today for a couple of hours.

"Mom, your finances will be fine. I had to transfer some money. You did a number on your checking account." She wasn't going to bring up the cause of that, all those checks to Todd Taylor. Even two to Elliot Ryan. Her mother had been the Bank for Exes. But no more. "Do you want me to check on things once a month or so?"

Her mother reached out to pat her daughter on the forearm. Darla tried not to wince at the scar on her mother's forearm, the one she's gotten when Todd slashed her as they fought the night he tipped over her chair. It was healing nicely, but she would always have a scar several inches long. Darla had a matching scar, although smaller, from where Justin had sliced her in their own altercation. Not the kind of mother-daughter outfit anyone would ever design.

"I think so," her mother said. "That would be a big relief for you to look things over. Sometimes I forget to balance my checkbook. I guess I got behind a little, didn't I?"

Darla nodded. She didn't think her mother ever balanced her checkbook, but if that's what she wanted to call it—getting a little behind—okay. "Let me know if you have any expenses, anything you want to buy that's out of the ordinary, and I'll see that it's covered."

"Or you'll tell me not to do it."

"I might."

They both smiled. Things were easier between them now. The police had warned away both of her ex-husbands. Her mother had even told both of them she wouldn't be doling out any more money. Darla fervently hoped she would stick to that.

It made her happy her relationship with her mom was better. Darla had been thrown way off balance by the secrets her mother had kept from her. She wondered if she was as relieved as Darla was to have gotten those out in the open. There couldn't be any more of these, could there? Darla would have to assume there would not.

In addition to feeling easier about her mom, ever since Justin Ryan's conviction for attempted murder, Darla had been sleeping well. He hadn't been sentenced yet, but he was incarcerated pending that. And he would be sentenced, she had been assured.

She would try to get back to where she'd always been with her mother, but she knew she couldn't, quite. Darla would always have, in the back of her mind, coloring their relationship, her mother had given a baby away and the baby had suffered greatly because of that. The past couldn't be changed, though. No matter how much Darla wished it could. That her brother could have had the life she had. Of course, she could never forgive him either, no matter what had happened to him, for what he had put her through.

Yesterday, she had gotten up and found she had forgotten to lock her front door. She didn't panic, as she would have before Justin was locked up, but simply chided herself and hadn't forgotten again since that one time.

Now, trying to keep her relationship with her mother a good one, she smiled. Someone knocked.

Lillian ran to answer the knock on the front door. She returned with Gin behind her. Her mother was getting two shifts a day, most of it covered by her insurance, once Darla had gotten that straightened out.

"Hey Darla, Mrs. Taylor," Gin greeted them.

"I'll be off." Lillian gathered her satchel. "Bye bye," she called and she went out the front door.

"You look chipper today," Darla's mom told Gin. "Are you wearing new makeup?"

Gin's laugh was bright and cheerful. "I feel chipper."

"I'm glad to see that." Darla was happy to see her friend smile. "What's new?"

"Well," Gin drew out the word with coy tilt of her head. "There's a certain someone."

"You're dating?" Mrs. Taylor asked, rolling toward Gin with an eager expression. "Details, please."

Gin glanced at Darla with—was it an apprehensive look?

"Yes?" Darla said, to encourage her to spill.

"I'm seeing someone." She looked at Darla. "Don't be mad."

"Why would I be mad?"

"It's Bobby."

"You're dating Bobby Abbott?" Darla blinked. She wasn't sure what to think about it.

"You're mad." Gin made a puckered face.

"No, I'm not mad. I'm just...surprised."

"It's okay with you?"

"Gin, we broke up a long time ago. I don't want him back. He's all yours. I hope you're very happy together." She wouldn't take him back for a million dollars, that was for sure. And she hoped he was staying sober now.

He'd been given leave from work at the hospital to enter a rehab program and, as far as she could tell, he had been clean for a few weeks now. Maybe it would last.

"I know he can't drink," Gin said. "But I don't mind stopping, myself, and joining him, to support him. He's really a nice guy."

"He is," Darla said. She meant it. Sober, he was perfectly fine. "I really do hope you'll be good for each and both of you will be happy."

"Thanks, girlfriend."

Gin gave her a hug. It felt so good. Maybe they would never be as free and easy as they had once been, but the tension between them was nearly zero now. Darla's return hug was heartfelt.

Darla left soon after, as Gin was chopping a hardboiled egg to make egg salad for her mother's lunch.

Fewer and fewer signs of the tornado remained. A first-time visitor might not even know it had happened. They might think there was just a lot of construction and renovation going on. An up-and-coming town.

Her phone chimed as she pulled into her own driveway. Moose was barking behind the front door, eager to see her. The call was from Detective Coleman.

"Darla, this is Wes."

"Yes?" *Now what?*

"I wondered if... I mean, I'm calling to... Okay. Can I take you out to dinner tonight?"

Her heart beat a bit faster. No, a lot faster. She had to make sure, though. "Um, you don't mean a date, do you?"

"No, no. Not if you don't want to call it that. I just want to get to know you."

She smiled. He would make a better male friend than a father figure, she'd decided. She had already figured that much out. And she did want to call it a date. "Yes, let's call it that. I'd like to know you better, too."

CHECK OUT THESE OTHER TITLES FROM ROWAN PROSE

Kaye George has had a prolific career spanning many years in the mystery genre, and also writes under the name Janet Cantrell. She has accrued four Agatha Award nominations, won a Silver Falchion, a Derringer short story nomination, as well as national bestseller status. She is a former reviewer for Suspense Magazine and a former columnist for Mysterical-E. She's also a violinist, arranger, and composer. She is a member of Sisters in Crime, the online Guppies chapter (where she was president), as well as the Smoking Guns Knoxville TN chapter, which she helped organize.
kayegeorge.com